Winter of Different Directions

Steven J. McDermott

Winter of Different Directions

Stories

STORYGLOSSIA PRESS

Winter of Different Directions

Storyglossia Press
Anacortes, Washington
www.storyglossia.com/press.html

Front and back cover photographs by Steven J. McDermott
Author photograph by Therese C. Rudzis

Some of the stories in this collection were previously published in slightly different form in the following:
"Tough Act" in *SmokeLong Quarterly*
"Swept Aside" and "Tools" in *The Angler*
"Blue Jeans and Black Leather" in *Red Wheelbarrow*
"Single Malts of the Olympic Peninsula" in *Word Riot*
"Crane Man" in *Scarecrow*
"My Summer Vacation" and "Seven Blocks North, Two Miles East" in *Carve*
"Nothingness" *in Aethlon: The Journal of Sports Literature*
"Oxygen" in *Passages North*
"Enter Wheelchair Man" in *Timbercreek Review*
"Go" in *Westview*
"Fresh Sludge" in *Thieves Jargon*
"Risk Factors" in *Storyglossia* under the pseudonym Wes Grey

ISBN: 978-0-6151-4280-7

Printed in the United States of America.
First edition. April 2007.

for Therese

Contents

Tough Act

I flinch and swerve as a snowball flattens on the door window, sticks like paint. I work the steering wheel, keep the car from sliding into the aluminum lamppost as another snowball hits the hood. Glancing back I see the kids out in the open, defiantly refusing to hide behind the shrubs.

I remember throwing snowballs from the same place when I was their age. Getting chased by irate drivers had been the highlight of our day. I turn around in a cul-de-sac and head back towards them.

Off to my right I see a flash of red and black in the bushes. A kid in a red cap leaps out onto the sidewalk and starts sprinting, his breath gushing out of his mouth. I see a dark snowball clutched in his glove and thinking rocks, tromp on the gas. I glance in the rearview mirror and watch as he slides to a stop in the street and throws.

Expecting the rear window to implode with the impact, I hunch down. The snowball hits, the window cracks, but holds. The aluminum lamppost is just yards away and I frantically steer. The bumper crumples with a metallic whine. The car rocks to a stop. I feel nauseous, shake my head to clear it, then open the door and get out. My knees go weak and I slip on the snow and fall into the ditch. I hear the kids laughing. I scramble up and they take off running.

I'm thirty yards behind and losing ground when they duck in between two houses. I'm out of breath and slow down to a jog. I round the corner of a house and see six of them, all teenagers, waiting for me.

The kid in the red cap says: Looks like you're outnumbered Pops.

The rest of the kids are laughing. They close in on me. This is not what I had in mind and I take a few steps back.

—What you going to do now, Pops?

I'd like to beat the shit out of the smart ass, but I don't think I can take on all six of them, so I bluff.

—You other guys can take off, I say, and point at the kid in the red cap. He's the one I'm after.

—Yeah right, Pops, like they're just going to hand me over.

The other kids think he's pretty funny. I keep walking backwards as they move towards me. One kid lunges at me and I knock him flying. Then they're on me, grabbing and punching. A blow to my neck sends me to my knees. Through the dizziness I hear the kids' voices:

—Come on let's get out of here.

—Danny, you okay?

—Billy! Don't!

A football-sized rock slams into the snow inches from my head. A hand pulls my hair back and I look into the glazed eyes of the kid in the red cap.

—Next time, asshole.

His kick into my ribs makes me retch and I double up as they run off.

It's two nights later and I'm waiting for my friends, Mike and Scott, to chase the kids to their hiding place. I hear vague shouts, boots crunching on the crusted snow, and then clearly: "Hurry up, they're on our ass!" They come cussing and sliding along the path between the two houses. A red cap rounds the corner and I clothesline him. His feet go out from under and I slam him to the ground as two more kids skid into the backyard with Mike and Scott right behind them.

Billy begins to gasp and struggle against my arms. I hold him down and say to Mike and Scott: Get them out of here. I want to teach this one a lesson.

—Fuck you! Billy says and spits in my face.

He squirms and kicks. Just when I think I have him pinned, he bends one of my fingers, forcing me to let go. He lashes out with his fists. I duck, but still catch a punch on my left cheek. I'm momentarily stunned, and he rolls away from me, trying to scramble to his feet, but slips on the snow. I lunge and tackle him, wrestle him onto his back, punch him, then pin his shoulders to the ground with my knees. He spits in my face again. I spit back, and he arches, tries to buck me loose. I slap him three or four times.

—Fuck you! he says.

I slide my knees off his shoulders, grab his parka, start thumping him into the snow.

—You don't look so tough now, Billy.

—You're the tough one, he says, beating up on a fifteen-year-old.

—Oh yeah? Listen punk. From now on, any other cars get damaged by snowballs, I'm coming after you, whether you did it on not. So tell your buddies to lay off.

—Woooooo, I'm scared now.

I punch him, over and over, until I realize he's stopped resisting. I stand up, feel the flood of adrenaline quivering my legs, and sink down to my knees. Billy sniffs, the sobs gurgling in his throat. His face is a mess, welts on his cheekbones, his lips split and bleeding. I grab a handful of snow and roll it into a ball.

—Fool, I say, and throw the snowball against the fence. Watch it disintegrate into millions of imperceptible flakes.

Swept Aside

I packed my two duffel bags and got the hell out of the house before I did something I'd regret. Sitting on the front porch waiting for the cab to arrive reminded me of when I got out of the army: everything I owned in two green canvas bags and thinking, *now what the fuck do I do?*

Behind me the door opened and Kym Lee stuck her head out.

—And another thing, she said. I cancelled the credit cards.

The door slammed shut. Earlier she'd told me about closing the other accounts and selling my truck to pay off her student loans and our credit card debt. Her lawyer told her to make a fresh start. So Kym Lee handed me $750—my share of what was left, Washington being a community property state and all—along with the divorce papers. Things were much simpler, she'd said, because we only rented the house.

Across the street a light came on upstairs and I could see a head peeking between the drapes. Ralph. Well this would prove him right. He always said my job in Singapore, one month on, two weeks off, would doom the marriage. At least Kym Lee didn't know about my account at the Malaysian bank.

The door opened again. Out popped her head.

—I already told Jackie and Steve, she said. They said it's about fucking time.

She slammed the door shut again. That wasn't an option anyway; they were *her* friends. The only other friends I had were *our* friends, which aren't any kind of friends at all. Not the kind that would help me move, or call me to ask how I was getting on. Not the kind that would give me a place to stay for a few days. That left Skeeter, my old army buddy. I'd have to give him a call, see if he'd let me hang out until it was time to return to Singapore.

The front door opened again. I didn't bother to look back.

—You want answers you selfish bastard? Do you? Go plumb your own fucking self!

As the door slammed I jumped up and tried the knob but she'd already locked it. I kicked the door, then turned around and looked across the street. Ralph's head was still watching from between the drapes. I unclipped the Swiss Army knife from my belt chain and went back to the door and started carving letters big enough for Ralph to see: F—U—C—K Y—O—U.

The cab pulled up to the curb and I grabbed the duffels. The cabbie helped me load them into the trunk.

—Sea-Tac, I said.

—Which airline?

—Just go to the strip, I said. I need a motel for the night.

As we drove off I could see them both watching from windows: Ralph on his side of the street, Kym Lee on hers.

Two days later, the Fourth of July, I was on the outskirts of Gresham, Oregon, having flown down to Portland on a shuttle flight. The rented SUV I was driving reeked of cigar smoke and Freon, which made it difficult for me to concentrate as I tried to find Skeeter's house. It had been five years since I'd seen Skeeter—a nickname he got after winning a skeet shooting bet one wild R and R weekend in Manila. A quick phone call, a line of BS, and there I was, leaving I-84, crossing over the railroad tracks, and prowling past mobile home parks and dilapidated apartment buildings with signs advertising Free Month's Rent and No Lease Needed! The sidewalks turned to gravel and then gave out entirely as I drove passed a stretch of wooded lots with 1960's style ramblers that looked as if they hadn't been cared for since they were built. None of the houses had numbers visible, but Skeeter had said to look for the septic truck, and that was how I found the place. A dark brown rambler with a shake roof covered in chartreuse moss and tufts of grass. A rusted chain link fence guarded the yard. What used to be a lawn was a couple of feet tall and gone to seed. The grass competed with five-foot high purple thistles. Foxglove grew in the open drainage ditch between the fence and the street.

I parked in the driveway behind the white truck with AA Septic Service painted on the back in red letters. As I walked up the driveway a 737 with its gear down roared overhead on its way to land at Portland International Airport. At the screen door I was met by a little kid in cut-offs with mud smeared on his bare chest.

—Mom, he yelled over his shoulder, a man's here.

—Let him in, mom yelled back from deeper in the house.

—You can come in, the kid said and ran off.

The house smelled of high-grade pot, fried chicken, and what might have been urine curdling in a toilet somebody had forgotten to flush. I went into the kitchen where Skeeter's wife Amalia was at the sink rinsing a plate.

—It's Rick, I said, and batted at a fly coming towards my face.

—Larry's out back, she said without looking at me. She grabbed another plate from the counter and dumped corncobs and chicken bones into an orange plastic garbage can. Beer's in the fridge, she said, help yourself. Her tone of voice was weary and made me think she'd seen a few too many of Skeeter's ex-army buddies.

Inside the house it was at least ten degrees warmer than outside and I missed the SUV's air conditioning. A drop of sweat slid into the gap between the waistband of my shorts and my back and down into the crack of my ass. Looking at Amalia, I couldn't help myself from thinking about Kym Lee. They were both short and dark skinned, although the similarities ended there. Kym Lee was Korean, Amalia probably Mexican. When Kym Lee and I had first met ten years ago, she was lithe and subtly athletic. Two years ago she'd gone hard-core, started working out twice a day—it helped to relieve stress, she'd said—until she was all muscles and bone, skin taut as stretched plastic wrap. I watched Amalia scrubbing plates, watched the roll of fat between her cut-offs and halter-top jiggle, alarmed at the way it aroused me.

I grabbed a couple of Dead Guy Ales from the fridge and headed outside. Skeeter, wearing a black and gray camouflage shirt that swelled over his gut—he'd easily put on fifty pounds since I'd last seen him—was helping his two boys arrange their fireworks for detonation. We hugged and backslapped, then sat in webbed lawn chairs and drank our beers. We got the old army stories out of the way first, then he told me about the septic business and I told him about working as a maintenance mechanic at off shore oil wells in Singapore. The kids got antsy when fireworks started going off around the neighborhood and Skeeter told them to wait until dark. Amalia brought us more beers and went back inside and I tried not to look at the sway of her ample ass, or at least not let Skeeter catch me looking. The volume of detonating fireworks kept escalating and Skeeter finally let the kids start in on the sparklers. We sat and watched the boys run around giddily spaying sparks. Then it was full-on dark and we lit the cones and firecrackers for them. When the boy's fireworks were all used up we sat back and listened as the neighborhood played at war.

—Doesn't exactly remind you of Desert Storm, does it? Skeeter said.

—No.

—So cut the shit, Rick, Skeeter said. What *are* you doing here?

—I don't know, I said. Guess I needed to see someone who knew me when.

Skeeter started laughing, big belly laughs. Oh, that's a good one, he said, and slapped his thigh several times. Tell me another.

—Just looking for a place to hang out, maybe get some advice on what to do about Kym Lee.

Just then a loud explosion went off nearby, followed in quick succession by three more.

—Whoa! one of the boys said. What was that?

—M-80's, Skeeter said. Now we're talking. But I can do better than that, he said, and went into the house.

A few minutes later he was back outside with a shotgun.

—That's the Skeeter I know and love, I said.

—Larry, don't be a fucking idiot, Amalia said from the patio doorway.

—Here, I said, and picked up a paper plate.

He laughed, put the stock to his shoulder, said, Pull!

I flung the paper plate like a Frisbee. Blam! Then the other barrel, blam!

—Take that, the older kid yelled as Skeeter reloaded.

—Do it again, daddy, do it again, the younger one yelled as he hopped up and down.

Skeeter let loose both barrels. BLAAAM!

The next night, I sat in the rental car, a new station wagon that smelled of vinyl, carpet gases, and cleaning fluid. I was parked across the street and down two houses from our house—my soon to be ex-house. At Skeeter's urging, I was there to work things out, but if you'd asked me, right then, what I had in mind, I couldn't have told you. Some vague concept of trying to open the lines of communication I suppose. Make one last stab at the whys and wherefores, one last attempt to pierce Kym Lee's defensive membranes. Except I hadn't a clue what to ask her, and even if I somehow figured that part out, I surely didn't know how to initiate the conversation, let alone what to do after that. And the last words she said to me—shouted, actually—weren't helpful. I mean what was I supposed to do with, *plumb your own fucking self?*

I wondered if all my travel was symptom or cause. I went out to the rigs when Kym Lee started on her MA. Which worked out great at first. The bucks I made covered a big chunk of her tuition, plus, I wasn't in her way for a month at a time so she had plenty of unencumbered study time. Coming back home was like honeymoon time all over again. But our relationship started going sour even before she began work on her law degree. As Ralph had said, I tempted fate by being away so much. I looked over at his house with only the porch light on, wondered if he was up there watching, same as me.

The depths of self I knew right then was embarrassment about my marriage ending as a cliché. I was ashamed that my life was turning into a fucking TV script. I couldn't understand that I'd been so out of touch—so truly out of the relationship—that I had no other way to conceive what had gone wrong—where *I* had gone wrong. At that moment I was utterly lost and contemplating god knows what scripted ending.

Skeeter had summed up my situation by suggesting I could try to repair the damage, make amends, beg for a second chance. Or I could concede defeat, move on, start over somewhere else. Or I could get even in a newsworthy manner, with guns blazing. But even drunk and wielding a shotgun, Skeeter gave me no odds on getting even *and* getting away. His last words of encouragement? You're down on your knees at the crossroads, buddy, is what Skeeter said. Ask the Lord to save you if he pleases, Skeeter said. But I do believe you be sinking down.

Up the street the lights in the house were out and she wasn't home yet. I waited, knocking back miniature bottles of whiskey. I polished off four of the six and wished I'd bought a pint, maybe even a fifth, instead. I considered my options. Back to the rigs in Singapore? One month on, and then two weeks to do, what? The brothels of Bangkok like the single guys, and even some of the married ones? No, I wasn't that much of a nihilist. Or maybe I could get transferred to somewhere else I didn't call home: Kuala Lumpur? Nigeria? The North Sea, where I could choose between Scottish or Norwegian wells?

I drank another whiskey, studied the house. I just couldn't believe she'd sold my truck. Easy enough to throw daggers of blame at her. But, realistically, where would that get me? She'd implied it was something I'd done. Or not done. Maybe it was those silences? Those moments when I was afraid to express how I really felt because I thought doing so would bring about the very situation we now found ourselves in.

A whirring like a car wash roused me and I saw in the rear view mirror that a street cleaner was working its way down the curb on my side of the street. The rig stopped directly behind my car and the driver got out and walked up to my door and rapped his knuckles on the glass. I turned the key a notch and powered the window down. He backed off a bit as a whiff of my booze breath wafted out.

—Mind moving real quick, he said.

—You kidding? I said. Go around.

—I've missed this stretch three weeks running, he said. Take me five seconds. Then you can park here for a month all I care.

—Forget it, I said.

—Look, pal, I've had a bad enough night as it is, so just move, OK?

—Fuck off! I'm having a shitty night, too, I said, and powered up the window.

He squatted, pressed his face hard against the glass so that his lips were mashed and his teeth tapped the glass with each word: Move the fucking car.

I mashed my face against the glass so we were lip to lip: Or what? I yelled against the glass.

He stood, kicked the door, and went back to street cleaner, mounted up. Before I could raise the seat he had rammed the bumper, engine growling like a bulldozer, and shoved the car forward. He pushed out a bit, and the back end of the car swung around until it was perpendicular to the street. He turned in, revved the engine hard, and shoved my car right up onto Ralph's lawn. As the car rocked to a stop I saw him raise the sweeper's brushes off the pavement. He gave me a big smile and the middle finger before shifting into a higher gear and driving off.

I sat there a moment considering the finger he'd given me—took it as the sign it was meant to be—until the lights came on in Ralph's house. I started the car, backed over the curb, and drove away from that street and those houses, which I'm both happy and sad to say I never saw again.

Tools

Corey watched Leann's ass wiggle while she buttered the toast; it reminded him of why he was there. The little bastards were out of control, as usual. Her two boys, Tommy and Timmy, seven and eight, couldn't eat without slopping cereal on themselves and the table. They fidgeted and squirmed as they ate, hyper. Tommy kneeled on the chair, trying to get a spoonful of Cheerios into his mouth, spilling it, finally, down his t-shirt. He clamped the spoon between his teeth while he wiped his hands on his shirt, laughing. Timmy, bent over, face practically in the bowl, was clanking the spoon against the glass and slurping and giggling. Leann seemed content with this cacophony as she prattled on about something that didn't quite register with Corey as he simmered amid Tommy's and Timmy's peals of laughter. Corey focused on Leann's ass in those tight 501s and retreated to his imagination for the silence he craved. He imagined how her ass had felt in his hands before the little bastards started pounding on the bedroom door that morning. He tried to feel once again each firm butt cheek in his hand as she rode him, tried to feel those long nipples on his lips, between his teeth. Corey tried to remember what he was there for, but Tommy and Timmy were playing their cereal bowls as if they were drums and Corey lost his focus.

—Shut the fuck up!

The drumming stopped. The little bastards lowered their heads, and Corey could see them trying to suppress their giggles. Leann turned from the toast and glared at him. She raised the butter knife and pointed it at Corey.

—I told you never to do that again.

—I just want some peace and quiet while I drink my coffee, Corey said. Is that too much to ask?

Leann grabbed another piece of toast and returned to buttering. Corey looked at the little bastards and mouthed, "Fuck you, fuck you," at each of them. They thought that was hilarious. To Corey it seemed they took perverse pleasure in his backing down, as if they knew the only reason he was there was to get a piece of their mother's ass.

Corey took a long drink of his coffee, filled his mouth, swishing it around, savoring the aftertaste before swallowing. He wondered what was wrong with himself. Why couldn't he live this life? Why couldn't he be Leann's husband, Tommy and Timmy's father? And not just theirs, but anyone's? Was there a gene he was missing? A screw loose? Something that made him detest taking on the husband and father roles? He wondered whether he was a worse person because he wouldn't subject himself to that kind of life, or because Leann was not the only one he was doing this with. There was Rachel. There was Jaycee. Corey put his hand in his pocket and fingered his keys. They were all there, Leann's, Rachel's, Jaycee's.

At times such as this Corey justified things for himself by remembering that he was entitled to have his needs met. Besides, it wasn't as if he'd coerced them—all three voluntarily gave him their keys, their bodies, and more. *More* was where things got messy. They were never content with a day here and there, the occasional weekend. No, they always had to have more. Corey's biggest challenge at such times was to not trip over his excuses, because, of course, none of them knew about the others.

He met Leann in a brewpub where he was trying to pick up her friend who wasn't having any of it. Leann didn't seem bothered that she wasn't his first choice; she was all over him on the dance floor, moving his hands from the small of her back to her ass. Telling him there was more where that came from. They'd gone to his truck, smoked a joint, taken hits from the bottle of McNaughten's he kept in the glove box, and then she'd given him an incredible blow job right there in the parking lot. And now three months later he found himself in her kitchen having breakfast with the little bastards. Corey knew he did not want to be a father to Leann's, or anyone else's, kids.

Most of the time he didn't need to justify things to himself. Most of the time he was proud of his situations, as he called them. Leann had the best ass, Rachel was the tit queen, and Jaycee, well, Jaycee was a stripper and she knew how to pull out all the stops. That was how Corey described things to the young punks working on the construction site. He was twenty-nine, could frame circles around them, and he was dicking three women at the same time. Even better, one of the women, Jaycee, was their general contractor's wife. They thought Corey was crazy, but they also idolized him. He played it up, bragging of his exploits and that he didn't have a place of his own—just went from girlfriend's place to girlfriend's place. He liked the idolatry because it made him feel as if he'd accomplished something with his life.

Leann put the plate of toast on the table. She placed her hand on Corey's back while she poured him fresh coffee. The little bastards fought over who would get the crust. Corey's cell phone rang, and he felt every nerve pinging with the rush of adrenaline. He looked at the phone's display; it read *Jack*. That meant the north end job site and he knew he'd be out of there quick and clean, no excuses this time. He answered on the second ring.

—Jack, buddy, how's it hanging?

Fifteen minutes later Corey was in Leann's garage gathering up his tools. He checked the canvas bag, making sure everything was there: hammers, chisels, metal rulers, hand saws, yankee drill, spirit level's, the pint of McNaughten's, the bag of weed, and the box of condoms. He was zipping the bag shut when Leann came into the garage.

—What's going on, Corey?

—Just getting my tools for the job.

—I thought you said this job was up in the north end.

—That's right, it is, he said and stood up.

—You never take your tools for north end work, you always use the one's you keep at Jack's.

—Well, I need some of these this time.

They stared at each other for a moment; then she said:

—You're not coming back are you? You're skipping out?

He didn't say anything. He'd seen this scene before and just waited to see which way she would go with it.

—It's the kids, isn't it? She said and crossed her arms under her breasts.

—I thought you were going to be different. Thought you meant it when you said you just wanted to have some fun and to get laid on a regular basis. But you're just like the others, looking for a daddy for your kids. Least you could do is be honest about it.

—So you could turn tail like every other guy? What in the hell are you so afraid of?

—Maybe all those guys aren't running from your kids, but from you. Did you ever think of that, Leann?

—You're not running from me, Corey. You're running from yourself.

—Hardly, he said and started laughing. You really want to know what I'm running from? Well, I'll tell you. You're losing it, Leann. Your prized possessions, your tits, they're sagging. And your once tight ass—

Her open hand smacked hard against his left cheek before he had a chance to react.

—Just get out of here, you son-of-a-bitch. Get out of here!

Her eyes were black, bulging in their sockets, and her teeth were bared as she moved towards him with both arms raised. He stepped around her as she screamed at him over and over to get out. He threw the canvas bag of tools up onto his shoulder and made for the door.

—Say goodbye to the little bastards for me, he said and walked out.

Corey got in his truck and peeled rubber out of Leann's driveway much the same way he had left his parent's driveway when he was seventeen. He'd gotten into a fistfight with his father over drug and alcohol usage. After picking himself up off the kitchen floor, Corey had gone into his bedroom, stuffed some clothes into his backpack, and then laid rubber from the rear slicks of his Firebird on the driveway. He hadn't been back home, or to Cleveland, or to Ohio, or even east of the Mississippi since then. A cousin was building condominiums in Colorado Springs so Corey headed west. He'd worked construction the previous summer and had a knack for framing. It was boom time in the west and over the next dozen years he'd worked in every western state but Arizona. From Colorado Springs to Jackson Hole, Albuquerque to Palm Springs, Las Vegas to Park City, Missoula to Boise, finally from Bend to Seattle, where he hooked up with Jack.

He'd stayed in Seattle longer than anywhere, almost two years. There was plenty of easygoing work, none of the breakneck pace of the other construction booms he'd worked. Finding Jack was part of that. Corey met Jack the same way he landed most of his jobs. Someone knew someone who knew a builder that needed framers. Jack built high-end homes for high-tech executives and programmers dripping cash. No square framed boxes for these guys; every house had impossible angles and rooflines. Jack was greedy, a greed that manifested itself by hiring teenage framers he could pay cheap. When he hired Corey he confided that he hadn't made any money on the last three houses, one of which had to be reframed after it failed inspection. Since then they'd built three houses together. Corey kept Jack in the game and Jack knew it.

Corey was not in any hurry to get to Jack's job site, so he bypassed the freeway and took the slow route from the south end of town through to the north end. He smiled at the realization that at least one hundred stoplights were between where he was and Jack's job site. Let him sweat, Corey thought. Then he had a better idea. He called Jack on his cell phone.

—Jack, buddy, how's it hanging?

—Where are you?

—Still in the south end, bud. Looks like I'm going to be awhile.

—Be here by noon. That's when we raise the roof trusses.

—No problemo. Give me time to stop by your place to grab some tools.

—Okay, I'll give Jaycee a call and let her know you're on your way.

—Thanks.

—You've got the key to garage, right?

—Yeah.

—Then you're set even if she's not there. So get your butt over here soon as you can. These punks don't know jack-shit.

They both laughed at his word play.

—No, problemo, bud.

—Hey, bring some.

—What?

—Bud.

Corey clicked off the call, thinking weed, knowing that Jack meant beer. Couple of tokes would set this mood just right, he thought and fired up a joint at the next stoplight. From Corey's point of view, Jack was an idiot. Because he hired mostly inexperienced punks so that he was forced to stay on the job site all day supervising. And he pretty much let Corey come and go as he pleased, a generosity Corey was only too happy to abuse. Not to mention that Jack let his wife strip at DeeDee's four nights a week. Given all that, Corey felt entirely justified getting some mid-morning action from Jack's wife. He stored tools at Jack's house just for that reason, and if Jack was too stupid to figure that one out, well, he deserved what he got.

With the weed settling deep into his brain, Corey drifted with the traffic from light to light, the steady low-end throb of grunge rock filling the cab of his truck. He rolled down the window, lit a cigarette, took a deep drag and flicked the ash out the window. It began to drizzle and Corey felt even less inclined to work. He drove by an apartment building that he and his friend Andy had framed the summer before. In the winter Andy had split for Arizona where construction was booming and there was plenty of work in the winter; and no rain. Andy had tried to get Corey to come down and join him in Arizona. But at the time Corey had a sweet thing going with a couple of big-titted blondes so he begged off. Andy hadn't come back to Seattle during the summer because there was too much work down there in the desert. And now, with fall's gloom descending and the ever-present rain sweeping in, the prospect of a another soggy winter working in raingear made Corey think that, just maybe, Andy was on to something down there in the Valley of the Sun.

He stopped at another light and realized Rachel's house was only ten blocks away. Usually she was off to work by now, but he decided to swing by just in case. He started getting hard as he thought about how she held her breasts up and squeezed them together as he thrust back and forth between them. She'd tell him to come like a freight train, and he would.

He parked the truck in her driveway and went to the front door and knocked. Rick, her German shepherd, started barking inside the house. Shut up, you stupid bastard, Corey said out loud. It's just me. The barking continued steady for fifteen seconds or so and then became more intermittent. Corey didn't knock again. He waited about a minute, but Rachel didn't answer.

The rain started pelting down harder so Corey went back to his truck and got inside. He grabbed the bottle of McNaughten's from the paper bag inside the glove box and took a long pull. He leaned his head back against the headrest, let the whiskey flame his brain, his throat, and finally his belly. He sat like that for a few minutes with his eyes closed, lamenting that he wasn't going to be able to throw one into Rachel. He let out a long sigh that added more mist to the steamed windows and put the bottle back in the glove box. He left the truck, went up to Rachel's garage door and unlocked it with his key. He sought out the canvas bag with his tools. The bag was right where he'd left it. He unzipped the bag, checked the contents to make sure everything was there: hammers, chisels, metal rulers, hand saws, yankee drill, spirit level's, the pint of McNaughten's, the bag of weed, and the box of condoms. He slung the bag of tools back over his shoulder, took them out to his truck, and then returned to the garage and picked up the cardboard box containing Rachel's brand new Teac stereo system and carried it out to his truck. She'd bought it a couple of days ago and had been waiting for Corey to help her set it up and run the wiring and the speakers into the bedrooms and the kitchen and the den. Corey closed the lid on his canopy, hopped behind the wheel and drove off.

By the time that Corey arrived at Jack's house the rain had let up, leaving a thick gray shroud of clouds that settled in like fog. He parked in the driveway and honked. Jaycee met him at the front door, and after he went in she shut the door and pushed him up against it.

—So Corey, babe, she said, it's a good thing you need your tools because I need your tool. She grabbed his crotch. That's my ready, Freddy, she said and kissed him.

—You know what I want to do? he said after she let him breathe.

—No, what do you want? she said and rubbed her hand up and down his button-fly.

—I want to tit-fuck you.

—Mmmm. Eat me first. I've been dying for it ever since Jack called.

Corey pushed the button on the garage door opener and watched the door climb up the rail, arch back, and reveal his truck. Looks like shit, he thought. Time was he used to have the truck detailed after every job. Kept it looking like new, his pride and joy. Not any more. The bug guard attached to the hood was cracked. The chrome grill was rusting everywhere it was chipped. You could barely tell that the paint was red through the mud and the dust and the road grease. Now's the time to spruce it up, he thought, so he could make a good first impression.

His canvas bag of tools was sitting on top of Jack's workbench, right where he left it last week. He unzipped the bag and surveyed the contents: hammers, chisels, metal rulers, hand saws, yankee drill, spirit level's, the pint of McNaughten's, the bag of weed, and the box of condoms. He heard the phone ringing inside the house. He zipped the bag shut and carried it outside. He went around to the back of his truck and raised the canopy, threw the bag of tools in with the others and closed the lid. He walked around to the front of the truck and was met by Jaycee. She handed him a six pack of Budweiser.

—Jack says to bring it with you. They're going ahead with the trusses so he's wondering where you are. I told him you were sharpening your tool.

—Did not.

—No, your tool is plenty sharp.

Corey opened the door to the truck and put the six-pack of beer on the passenger seat.

—You coming back for dinner tonight?

—Maybe, he said. If Jack asks me.

The next door neighbor's garage door started to go up so that saved Corey from an affectionate goodbye.

—Okay, see you later, she said and blew him a covert kiss.

Corey got in the truck, closed the door, and started the engine. Jaycee was walking into the garage. He backed out of the driveway. As he was driving off he looked back and watched the garage door going down until it was closed.

Four hours later, as Corey crossed over the Columbia River from Washington into Oregon, he felt something give way inside himself, felt like he was both coming and going at the same time. He left the freeway at the first Oregon exit and immediately started looking for a car wash.

A mile or so off the freeway he spotted a BP station with a self-service car wash and he turned and parked in a stall. After converting a five dollar bill to quarters at the change machine, Corey started spraying down his truck. He soaped it into a thick lather and scrubbed at the grime until the paint was once again a lustrous crimson and the unrusted chrome shone. He drove forward to the vacuums and spent another ten minutes removing garbage from the cab and vacuuming the seats and the carpets. When the interior looked presentable, he drove away from the vacuums and parked.

He opened one of Jack's Budweisers and drank half of it down. By now they'd be wondering what had happened to him. Jack would be pretty pissed, trying to get those trusses set in place without Corey's help to keep those young punks in line. Corey knew that Jack would be cussing him for the right bastard that he was. He looked at the cell phone on the seat beside him and thought about calling Jack. But that had never been his style. He looked back through the cab window into the bed of his truck and saw the backpack full of his clothes and Rachel's stereo. He stared at the three canvas bags of tools for a long time. He wondered how many of them he would need in Arizona. Most of the houses down there were built with stone or stucco and Corey was pretty sure he'd need new tools.

Blue Jeans and Black Leather

I lock the last of the beer and wine doors and head back to the cash register. Our clocks are not on bar time so I only have a few minutes. I check the till. A stack of ones and three fives. Enough to break a twenty, but looking bare. The parking lot's empty. The air conditioner rattles until the fan picks up speed and evens out. I rinse a sponge in the sink and start wiping down the counters. I took this job because I thought I could study at night. It's been six months and I've yet to crack a book. I swap filters and brew a fresh pot of coffee. The nacho cheese has crusted over in the dispenser so I stir it with a plastic fork. It's free for you, the manager said when I hired on, one of the perks. You couldn't pay me to eat this late-night favorite. Headlights sweep the inside of the store as the pickup truck turns into the lot and parks in the stall in front of the door.

I'm back behind the counter when they come through. The first one, judging by the measuring tape along the doorframe, is 5'6" tall, but he's wearing thick-heeled work boots. The blue is gone from his jean jacket, except at the seams, where the orange thread gleams in the fluorescent light. His jeans are ripped at the knee, one a white net, the other all flesh. His flannel shirt is blue and white. He's color coordinated. Blonde hair bunches around his collar like fur. He avoids eye contact and heads for the coolers. The door opens, buzzes, and the driver, a six-footer, steps just past the electric eye, takes a deep drag on his cigarette before flicking the butt through the gap as the door swings shut. Black leather jacket over a gray sweatshirt with the hood hanging out. Motorcycle boots with straps and buckles. Dirty jeans stained with grease and grass and mud splatters around the ankles. His black hair is shoulder length, thick and wavy. He might be part Indian, but not from one of the coastal tribes around here. I haven't seen either of them before and glance at the truck, a black F-100. Out of state plate—Oklahoma. I wonder what they are doing up here along the border of Washington and Canada.

Blue Jeans is working the cooler doors against the locks. I keep my eyes on Black Leather and call out: It's after two.

That's fucking bullshit, Blue Jeans says. He yanks hard on the door handle, metal clanking against metal, then turns and disappears behind the shelves. In the mirror I pick him up in the chip aisle. Black Leather and I lock eyes—he's all pupils. Blue Jeans is up front again and Black Leather is on the move. They converge on the other side of the counter from me. I'm standing just to the left of the cash register, open countertop between us.

Blue Jeans has thick lips and the left side curls back unevenly, pulled toward the cheekbone by a ribbed scar. He's all pupils too.

What say you unlock that cooler, Blue Jean says. Sell us a half-rack.

He's drunk plenty already, and it smells like he's been eating pepperoni sticks and those pickled eggs. Attitude's everything here, but I hope someone else pulls into the parking lot just in case. I keep my hands flat on the counter. Blue Jeans sways a bit. Black Leather is studying me, gears turning, calculations being made. I turn my own gears. I've probably been asked to sell more booze after hours than I've made legal sales before lock-up. Only agreed once, to a redhead who promised me an unbelievable blowjob and then delivered. Broke a guy's nose once, too. He ran into my fist and hit the floor faster than the two bottles of wine he was trying to steal. I can only see one of Black Leather's hands. The other is in his jacket pocket.

If it were up to me, I say.

Blue Jeans says: But it ain't.

I can take that either way. His eyes are drilling me now. I shrug, say: I need the job. They've busted me before. Next time it's a $500 fine. I can't risk a sale. They keep an eye on me.

Do they? Blue Jeans says. He looks at Black Leather, who is impassive.

I feel a chill and don't like myself for what I'm about to do, but I do it anyway.

There's a Circle-K at the crossroads, I say, by the refinery. Less traffic out there. If you know what I mean.

That so, Blue Jeans says. He laughs, sways.

I'll take a pack of smokes, Black Leather says suddenly. Marlboro red. Box.

There's nothing behind his pupils as I reach down for the carton under the counter. I grab a pack and look for the hammer. It's right there on the shelf, less than six inches from my hand. They are both watching me, but haven't moved, so I place the pack on the counter.

Two-forty-five, I say.

Black Leather reaches into his jeans pocket and pulls out a wad of bills and drops them on the counter. His other hand is still in the jacket pocket. I uncrinkle the bills, take three and leave the fourth lying on the counter. I ring it up. Place the ones in the till and get his fifty-five cents. I leave the cash drawer open. Make sure they see it's light. Make sure they see the empty slots. I put the two quarters and the nickel next to the dollar on the counter. I close the drawer. Black Leather leaves the change sitting there with the pack of smokes. His gears are turning again.

Matches? I say.

He nods. I get him a packet. Set it next to the smokes.

Do you believe in God? Black Leather asks.

Out of the corner of my eye I see Blue Jeans tighten up his swaying. The other side of his lip curls back in a sneer. So here it is. The ice cream case shudders as the refrigeration unit kicks in. I can smell the simmering nacho cheese and Blue Jeans' beer breath. The rotisserie grinds, winching the hotdogs around and around under the heat lamp. Black Leather's eyes are flat. I realize everything's at stake and lock my knee before it starts shaking.

Been down that path, I say. Look what it's got me, I say, spreading my palms to encompass my chain store smock, the store, this situation, my life. So, no, I don't.

The hand rustles a bit in the jacket pocket. Blue Jeans smirks. I gauge my odds of getting to the hammer. Black Leather's brow pinches, then he picks up, one at a time, the nickel and the two quarters and puts them in his pants pocket. He picks up the dollar bill, holds his hand out palm up, and wads the bill tight. He stuffs it into his pocket. His eyes are locked on mine and I hold the gaze steady, give him nothing. He snaps his head toward the door and Blue Jeans laughs, turns, walks away. He shoves out against the door with both hands as the buzzer goes off. Black Leather taps the box of smokes on the counter half-a-dozen times, then out he goes, lingering on the buzzer for an extra beat. He gets in the truck, revs it, hits the lights, backs out, and they drive off.

I go into the cooler, rest my forehead against a strut of the steel shelving. The cold metal bites my skin. I close my eyes and breathe hard. The Freon stings my nostrils. The quiver in my legs quiets. I pull a 22-ounce bottle of Heineken out of a cardboard box. I lean back on the cinderblock wall and slide down until my butt is on the concrete floor. I twist off the bottle cap and sniff the skunky aroma, then chug half the bottle, burp, and chug the rest. The door buzzer goes off. I peer out through the milk and juice and butter and eggs into the lit store. The light wavers as shapes move through it. I can't tell who it is.

My chin sags towards my chest and I stare at the corporate logo stamped in a checkerboard pattern on my smock. Clanking reverberates off

the concrete in the cooler as the shapes try to open the beer door. I bop the
back of my head against the cinderblocks three or four times, then stand up.

Single Malts of the Olympic Peninsula

Ralph, Danny, Shay Lynne, his father—each had their slogans with which to prod him. Crock of platitudes, Gregory Anderson thought as he drove his van out of the liquor store parking lot and onto highway 101 heading for the coast with a bottle of Bowmore squeezed between his thighs and a bottle of Glenrothes on the passenger seat. What had Danny called it? Getting laid by blame; finding someone to take the fall. Of course he could take the blame himself. No, that's getting reamed. Twelve million steps with no end. Forget that. He'd confront his demons. Go back to Forks, to the old homestead, to the scene of the crime. Slay the fucking dragon in its lair.

Heading north on 101 he crossed the Hoquiam River and cracked the cap on the Bowmore. Dusk was cleaving into darkness as a wedge of clouds, the storm's leading edge, plowed into the Olympic Mountains, and more clouds, the froth and frenzy of the storm, shoved ashore from the Pacific Ocean. He took the first swig of the Islay single malt as the highway weaved through clearcuts, logging yards, and trailer parks. The Bowmore was young, flavors not yet melded, but he liked the iron, the peat, the iodine oiling up his mouth. He preferred the twelve-year, which was like drinking a tide pool, but the liquor store didn't have it. In fact, the store's selection of scotch, except for the usual Glens he steered clear of, Glenlivet and Glenfiddich, was almost all blends. The store didn't even have the passable Glenmorangie or Glenfarclas. Just the $100-a-bottle Macallans. But he didn't want a sherry-malt, wanted something with bite, the pepper of Talisker, the phenol of Laphroaig, or the tar of Ardbeg. The store had none of those, so he made do with young bottlings of the Bowmore and Glenrothes malts; seaweed and spice, the long deep after-burn either way. Iodine and licorice. Close as his palate would get. He filled his mouth, swished the Islay, teased up the seaweed, swallowed, let the brine and iron rise. Glugged some more.

Into the teeth of the storm Gregory goes, with his addictions, with his pain. Ralph, his sponsor, had said: You can run but you can't hide. Wherever you go you take yourself with you. Time to get to the bottom of what you're made of. Gregory wondered whether the truth really was any better than self-deception. His failings, as Ralph was only too happy to enumerate, added up to deception. This is how I've got you pegged, Greg, Ralph had begun. You can't achieve emotional distance from your past. Each painful experience remains an open wound in your memory. You can't treat experience as experience, as something to learn from. You let your memories become searing pain in the present. You choose alcohol as a form of self-medication to blot out your memory. Those were the words Ralph used to peg Greg. Even so, all he offered in the way of a cure was a crock of platitudes. Gregory knew that truth was slippery. Sometimes he did drink to forget. Sometimes. Most of the time, though, he drank to remember, drank to put himself in the right frame of mind to chase down the synapses of pain. Like the way the iron and copper finish of the Bowmore reminded him of his father's fist.

Finally trees. The highway flexed its muscle, curved right and left through groves, as light slipped away, gusts rose, and the rain sent his wipers from intermittent to low. *Alnus rubra, Acer macrophyllum*, patches of *Tsuga heterophylla* in between clearcuts, and then he was into the Olympic National Forest with stands of *Psuedotsuga menzeisii* bordering both sides of the road. Shay Lynne gave him that, at least. She was the botanist, the nature girl. Took him backpacking, taught him the names. Latin. Latin only. Genus and species. No common names. No Devil's Club. Only *Oplopanax horridum*. Teach him on the way in. Quiz him on the way out. What's this? *Cornus canadensis*. What's that? *Trientalis latifolia*. This? *Ribes sanguineum*. That? *Acer circinatum*. Then pointing. *Holdis discolor*. Point. *Gaultheria shallon*. Point. *Montia sibricia*. No, the one next to it. *Vancouveria hexandra*. Good. Make a botanist out of you yet.

He popped in a Steely Dan CD, cranked the volume, saturated the inside of the van with saxophone and guitar riffs. A newly resurfaced stretch of blacktop glistened in the van's headlights. The freshly painted side and centerlines dazzled his eyes. The wind pulsed against the van, pushing it towards the shoulder; he steered to the middle and then the gust sagged and he swerved across the centerline and back. Leaves and branches pocked the road with debris.

Into the reservation. Indians raping their own land. Shit, at least the lumber companies replant. The old-growth nearly gone. Nothing but quick-wood. Lumber farms. That last apartment complex he worked on with Danny. Warped two-by-fours quickly hid under wallboard and siding. The knots exploding under the nail gun. Didn't anybody hand-nail anymore? Even the cabinets were shit. So out of square he'd had to use a scrub plane to raze an inch off the mounting trim. Was it Danny's technique or the bad lumber? The tribe might as well sell it all, log off their entire triangle of old-growth, bring good wood to market, and build themselves a city somewhere with the booty. Build a casino like the others. Okay, they made an attempt to replant here, *Tsuga* and *Thuja* in the wide open. Fuck, don't they have any botanists? Don't they have anyone who knows that *Tsuga* and *Thuja* need shade to grow, that you have to grow the *Psuedotsuga* in the sun and wait fifty years to grow the others underneath? Everything they've planted here is going to die.

Of course, if it hadn't been for all those poxy European explorers and settlers and their voracious industrialized appetites the natives might still be fishing and hunting and never think to log what they couldn't use. Each storm producing enough deadfalls, windfalls, to support five times the population. But we did take their life away, their means of support. Poor trade for pox. Gave them their land back though. Let them log it to a market ready made. The old ways are dead; let's see what they make of the new. Hope they hire a botanist. And don't I know one? Course Shay Lynne's allegiance always was with the bureaucrats; the only way to save the trees, she'd said. Judging by this logged-off reservation, maybe she was right. Better hire a botanist quick before it all sluices into the ocean, erodes right up to the glacier. What would it be if it wasn't a rain forest? Welcome tourists to the beautiful Olympic National Clearcut. If they stick to the road that's all they'll see anymore.

That's not fair. Still, something's changed. When he was growing up in Forks the tribes were complaining about the clear cutting. Now they were doing it on their own land. His family didn't live near the reservation though; they lived in logger country. His father ran a small shake mill, splitting old growth *Thuja* into shingles. That was before the environmentalists put an end to all that, turned the mill into a rusting hulk. That was before his mother, who'd taught English and history at Forks High School, ran off to Port Angeles with the science teacher. Maybe she too, had been familiar with father's fist. Last he heard from her she was living in a geodesic dome in Prescott, Arizona, trying to channel some fifth-century B.C. warrior goddess's spirit, or maybe it was just the tourist money she was after with those psychic readings. Back then, though, his father was so busy he'd had to shut down the mill whenever he wanted time off to build furniture in the barn he'd converted to a workshop.

Tunneling through the corridors of trees, headlights sweeping on the corners like a lighthouse torch, he slugged down another mouthful of Bowmore. The whisky hit like a punch, snapping his head from side to side like his father's fist. Even the same coppery aftertaste, the same long overpowering finish—thick, scalding, gluey, just like the blood. One drink and you're through. That's what Ralph said. You'll never be able to stop.

You'll just keep drinking until you drop dead. Well, Ralphie, sponsor this, sponsor this, pal. He upended the Bowmore. Shook his head like a Labrador emerging from a lake. The Bowmore was half-gone; he'd drunk it fast and the buzz hadn't peaked yet. He poured in more fuel. Whew! Getting in the right frame of mind now. Binge, baby, binge! Make that persona twinge.

He'd intended to wait for a significant day. The anniversary of his father's fist actually. Still a week away. But the storm was here now, and he wanted to be in a storm, was in a storm, heading for the eye, hoped his would blow itself out with the weather. Been thinking about it long enough, time to get it done. So he bolted from the meeting and took off for the coast mid-morning as the storm came up. He hit the liquor store when he got to Hoquiam.

What was it the discussion leader said? Write a memoir, a story of your past, she said. Come to terms with your past; write its history, she said. Get it out of your head, make it real, she said. As if writing it down was more an act of imagination than thinking or remembering. *Scripto ergo sum? Cogito ergo sum? Commoneo ergo sum?* How about *Bowmore ergo sum! Uisge beatha* fill my veins. The malt exploded on his tongue like a depth charge.

He was nineteen when his father kicked him out of the house. I've been carrying you longer than I should have, he'd said. Danny was out of here when he was seventeen, so you're long overdue, he'd said. You're doing more damage than you're helping, he'd said. Don't come back until you're a master cabinetmaker. Gregory had been tuning up a new plane and had forgotten to remove the frog, to file off its upper face, so that the blade was sticky when adjusted, imprecise. Blade chatter and tearout betrayed him and his father came unglued.

After leaving Forks he'd gone to Tacoma and signed on as an apprentice with a Norwegian cabinetmaker. Which got him four years of listening to dogma dating from the guilds in the Middle Ages. The Norwegian believed in the arduous path of apprenticeship, whose main requirement was sacrifice, sacrifice at the feet of a master. The apprentice first had to learn the rudimentary skills, had to learn the feel and task of each tool. Had to learn you plane when you needed to shoot a perfect edge joint. You scrape to leave a smooth sheen without tearout when working against the grain. You file to clean end grain. You rasp on the forward stroke to cut quick and leave a rough surface. You hand saw to cut compound-angle tenons. You power saw to mill raw lumber. These techniques, though essential, gave the apprentice no satisfaction, no feeling that his goal of becoming a master was getting any closer. Yet that was the test of mastery— devoting the long years of sacrifice to the fundamental techniques so that, later, art could bloom. Without such sacrifice mastery could not be achieved. This the Norwegian knew; this he passed down to Gregory as it had been passed down to him, passed down generation after generation.

Gregory had felt that because of the many years he'd spent under his father's tutelage he should have been allowed to start further up the scale, maybe not as a journeyman, but at least given a chance to show what he could do. The Norwegian made Gregory start from scratch, and in the process Gregory learned that although his father was a good craftsman, he was no master, that he had in fact taught him many shortcuts. And that knowledge led to the fist, the straight left jab, the anniversary of which was almost upon him.

The CD hit "Deacon Blues," his favorite song, and he tried to sing along, but he'd drunk too much scotch already. Die behind the wheel? That he could do. And he wanted a name when he lost. Lose, schmooze. This isn't about losing. His father's fist. Now that was losing. Flipping over the porch railing and landing in the *Mahonia aquifolium*. That was losing. He filled his mouth with Bowmore, held it until the seaweed and iodine stung his gums. Least he could have done was come up with a better name to call me than Loser. He pushed the rewind button on the CD player and kept trying to sing. Come on, Dad, couldn't you have come up with something better? He glugged the last of the Bowmore, pitched the bottle over his shoulder, so that it plunked around on the floor of the van.

Closer to the ocean the vegetation morphed. *Pinus contorta*, with galls the size of beach balls, on the ocean side. *Thuja plicata*, grizzled with dead wood, on the inward side. Both roadsides clogged with mounds of *Gaultheria* and *Mahonia*. Wipers on full, from stun to kill, as the rain lashed the van's windshield. Briefly, through gaps in the trees, his first sight of the ocean, whitecaps in the night. Gusts funneled through the same gaps in the trees and the van was pummeled with each one so that he proceeded along the highway swerve by swerve.

He approached Kalaloch. Sounds like a single malt when pronounced correctly. The van slowed as the trees gave way to the lodge and the wind had an unimpeded shot at him. Then into the trees again. Branches and cones battered the side panels and roof. Snatches of ocean. Gusts. Back inland, away from the beach, up on the ridge top. He starts to lose sight of the road as it heads back down toward the beach and the storm's fury. Yellow line separates, becomes two. Follow which one? Close an eye. The lines braid, become one and the same. There's Ruby Beach. Fuck, look at the waves! He swerves through a gust, dives down the hill toward the bridge at Cedar Creek. Too fast for the corner, he pushes into the brake pedal. Whoa Nellie! Too late, drive it through, foot on the gas. This road's like Galloping Gertie. Gotta get offa this bridge.

Centrifugal force takes over the van, leans it over on two wheels like a catamaran tacking toward the creek, until the van hits the guardrail, flips over, launches into a slow roll, thwumps into the alder trunks upside down, slides along the trunks, the van's roof crumples as it snaps through branches, then the van tilts, dumping Gregory onto the rear doors, his weight popping them open, and he falls out, smashes through branches, bounces off tree-trunks, and lands in a mingled patch of deer and sword ferns.

He came to with the rain pelting down and the wind howling through the branches. Sprawled on his back in the ferns, he looked up at the van twisted around the trees, its lights shinning up into the rain, the raindrops like bullets caught slo-mo in a strobe light, before splatting on his face. The sting in his chops telling him he was still alive, even if the wind was a whirling dervish within the woods. So how'd I get into the wood, into this forest, my face in the ferns? *Blechnum spicant*, picante sauce, she salsa, she salve, a botanical.

The trees went knock and creak, then crackle, thump, and whump, as one came down behind him. He could use a Knockandoo, but knew it was no can do. He remembered putting up those roof trusses on that Bellevue condo; he and Jack had been knocking back belts of Knockandoo while Danny went to reload the nail gun. Raspberries and licorice, can't knock that, although Jack took a knocking when he slid off the roof. Jack was lucky to have landed on the stacked pallets, which broke his fall; just the way these ferns had broke Gregory's. Broke? He took inventory of his limbs, his cordwood. Right arm? Righto. Left arm? Trim and top shape, sir. He saluted. Right leg. I can't do that, Dave. He slumped back into the ferns. Shit! This is how wood feels getting planed against the grain. He felt the sole of the plane working back and forth on his shin, the chipbreaker chunking out shavings. Watch the fucking tearout, will you! Broke. Brackla, now that was a sulfurous malt, burnt and smoky. Take a dollop of that molasses on my tongue right now. His right leg was a pile of shavings and wood chips, take a few c-clamps and pinch dogs to hold it together. He couldn't feel his left leg and was afraid to wake it up. But he could see the slashed and bloody jeans and it looked like he'd been mauled by a grizzly. With a sharp-breathed pain he realized that something in his ribcage, where his heart knocked, wasn't right.

Widow makers falling. Ha, no widow to make. The widow he woulda made was Shay Lynne. Focus on the future; forget the past, she'd said. Where was she now? Why'd he chase her off? Can't look at a plant without thinking of her. Need something to drink. Got to move, or die shivering. He props himself against a deadfall, sees the creek ten feet away, drags himself hand over hand to the creek side, collapses with his face in the muddy bank.

Drink something. Not the water. Touch of giardiasis. Kill that in the still, the copper kettles. Really am up shit creek. What's that malt called? Glenfeces. That parasitic fist with its bloody finish. Glenfist. Nobody wants to drink a single malt that tastes Latinate. *Polypodium vulgare. Oxalis oregano,*

Symphoricarpos alba, don't pass the mental taste test, but licorice fern, wood sorrel, snowberry, those are bottles hoarded rather than shared. Screw the giardiasis. If he gets out of this, they'll get it out of him. Glenfeces it is, he thought as he slurped from the creek.

As he looks up into the trees and sees the van hanging there, its lights still on, illuminating the drenching rain, he realizes just how fucked he is. He raises from the creek bank and starts crawling toward the bridge, a way out. His chest feels like a rip-toothed saw is ripping its way across his ribs. A branch drops, snaps, crackles, pops a few feet behind him. He crawls faster, the wind slapping his face with *Polystichum* fronds. He swims through the ferns, shoving off with his left foot, dragging his busted right leg behind. On the other side of the ferns he slides into muck, into a patch of *Equisetum arvense* and *Lysichitum americanum* growing along the edge of the creek. Pollinated by carrion beetles, not the birds or the bees, hard-shelled carnivores. Lesson there. Where? Be a carnivore? Keep a hard shell? Follow the stink?

The swamp is no way out, not the place he wants to die, not as beetle food. The way up to the road is choked with *Rubus spectabilis, Rubus parviflorus*, and *Oplopanax horridum*. Fucking Devil's Club! But if he could get through all those thorns and onto the slope, the way would be easier: remnants of *Adiantum* and *Pteridium* ferns, *Sambucus racemosa, Vaccinium parvifolium*, and *Acer circinatum*.

Off he goes, into the *Rubus* patch. He's getting scratched and scraped, planed down as he crawls through and under the brush. It's like he's being abraded. Ah, give me a good rasp. Danny where'd you fuck off to with all my favorite tools, you son-of-a-bitch. No, you're a bastard. Just like the old man and his fist, you had to kick me when I was down. Stole my truck and my tools with it. Your own fucking brother. What did I ever do to you? You were the fucking favorite, not me. Asshole. Least you let me stay with you when I showed up, I'll give you that. What's a brother for? you'd said. Someone to stick it too, Gregory thought on the other side of the *Rubus* and staring into the inch-long thorns on the *Oplopanax* stems.

Stuck there, between the thorns he'd been through and the thorns yet to come he lay with his face in the *Oxalis*, the rain spattering his back while branches clattered overhead. His father had told him that he'd never make it in woodworking because he never finished what he'd started. Was that his crime in the barn? He heard his father yelling at him. You can't stick to anything. You never finish anything you start. Your problem is you have no stick-to-it-ness. He ducked his head, dug his elbows into the *Oxalis*, and started crawling, thorns stabbing like an awl, marking him for nailing.

He slithered through decaying *Adiantum* and *Pteridium* ferns, their brown stems and fronds clinging to his hands and face, until he bumped into a fallen tree trunk. Panting, he rested. Overhead branches rubbed together, sounded like a baby crying. Or was that him? The chattering was not a bench plane, but his teeth. He knew that and clamped his molars together and shivered against the trunk's bark.

The rainwater dribbling into his mouth made him crave a whisky. Why should Scotland have the corner on the single malts? This peninsula could be as just good as the highlands of Scotland. It has all the ingredients: water, plants, mountains. And the names. You've got the rivers: Soleduc, Bogachiel, Calawah, Clallam, Hoko, Waatch, Queets. But steer clear of the muddy Wishkah—unless you want that clearcut sludge mixed with two-cycle chainsaw oil, logger sweat, and tobacco juice. The finish is bitter and long, definitely oily. Could the Glens compete with that? And the beaches: Rialto, Shi Shi, Mora, Kalaloch, Bohobohosh, Kayosita. Seaweed, driftwood, starfish, sand dollars, razor clams, geoducks, salt brine, and gull shite. Give those Islays a run for the money. Of course each of the coast tribes—Hoh, Quinault, Quillayute, Makah, Ozette—would have a distillery; the alcohol revenge even better than the casino's crap tables. The Hoh. That's a river too. Milky, the flour of glaciation, ice age grist, a chalky malt, flowing through the Hall of Mosses, an epiphytic malt if there ever was one. The highlands don't even have trees, so how the hell are the Scots going to compete with this? I'll see your *Erica* and raise you a *Picea sitchensis*. He thought of them all, the single malts of the Olympic Peninsula.

The van's lights were dimming as the battery drained; he knew he had to reach the road before there was total darkness. He heard trees falling somewhere deeper in the forest. His path to the road was over the tree trunk. If he could do that, the ground hugging branches of the *Acer circinatums* would get him the rest of the way. He dug his fingertips into the thick bark furrows and chinned himself, pushed up, heaved on top of the trunk. The pain in his ribs sent his breath out with a whoosh. He felt the jaws of the vise tightening and slid over the trunk and fell into a spiny-leaved bush. *Mahonia aquifolium*. He tasted the blood. Gasped for breath. Gregory lay in the *Mahonia* knowing he'd stuck it out, did the four-year apprenticeship, become the master craftsman, returned home, and been welcomed by his father's fist. It wasn't the branches. It was him crying now, he was sure of it.

Spider webs everywhere, draping him like a mossy maple. Soon mushrooms and epiphytes would sprout from his decaying body. He'd become a nurselog, birthing *Tsuga*, *Picea*, and *Thuja* seedlings. Smell of something's dung, a grizzly's? Or is it him? What if it's him, rotting? He could see it now, the carotid beetles, digging out his eyes. Of course, if it is the grizzly's dung, the undigested berry seeds would be good for the malt. Another carnivore that follows its nose. No hard shell. Has the thick grizzled hide. Hibernates in winter. Lesson there. He watches the van's lights go out, the forest go black, and still the rain descends drop after hypnotic drop.

He dreams he's following the grizzly bear. He's running through the woods, right on the grizzly's heels. He's trying to learn what it feels like to be a grizzly. Then they are out of the woods, running along the beach, jumping over tide-pools. Every now and then the grizzly turns and growls over his shoulder and nips at Gregory to keep up. They've stopped and the grizzly says to him: You are too high up, you have to get down on all fours. So Gregory starts crawling around on all fours, following the grizzly across the beach. Then the grizzly stops and says: You need the grizzly bear costume. Gregory starts trying to put his feet into the costume but the grizzly insists on showing him how it's done. Gregory says he doesn't need to be shown, that he knows how to put on the costume, but the grizzly takes the costume away from him and starts pulling the costume over his own grizzly hide.

Gregory tastes blood as he drags himself hand over hand along the branches of the *Acer circinatum*. He's on his back, pulling himself toward the road. Red and blue lights flash, strobe the white car in and out of shadows. The state patrolman reaches down, and, grabbing Gregory's collar, says: Okay Buddy, I got you now. Then he drags Gregory up onto the gravel shoulder of the road. Whoa! You're a mess.

Crane Man

Inside my high-rise studio apartment there are only three locations where Crane Man can't see me. The bathroom is one—although he watches me go in and he watches me come out. Crane Man does a lot of watching. Sometimes it seems he spends more time looking through his binoculars than he does operating his crane. I suppose it's the nature of his work; all the downtime waiting for trucks to arrive and unload the bundles of re-bar, mixers full of concrete, porta-potties, ducts, pipe, and all that lumber. He's stuck for a ten-hour shift of which three hours max is spent swinging the boom, raising and lowering cabled-loads.

Crane Man spies on me through a picture window, to the left of which is my desk. That's the second location where Crane Man can't see me. But even though I'm hidden from him while working on the computer and surfing the web—ah, the places I go when Crane Man can't see me—I can feel him watching, staring hard into his binoculars, waiting until I'm visible again. I can't leave the desk without risking his gaze.

In the kitchen, on the counter against the wall and across from the refrigerator, is my espresso maker. There's twelve inches between the wall and the picture window he looks through. It's not much, but it's all I have. When I'm standing there making coffee I can't see the crane. I may be wrong in thinking this, but I figure that if I can't see Crane Man, Crane Man can't see me. That's my third place of refuge.

I know—shut the drapes for Christ sakes! And sometimes, when I can't take his gaze any more, I do. But then I feel trapped, a prisoner in my own apartment.

Over time I became as curious about Crane Man as he was about me. I decided to look in on him at *his* home. First I hung out near the construction site and waited for him to climb the ladder down from the crane's cab. I waited across the street, over by the fish-n-chip bar, because I was certain he'd recognize me if I got too close. I followed him two blocks over to the construction worker's parking lot where he got into an old gray jeep, one of those that pre-dated the whole SUV craze. The jeep's rear bumper was rusted and the side panels were splotched with primer. I liked Crane Man better because of his choice of wheels.

The next day, when Crane Man's six-o'clock quitting time came, I followed him home, parked on the next block, grabbed my rucksack and walked up the alley behind his row of houses.

From the alley I could see into several of Crane Man's windows with my binoculars. In the kitchen window a red-haired woman wearing a paisley apron peeled potatoes, shaving the skins into a brown paper bag sitting in the sink. So, Crane Man had himself an Apron Lady! I watched as she worked on the potatoes, her brow sharply fretted, her hands rotating and peeling, rotating and peeling. When she was done she rinsed the potatoes under the tap and carried the pot over to the stove. She left the kitchen then and I panned over to the dining room and watched her set the table.

No sign of Crane Man yet, so I shifted to a spot further up the alley where I could see into the windows along the side of the house. Crane Man was sitting in a black leather recliner with his feet up. In one hand he held a remote controller and in the other a tall tumbler with ice and an amber liquid that looked like whiskey. He wore slippers now instead of work boots, a pair of those tan imitation sheepskins with the white fuzzy turned-over lining. He drank from the tumbler and pointed with the remote, jabbing his thumb at the button. He didn't pause to watch anything; it was just jab jab jab, drink, jab jab jab. After about five minutes of channel surfing he seemed to call out. A moment later Apron Lady walked up to him and took his glass. As she turned to leave he reached and pinched her rear-end. She jumped, slapped at his hand, laughing, and skedaddled. He leaned his head back and had himself a good laugh, too. Crane Man started jabbing the remote again until the Apron Lady brought him another drink. He set the glass and the remote down on the end table and reached up and pulled her into his lap.

Excited now, I put the binoculars in my rucksack and pulled out the camera case. I attached the telephoto lens and aimed it at Crane Man's window. They were making out. Apron Lady sat crosswise in Crane Man's lap with her legs over the chair's armrest. I zoomed the lens and snapped a picture of their tongues twinning. Apron Lady wiggled her high-heeled shoes. Click. I continued taking pictures as their snogging intensified. Crane Man started caressing her right breast and then, as easily as he controlled his crane, his fingers deftly undid the top buttons of her blouse and pushed the fabric aside. Her bra hooked in the front and Crane Man undid the clasp one-handed and popped the milk-white blue-veined breast out of the bra's cup. His fingertips teased the nipple erect and Apron Lady worked her tongue in Crane Man's mouth. Click. Click. Click.

Half-a-dozen glossy 8x10s and a slightly grainy two-foot by three-foot poster of Apron Lady, her head arched back, neck exposed, and with her nipple tugged taut between Crane Man's teeth. Low in the foreground and blurry were the high-heels, which had been wiggling.

I was up early the next day preparing my surprise for Crane Man. First I spread a black tablecloth over the table. I propped the poster in the middle and flanked it with a couple of the 8x10s. One showed Crane Man unhooking the bra, the other showed him knocking back a tumbler of booze. No shrine would be complete without candles, so I arranged a dozen votives around the pictures. I have to say it even creeped me out a bit.

How to see Crane Man's reaction without him seeing me? Duck hunters use a blind and that seemed a good approach. I made mine on the kitchen counter by loading up the dish rack with every pot and pan I could stack on the thing. Then I placed a chair behind my blind. It was 6:45 AM and Crane Man would be arriving for work soon. I drew open the drapes. From my blind I leaned forward and looked through the binoculars and focused on the crane's cab.

I only had to wait another ten minutes before I saw Crane Man climbing his crane's ladder. He rested for a few seconds on the platform beneath the cab, then scurried up the last rungs. He took off his jacket and sat down in his control chair. He poured a cup of coffee from his thermos and then did what I'd been waiting for—raised his binoculars and began to scan the buildings.

I hunkered down and focused my binoculars on Crane Man with his binoculars. I wanted to see the expression on his face when he saw the poster of himself nibbling Apron Lady's nipple. I watched as he swung toward my building, methodically working his way up and across floors searching for his voyeurism fix.

And then he saw the shrine I'd built for my Crane Man. He lowered the binoculars, seemed to mouth the words *no fucking way,* then refocused. He continued staring through the binoculars, no doubt wondering how I'd gotten those pictures of him. He chewed his lower lip with those same teeth that had tugged Apron Lady's nipple. Then he said something that looked like *who the fuck does this creep think he is.* But he didn't stop looking into my apartment. I could see him making micro focusing adjustments as he scanned the room. For the first time since Crane Man began watching me I felt safe. He'd be checking his rearview mirror on the drive home. He'd pull his drapes. Maybe take a walk up the alley just to make sure I wasn't watching. Would he tell Apron Lady? That's what I wanted to know.

My Summer Vacation

I run the compiler for the twenty-third time, setting the break point in the debugger so it stops at every line. It's a sixty-line program and I've been trying to compile it for three hours now. I start clicking through the lines of code one at a time. Again the program blows up at line forty-seven. I resist the urge to heave the monitor against the wall. I've scrutinized each character over and over and I can't find anything wrong. I shake my head trying to clear it. I squeeze my temples. I've been working fourteen hours straight, trying to meet the deadline for this week's build, and I feel done in by this program that should have taken me fifteen minutes to complete. I close my eyes and rest my head on the wrist pad in front of the keyboard.

I wake up with the computer's speakers spewing beeps. My head had depressed the space bar and typed enough spaces to fill the buffer. I delete the spaces and decide to take a break and read my snail-mail. I skip over the C++ developer's journals, read a couple of brochures for internet security conferences, then open my brokerage statement from Fidelity Investments. Good news on the stock-option front; a big block of shares has vested. The stock's rise in the past month has pushed its price near $150 and it's going to split 2 for 1. Fidelity calculates I'll have 30,000 shares vested at an average option price of $25. Christ! That's nearly $1.5 million.

Unbelievable, a million and half dollars. They told me this would happen. That was their pitch in the recruiting interview four years ago when they gave me all those options as a signing bonus. I never really believed it. Never went on a credit-card spending spree like some of my friends. I still live in the same apartment I did when I moved to Redmond.

A ruckus is building in the hall and I look in the rear-view mirror stuck to the top left corner of my monitor. It's aimed at the doorway of my office. I can't see anyone but I can hear them talking about going to see a movie over at the Cineplex. Might be just what I need. And then I hear:

—Should we ask Paul?

—What for? He's never gone before.

—There's already five of us. The car's full.

—Okay, let's book.

As I watch in the mirror they flash by the office door and then are gone down the hallway, laughter echoing. I swivel my chair around, stare at my mountain bike propped between the futon and the desk. I don't even have a car—I still bike the four blocks to work. I kick at the bike tire but miss and wedge my sneaker between the spokes. Jerking my foot back I kick the tire so hard it bangs back and forth against the futon and desk. I glance at the brokerage statement and that number again: $1,497,686.23. For the first time I feel it starting to sink in. I'm twenty-seven-years old and one of those Microsoft millionaires. So why in the hell am I working sixteen hours a day in this dark office? I fling the statement against the wall.

—Temper, temper.

—F-you. I say, and then swivel to see my boss, Dean, silhouetted in the doorway.

—I'll pretend I didn't hear that, he says and leans a shoulder against the door frame.

—Too bad.

—Guess that means you still haven't got that code checked into the build.

—Nope.

—Well, you lucked out this time, Paul.

I feel the first rush of panic.

—Don't tell me, I say. We're slipping again.

—Yep. Henderson decided to slip the schedule another month.

—Shit! I bang my fist on the desk causing a stack of magazines to avalanche. We have to ship this thing sometime.

—The browser team is still struggling.

—If we'd built our own in the first place instead of buying that crap code we wouldn't be in this mess. They spend all of their time fixing the bug fix to the fix to the fix.

—Preaching to the choir.

I stare at my computer, scowl at my program stalled in the debugger.

—Look at it this way, Paul. Now you have time to get some of those new features in.

—You've got to be kidding.

—Didn't you tell me last week that we need to wrap the remote sessions with the new memory protection code?

—Well, I'm exhausted now, I say, and glare at the debugger. I just want to get this program completed and then take it easy for the next thirty days.

—You know Henderson, Dean says. Just because one group is in trouble doesn't mean the rest of us get to sit around and drink beer. He wants us to get all the priority one features into the next build.

—That's fucking ridiculous! We'll slip another thirty days trying to get everybody's new features to work together. Dammit, Dean, I've been on this death march for nine months already. All this slip means to me is another month of sixteen-hour days. When is it ever going to end?

—Henderson insists this is the last one. Get the browser code working, drop in only clean features, and then ship the sucker and party like it's 1999.

I feel the depression sink deep into my gut.

—I've heard that so many times before and I'm sick of it. I don't think I can take it anymore.

—Hey, Paulie, you're just burned out

I grab my brokerage statement; wave it at him.

—As of last week I've got a million and half reasons not to take it anymore. I'm thinking about cashing in and getting out.

—You don't want to do that, Paul. Burnout is something that we all go through. Take a few weeks off and recharge your batteries. Go somewhere you've always wanted to go. Then come back and we'll kick some AOL ass.

—I don't know, I think I'm done.

—Just chill out, okay? I'll go talk to Henderson, see what I can do. Think it over. We'll talk later.

He leaves my office. I think about taking a vacation. But I don't have a clue about where I'd go or what I'd do. The only place I've ever wanted to go is Disneyland and I've already been there. All I've done for the last four years is work, and I realize I haven't thought about much else during those four years. Some of the guys go off on golf junkets to Scottsdale or backpacking trips to Nepal. But I don't golf and I don't backpack. Don't do anything but work. Programming is the only hobby I've ever had, besides video games. That's what I did before I got into hacking; I was the video game master. So it's not like I have some vacation in mind just waiting for a time like this, it's not like I'm going to head off to the Serengeti for three weeks the way the executives—Gates, Myhrvold, Silverberg—do.

Dean is back in my office in less than five minutes. He's got Henderson with him.

—Paul, what's up?

—I've hit the wall, Frank. It's taking me sixteen hours to do eight hours work.

—I hear you, Paul. Loud and clear. This is what I did. Got me a boat. Beautiful sixty-foot cruiser. Moor it up in the San Juans. Friday comes; I'm in the Ferrari and off like that—vrroom. No pager. No cell phone. Gone. Then I come back in Monday morning ready to kick some Linux ass. That's what you need to do, reclaim your weekends.

—I don't see that happening as long as we keep slipping the schedule and cramming features in.

—This is it, Henderson says. Hang in there on this one and then we'll work to scale back your projects. Won't we, Dean?

—Absolutely.

But his sheepish look tells me he'll cave later. I hold up my brokerage statement.

—I think I'll cash these in and sleep for a month.

—Whoa! Whoa there, Paul! No need to do that, Henderson says, holding up his hands. Take a few weeks off before you make that kind of decision. We need you, Paul. Windows 2000 final push. You've been through the wars, know how to get it shipped. Take a couple of weeks off and I'll have a glory job for you when you get back. We're going to kick Linux ass, that's the next battlefield. You can be right in the thick of it.

Thing is, I don't know if I want to be in the thick of it anymore. Don't know if I want another glory job. Don't know if I want to be part of the Windows 2000 final push. I've been on those death marches before. Lined up in the hallway to get my dinner in the conference room that had been converted to a buffet. Slept in my office night after night. Windows 95. Windows NT 4.0. Windows 98. Now Windows 2000? I don't know. The other thing is, I really don't feel like kicking Linux ass. Don't see how that is any different than any of the other ass we've kicked. IBM ass. Apple ass. Novell ass. Sun ass. Netscape ass. After awhile it's like, what's the point? Where does the ass-kicking end?

But I really don't know what else to do. I joke about quitting and sleeping for a month. That would last less than a week before I'd get bored and start building a new web site or crank out a web version of some game. As much as I'm fed up with the crushing grind, I haven't the slightest idea about what I'd do with myself if I quit my job. I decide to take the vacation, see if it will recharge my batteries.

—Okay, I'll take some time off.

—Great! Henderson says.

—On one condition.

Dean and Frank look at each other, then back at me.

—It starts right now. I'm off this death march. I hand off my code and get a new project when I come back.

—That's our Paulie, Dean says.

I'm not a Serengeti kind of guy. I go to Los Angeles. Hit Disneyland. Knott's Berry Farm. Universal Studios. I end up at Venice Beach and immediately find myself out of my element, overwhelmed by the sudden welter of life. Amid the crush of people I walk down the boulevard dazed by the sheer variety. I can't imagine where the ideas to live like this come from. Beachside street-people hawking tattoos, piercings, massages, and tarot readings. Impromptu booths selling bracelets, earrings, sunglasses, shoes, luggage, bongs, African carvings, pop-can airplanes, and pepper spray. Artists pushing their drawings, caricatures, and air-brushed paintings. Musicians playing their fiddles, banjos, guitars, and drums. A girl wearing psychedelic bell-bottoms and a fringed buckskin jacket like she's still in the 60's is playing guitar and singing Dylan's "Tangled up in Blue" and I stop to listen to her. She locks her eyes on mine as she finishes up the verse.

—Can I play you a song?

I shake my head.

—I'll play you anything you want for a dollar, she says and leans towards me wafting alcohol and sweat.

—No thanks.

—How about a blow job then? Twenty-five bucks and I'll play your skin flute.

I back away from her and turn into the crowd.

—Chicken! she yells after me and starts making clucking noises. The crowd around her starts laughing and I shove through and away from them.

I leave the boulevard, cut across the grass and make my way out to the Santa Monica Pier and find myself among the people that fish all day. I walk to the end of the pier, counting. One-hundred-forty-seven. Fishing. They are there for the duration. They have their chairs, buckets, knives, nets, newspapers, books, thermoses, ice chests, cans of pop, booze in paper bags, plastic bags with fish, sardines on Styrofoam trays. Some have half a dozen poles going. I hear they do this all day. I don't know if this is work or fun for these people, but it's clear that they fish the way I write code. I've never been fishing in my life, and it's a revelation that so many people could make it their life. How does that happen?

At the end of the pier I stop and lean against the railing. I recognize this place from the movie *Falling Down*, the one that starred Michael Douglas as a laid-off defense industry engineer having a bad day. The movie's climatic scene takes place on the pier. I walk to the spot where Michael Douglas's character was shot and killed by the retiring policeman. The irony of finding this location hits me hard. Back in my office in Redmond I have a picture over my desk that was taken from the movie.

The picture is a close up of M.D. with his jaw set and his lips tight and an angry stare cutting right into you from behind his glasses, glasses which have one lens shattered and cracked, although still intact. His buzzcut so perfectly trimmed and so stark a contrast with the shattered lens of his glasses. Meaning burns intensely in those eyes. It's not just anger and despair; it's loss of hope without depression, the horrific terror of displacement. He's an image of someone molded into a role, nurtured to excel at that role at the exclusion of everything else, who is tossed out one day with nowhere to go, tossed out and told that his role isn't needed anymore. Tossed out and told not to come back anymore. Tossed out because they are done with him. No gold watch, no pension, not even an attaboy.

And back in Redmond, on those Friday night beer bashes, when we took a rare couple of hours out to blow off steam before heading back to our offices and our code, *Falling Down* was one of our favorite movies to watch. We laughed at his buzz cut and white shirt and tie. Laughed at the pitiful briefcase, empty except for a sandwich. Laughed as we realized that he had been laid off for months and had just been pretending to go to work when really he was going out the door to nothing. And then we cheered as he mugged the muggers, out shot the drive-by shooters, and shot up the fast-food restaurant because they wouldn't serve him breakfast at lunchtime. We cheered as he kicked ass. And then we fell silent, not laughing, not cheering, as he sprawled on the pier, shot by the retiring cop, who was himself heading for certain death in his adrenaline-less retirement. Our silence was brief though, as embarrassment rose and the jokes spilt forth. Then it was back to our dark offices we went.

I'm not the only one who has that buzz-cutted, shattered-lens picture on my office wall. Someone downloaded the image off of a web page, and it circulated among the team like contraband, until the anti-hero of *Falling Down* became our icon.

There on the pier, the scene of his final falling down, I don't understand the displacement he felt. Microsoft just keeps throwing more glory jobs, more stock options, my way. That's what awaits me when I get back. Whatever part of the Windows 2000 kernel is most in trouble will be mine to rescue. I can go in fresh, be the hero, kick some ass. Collect another five thousand options. It doesn't end in falling down.

I hear the sound of skates and look over my shoulder. A cute blonde in jeans shorts and yellow-bikini top skates up to the railing next to me. She stands there looking out at the water. She catches me staring and, embarrassed, I blurt out:

—Hi, do you skate here a lot?

—Yeah, she says and looks away.

—Live nearby?

She sniffs and gives me a disgusted look.

—Well, you could be from out of town, here on business or something.

—Like you? Forget the pick-up lines, she says and pushes away from the railing, skating backwards. I'm not into men.

She starts laughing, then pivots and cruises off down the pier. I shake my head and lean against the railing of the pier and watch as two jets take off simultaneously from LAX on parallel runways. One's a 737 and lifts into a steep ascent, banks sharply back over the city. The other is a 747, slung low, barely climbing out over the water, seeming to make no effort to get up to its 40,000 feet cruising altitude. It heads due west straight out into the Pacific. No land for 4,000 miles. Fully loaded with fuel and passengers, close to a million pounds. It takes fifteen minutes until I can't see the 747 any longer. At least twenty other jets take off during that time, fanning out in all directions. The range of possibilities is staggering: vacations, funerals, weddings, business trips, job interviews, and family reunions. So many lives on the move to so many places.

I walk back down the pier. I'm tempted to stop and talk to the fishers. Ask them how they do it all day. Ask them, why? What's the point? But I don't. I leave the pier, cross the boulevard and go into a store and buy a Coke. Just outside the store's front door stand several racks of free magazines, mostly real estate listings. One magazine catches my eye. A couple is smiling and hugging on the cover. Under their smiles, in big white letters on a red background, it says: "Los Angeles' Guide to SUMMER FUN." Fun is in letters two inches tall. I pick up the magazine. It's a continuing education catalog. I open it and find dance on one page and sports on the other. African dance, Latin Salsa Dancing, Ballroom Dancing, Argentine Tango, Swing and Jitterbug. Rollerblading, Golf, Tennis, Horseback Riding. I flip through the rest of the magazine, fifty pages of classes. Intrigued, I take the catalog and the Coke and head to the beach. I find a place on the edge of the sand. A bit of lawn, a palm tree to lean my back against. The pier stretching out into the surf. Bikinis and bellies litter the sand.

I open the catalog, began reading, rapt, blown away by the range of experiences I could learn and do, life outside the Redmond campus, life outside code, life not about kicking AOL ass or kicking Linux ass. Life not about Windows 2000 or Windows 2002 or Windows 2005. I count the class offerings; 216 different classes. Everything from "Using Your Psychic Energy" to "Mastering Windows 98." The possibilities seemed endless, and right there on page one they begin to unfold.

HOW TO BREAK INTO ADULT VIDEO with porn star Nina Hartley. All right! A chance to meet a porn star—and a nasty one at that—in person. The blurb says she is the star of "400 sexvids," and I believe it. I've downloaded off the internet enough pictures of her to fill up a 100MB Zip-

Disk: pictures from magazine spreads, freeze-frames from movies, even video clips. There's nothing she doesn't do; from oral to anal to vibes. She does girls, guys, threesomes, foursomes, orgies, and gang-bangs. I've got it all on disk. I hope they've booked an auditorium; this class will break attendance records.

I flip pages and another one catches my eye: HOW TO HAVE AND OUT-OF-BODY EXPERIENCE. The subtitle promises that I'll learn astral-projection techniques. The description ensures me that an OBE is "safe and fun." I don't know if I'm ready for that yet; I'm still trying to get used to my ORE—my out-of-Redmond experience.

Cool, here's one I know something about: HOW TO MAKE MONEY DOING CHARACTER VOICES. When I'd get coded-out back in Redmond I would go around and lurk over other programmers shoulders and say in Bugs Bunny's voice: "What's up, doc?" I also do Roadrunner, Snagglepuss, Yogi Bear, and Scooby Doo.

Oh, here's a dream job: BECOME A CELEBRITY PERSONAL ASSISTANT. I'm curious about what will be revealed when they discuss "what's expected of you once you're hired." And also what are the "not-so-glamorous aspects of working for a celebrity?" I imagine following behind the celeb, pooper-scooper in hand, as they walk their dog. I think not.

Bingo! MIND OVER METAL. Psycho-kinesis, cool! Bend a spoon with my mind. This is something out of Star Trek. Guaranteed to make me a star at Redmond, and not because of my programming prowess.

And then I could wow them with the power of style after I've learned HOW TO GO FROM GEEK TO CHIC. No more t-shirts from developer conferences, no more shorts stained with pizza, no more bad hair days.

BEGINNING BLUES HARMONICA promises that I'll be dazzling my friends "in just one evening" with "entire blues riffs or even entire songs." I wonder how playing the harmonica compares with playing the kazoo. During code regression testing I play a kazoo version of Camptown Races at the bug triage meetings. Every time someone's bug fix introduces a new bug I play a chorus of doo-dah. It turns into a regular sing-along.

Here's one that my Redmond chums who collect action figures will love: HOW TO MAKE LIFE-SIZE 3-D REPLICAS. It's a hands-on lab with body casting using a live model. Maybe Nina Hartley could be the model. The special note says: "be prepared to get messy." I can see how a handful of clay and a nude model could really make my day.

Ok, here's one for a geek like me: HOW TO DATE OUT OF YOUR LEAGUE. This one is for men only. Guess women already know how to date out of their league. I'm out of my league with anyone I date. If I dated that is. After four years of sixteen-hour days working at Microsoft—

you get the idea. Well I did have one date with a girl geek. Linda. Over in the Search group. She's on that elite team, all experts in Bayesian mathematics. We went out for pizza and beer and she talked practically non-stop about statistical probability and game theory and how they were trying to kick the ass of the British startup company Autonomy, which had a head start on Bayesian searching. She was certain we'd win because, of course, Microsoft has all the best mathematicians. "Like *moi*," she said. She e-mailed me a couple of times after the date, but I told her I was in the middle of a death march and couldn't go out. That was a year ago.

No better luck on my project. There isn't a single girl geek on the development team. The test team has a couple of Taiwanese girls, but they keep to themselves. The only other women on the project are on the marketing team—all ex-sorority types. Now that would be dating out of my league. The class description says: "She could be your ideal woman. But you're frozen in place." Ouch, that's me. The Redmond campus has plenty of women, but I don't know the first thing about how to meet them.

Last Christmas I went home to Minneapolis and my not dating became a dinner topic. My mom said: "How are you going to meet any girls when you work sixteen hours a day?" "Oh, leave him alone," dad said. "When he's a millionaire he'll have a girl on each arm." "Yeah, even if he has to buy them," was my brother's contribution.

I used to get girl advice from my sister, but since she's been gone I really have no one to talk to about dating. I know it's something I need to get over, but it's easier working than trying to find a woman to go out with. Maybe I should take one of these classes. It can't be any worse than the chat rooms, and it has to be better than downloading porn from the internet. Fortunately, there's plenty of help for me on the next catalog page: HOW TO BE WILDLY SUCCESSFUL IN ROMANTIC RELATIONSHIPS. ATTRACTING, DATING, AND UNDERSTANDING WOMEN. 10 FATAL DATING MISTAKES. THE ART OF EROTIC TALK.

Score. HOW TO TRANSFORM YOUR RELATIONSHIP WITH NLP. That's neuro-linguistic programming. Sounds like something I can master. Except I don't think I like the bullet "How to neutralize painful memories." Before you can neutralize you have to remember first. I decide I'd rather spend an evening with the "Goddess of Aural sex" so I can learn to make erotic talk that doesn't break the mood.

I turn the page again and find a MOONLIGHT HIKE in the Santa Monica Mountains. The course description cautions that students should bring "water, insect repellant, a flashlight" and that "sturdy shoes" should be worn. I've only been hiking once. My sister tried to get me interested in backpacking so I went with her one time. I guess I didn't have the right shoes because I got blisters so severe that we had to turn around and go back before reaching the lake.

Although sturdy shoes didn't save Sis, didn't keep her from mis-stepping and slipping off a trail and falling 350 feet. Her boyfriend had been just in front of her. One second she was right behind him and then she was gone. He said he heard the scuffing slide of her boot and turned around but she was already tumbling down the rocky slope. She didn't even have time to scream.

I don't let myself think about it much anymore. For several months after it happened I couldn't stop thinking about it. Even though the Medical Examiner said that the first time her head hit the rocks it probably knocked her unconscious I still imagined her terror and pain as she bounced uncontrollably from rock to rock to the base of the cliff. It was too steep for Jack to get down to her without ropes so he had to leave her and go for help. By the time he got back to the trailhead and drove to a phone it was already dark. Search and Rescue had to wait until morning to make the dangerous descent to where she lay crumpled on the scree. The Medical Examiner assured us that she was already dead by the time her fall came to a stop. Still, I couldn't help imagining her lying there alone in the dark, her body smashed, shivering in shock, terrified, and slowly dying.

I quickly flip through the last few pages of the catalog. It's all geek courses. MAKE MONEY AS A WEB DESIGNER. ADVANCED WEB-PAGE DESIGN. LEARNING TO PROGRAM FOR FUN AND PROFIT. Those classes should come with a warning label from the Surgeon General: "Taking these classes may lead to a workaholic career in the high-tech industry. Side effects include, but are not limited to, ulcers, sleep-deprivation, near-sightedness, and high-blood pressure. If you are married, it will lead to divorce. If you are single, terminal loneliness."

I wonder what Sis would have suggested to me. She was always encouraging me to try new things, to not get stuck doing just one thing. "People who do just one thing are boring." That's what she was always saying to me. Then she'd ask: "You don't want to be *boring*, do you?" I bet she'd tell me to kick ass on this catalog. And maybe I should take them all, or as many as possible. Most of them are three-hour/one evening classes. There are classes every day of the week all throughout the summer. An idea starts taking shape. I decide to see how many classes I can take if I try to take every possible class that doesn't overlap or repeat. With no time or money constraints, what can I do?

It takes me two hours to build a list of classes. I've got a class scheduled every day from the Fourth of July to Labor Day and I'm ready to enroll for a summer of fun. I study the list, know it holds some answers. I wonder if it will kick my ass, lead to my falling down. I wonder if it is a great summer vacation or the beginning of getting a life. $2,250 seems an absurdly low price to find out; that's less than fifty shares of stock. This is an entirely new kind of algorithm, one that will take all summer to compile. I head back to the store to check out those real estate listings.

Nothingness

I decked the lad from St. Andrews with a head butt, sent him reeling backwards until he hit the pool table and spread across the faded green felt like a spilled pitcher of beer. He twitched, as if zapped by a cattle prod, and his right arm cocked at the elbow, released, crisply backhanded the thirteen ball, which banked off the end cushion and neatly cut the eight ball toward the corner pocket, where it teetered, fell, rolled down the interior chute, clack-click, stopped. Everyone turned to stare at me. Someone clapped, everyone clapped, followed by whistles and whoops. Cheers filled the room as if I'd just won the World Billiards Championship. The publican was banging an empty mug on the bar as if it were a gavel and he a high-court magistrate.

—Quiet up! Quiet up, lads! he bellowed. When they did, he said: 'Twas a nice piece of work, Yank. He was interrupted by a rowdy chorus of cheers. But I'll have no fighting in my pub. Drain yer pint and oot ye go. A refrain of jeers. Ye all ken the rules, lads. I'll have no fighting in my pub.

I guzzled my beer, left. The pub's door swung shut behind me, sealing off the music and laughter. Standing on the stoop, bathed in the eerie jack-o-lantern glow of the street-corner fog lamp, I felt like I'd just been sentenced to solitary confinement. Walking down the village's main street toward my cottage, I marveled at my tendency to commit the same mistakes over and over as if they were koans I needed to learn.

I'd planned to stop in the pub for a plate of fish-n-chips—a quick dinner before going to St. Andrews for a late round of golf. The British Open was only a couple of weeks away, and I needed to practice, needed to work on the swing changes Hamish, my teacher, had pushed me to make. Half a dozen pints later I was being kicked out of the pub for fighting. As I reached the hill at the end of the street and descended into fog, I was thinking I needed to change more than my swing.

—Yank? A man called. Ye still oot there?

—Wait up, we're loaded with take out! another man shouted.

I stopped on the bridge, waiting and swaying. And then my friends, laden with armloads of beer, were all around me.

—That was a right cracking header, Ian said. Ah didnae ken ye were a footballer.

—Teach that wee shite ta come doon here, Jimmy said.

—Pity though, Rab said, Jock banishing ye like that.

—Oh, he'll let me back in tomorrow, I said. You guys didn't need to follow me out.

—The fuck we didnae, Ian said. One for all, and all for one. And yer one a us like.

—I'll drink to that, I said and we started opening the cans of beer.

The next day I woke up feeling as if someone had used my head for a chopping block to split a cord of wood. I was not in my bed, but on the couch, and still dressed. At my feet lay a fragmented cassette player, the plastic pieces of its shell scattered as if it were a jigsaw puzzle. The tapes themselves were unraveled, curlicued, knotted, strung, along with toilet paper, from lamp to lamp like streamers. The predominant decorative features of my living room were, however, beer cans. Beer cans on the windowsills, tables, and chairs, beer cans with me on the couch. Beer cans on the floor, crumpled, squashed, sideways, upside down, and even a few right-side-up beer cans. A cornucopia of beer: Tennant's Lager, MacEwan's Export, MacEwan's Pale Ale, Guinness Extra Stout, Tartan Special, even an unopened six pack of Budweiser. Taken as a whole, along with the cigarette butts, potato chip bags, and the derelict on the couch with a blistering hangover, my living room was a classic of postmodernism, a Johnsian pop art sculpture: "Beer Can."

When the pressure on my bladder neared the pain threshold I stood up, swayed, sat back down, stood, swayed, steadied, and with my head spinning like a stripped ratchet, took my first steps. I paused to kick a can of Guinness out of the way; it spun lazily, spewing black beer into the carpet. The hallway was decorated with toilet paper stuck to the walls with dried puffs of shaving cream. I staggered to the bathroom. Someone had thrown up in the bathtub and I focused momentarily on the chunks of meat in the yellow bile, then spun like a discus thrower and vomited in the sink.

I washed my face, took a long and painful piss, avoided looking at both the mirror and the bathtub, went back to the living room, sat down on the couch and tried to reconstruct what had happened. My fat lip, cut knuckles, and the knot above my right eye brought back the pub fight. I remembered walking home in the fog, shouts of "wait up," and half a dozen beer-clutching friends. But that was all I could remember. I looked at the tapestry of beer cans, the party wreckage, and thought: this is not why I came to Scotland.

I'd shot four rounds in the 60's when I won my state amateur. I'd once had a streak where I'd gone fifteen straight rounds without missing a fairway. I had a shot for every sucker pin. Then a couple of snap hooks down the stretch at Q-school and I was back to eking out a living as an assistant club pro. Four years of late-night card games and last-call nightclubbing and I was trying to live with the new reputation I'd acquired. My golf pro friends, resentful of my talent on the way up, flocked around me on the way down. They offered swing tips. I listened to everything, tried anything, and turned my swing into a pretzel. But there was always a party, always the consolation of alcohol. I'd overheard the locker room talk at tournaments—"He drinks better than he plays"—and didn't like being labeled a loser.

The turning point came, I'd thought, when I quit my job and moved to Scotland. I felt that getting back to the origins—the dunes, the gorse, the turf-walled bunkers, the two-foot-high rough, the Road Hole—would rekindle my passion for the game. So I went to Scotland brimming with hope and determination: hope that a new environment would allow me to change my behavior, and determination to turn my natural talent into something I could be proud of. But when I looked around my living room the wreckage was too familiar to be a new low.

I removed myself from the artwork, headed to the kitchen for medicine. I started back to the living room for a can of Tennant's lager, only to remember that I'd begun the night drinking Stella Artois. Stella's a fortified beer—three pints are a mule kick. I drank at least six before being banished from the pub. I searched through the refrigerator and found the emergency bottle hidden behind the malt vinegar and the canned asparagus spears. I poured the Stella over the cornflakes, waited until they were soggy, then started spooning in the hair of the dog. After a few mouthfuls I again became familiar with nausea, pushed the bowl aside and slumped over the table, my cheek wincing at the chilled Formica as if it were a stainless steel tray in the morgue. Changes had to occur. Like most people I kept a secret life; only my bouts of drunkenness wasn't it. My golf career was my secret. The life my friends from the night before knew nothing about. Oh they knew I was golf pro, all right, but they didn't know what I'd been, or what my aspirations were; they didn't know about all the time I'd been putting in with Hamish.

Just like every assistant pro in the British Isles, I came to Scotland wanting to work at St. Andrews. I ended up at a course ten miles farther south that was perched on a promontory jutting into the North Sea. The head pro, Hamish Johnstone, took me on more as a novelty than anything: he thought he could make some money by having an American pro on the premises. My duties consisted of running the pro shop when Hamish was at the pub and giving lessons when he didn't feel like it—or when someone requested lessons from the Yank pro. However, I wasn't just there to teach, but to learn as well, and I bought Hamish at least a hundred double whiskys before he finally agreed to take a look at my swing.

The practice ground where we gave lessons was back behind the pro shop. Hamish's usual style was to sit there in a wicker chair with a can of Tartan Special and bark instructions like a drill sergeant. He never gave me that treatment, however. The first time out it was: Go ahead, laddie, warm up and show me your best.

I hit some long irons just to get the feel of my clubs, then began hitting four woods, adding more clubhead speed with each swing. Hearing soft explosions of air behind me as Hamish snorted and burped in response to my shots, I became more determined to impress him. Taking my driver out of the bag, I made a couple of big looping swishes, then teed a ball and let rip. I caught the ball flush, and it took off with a sharp crack, low then slowly rising, arcing higher and higher, hanging at the apogee for an instant before going up and over like a rollercoaster. It was one of the longest drives I'd ever hit. Hamish wasn't impressed. So I hit about ten more just like it, all of them cannon shots.

—Okay, I've seen enough, Hamish said. Stop punishing the wee buggers.

—So what did you think?

—It's obvious you're going aboot it all wrong.

—But you saw the results.

He spat, got up from his chair, traded his beer for my driver and teed a ball. He was short, stooped, and stubby legged, with long orangutanian arms and a head the size of a basketball. He had bushy grey eyebrows, cauliflower ears, raisin eyes, ruby rose petals for cheeks, a peanut nose, and no lips. Wispy white wings of hair sprouted from beneath the red and green tartan tammy perched atop his head. He made about twenty waggles, wrists hinging the club until it was parallel to the ground, back and forth, back and forth like an unlocked garden gate. Then, with a flat, shoulder-height backswing, he hit the most amazing shot I've ever seen. It was a cliché: a line drive, a rifle shot, a clothesline pass, straight as a string. The ball never got more than fifteen feet off the ground, just sizzled along at its appointed altitude like an F-14 Tomcat trying to avoid radar. Streaking past where my longest drive had stopped, the ball skimmed a swale, took three waist-high bounces, and rolled out of sight.

—Och! Hamish said, I got under that one a wee bit.

He handed the club back to me, took a swig from his can of beer, then said: But that, laddie, is how you're supposed to hit the driver. When ye can do that, I'll give ye a lesson.

—How in the hell do you expect me to hit a drive like that? I said. I've never seen a golf ball do what that ball just did.

—It's obvious then that there's things ye don't ken aboot the golf swing.

—There's nothing wrong with my swing.

—Is there no? he said, then brayed like a donkey. I wasn't going to tell ye, but since your ignorance is so persistent. Your hands are too high for one thing. Your elbows are too far away from your body for another. And you're standing too upright.

—Oh, is that all.

—As a matter of fact—

—Forget it, just forget it. I don't want to change my swing, I just want to fine tune my game.

—Oh, is that all, he said and guzzled down the rest of his beer. Well forget it, just forget it, he mimicked. If ye cannae hit the ball long and straight into the wind you're nae golfer. And that rainbow tee shot of yours will go naewhere in a gale.

—Listen, Hamish, I've won tournaments with that rainbow.

—Aye, so what are ye doing here, laddie, what are ye doing here?

It had taken me a couple of months to accept what I had, of course, known all along; that I had to change my swing. In the heavy winds that were normal for Scotland—fifteen miles per hour was called "a wee touch of breeze"—my booming rainbow drives turned into pop flies. So I'd adjusted to the environment, completely revamped, without any help from Hamish, my whole swing; and played worse than I ever had in my life. Finally, out of pity, Hamish pushed me with cryptic one liners, pointers designed to enlighten, but as the British Open drew closer, the practice ground was my only hope of salvation; and I'd been squandering what little time I'd had left.

Rising up from the Formica, I began again to spoon in the soggy Stella-saturated cornflakes. Even under the influence of a crushing hangover, I knew I had to practice, had to make up for the time I'd lost to drink the day before. So with my head marginally clearer, I rescued my golf clubs from the living room sculpture, abandoned the mess, and drove into St. Andrews intending a serious practice session.

It seemed no coincidence that the Scots invented both golf and whisky—my theory is that because their lives were so miserable they needed some leisure activity that was more difficult, some sport which would make their lives seem easier in comparison. And then they had to come up with whisky to blot out the horror of what they'd unleashed upon the world. I understood the connection between game and life all too well and the hallowed links of St. Andrews seemed fitting terrain for a down-and-out American pro seeking renewal: along with the pubs it was my home away from home.

The practice ground at St. Andrews was not like American driving ranges, where you get a bucket, belt the balls, get another, and keep on until your hands blister. You had to bring your own balls for one thing. And then go out and shag them before you could hit again, so there was some incentive for accuracy. Particularly as the other golfers kept hitting their balls while you picked up yours. When I arrived at the practice ground around noon there were only a couple of others hitting balls into the salt breeze. I claimed my usual place near where the mossy stonewalls came together at right angles. As I stretched, I surveyed the consecrated landscape. The practice ground was about seventy yards wide and 230 yards deep, bordered on the far end by the seventeenth fairway of the Eden course. Both practice ground and course resembled—just as Sam Snead had once blasphemed—a cow pasture. Still, that cow pasture is sacred to the Scots and I always felt a bit shaky at the start of a practice session.

I hit balls for thirty minutes, the only purpose being to help the mind and body remember what a golf club was for. The balls weren't going where or how I wanted them to, but it felt good to be drenched in sweat, to breathe in the alcoholic steam rising off my body. I cracked a beer, got serious, and spent another hour trying to groove arcane body movements into a smooth swing. Frustration became an intense high. Hamish had repeatedly said I tried too hard and would admonish me with sayings like "You're over controlling the wee bugger" or "Ye've got to feel your inner body." Lately Hamish had been trying to get me to feel my swing, or paradoxically, not feel it "Ye have to let the nothingness into your shots," he'd say, then wink with a raisin eye.

I'd never had any luck at feeling my inner body in the past, but nothing else was working so I tried again. After an hour I could feel a toenail cutting into another toe and the blister forming on my left thumb. Inner body? No way. It didn't really matter though, because feeling my inner body seemed a contradiction of what I most wanted to do: let the nothingness into my shots. Ah, the magic of that phrase. I chanted it to myself before each shot: let the nothingness into your shots, let the nothingness into your shots, let the nothingness into your shots. But I was still too caught up in trying to make the ball go where I wanted. I worked on it though, ball after ball, hour after hour, like some Faust of the links. I imagined returning to America to face the question: "So what did you do in Scotland?" and saying: "I sold my soul to let the nothingness into my shots."

Evening arrived, a gloom descended as a bank of clouds oozed from the Lomond Hills toward the North Sea. The practice ground was deserted except for me. I'd just finished hitting a lengthy series of bad shots, and as I picked up the balls I was ready to go—the pubs were opening and my friends would be waiting. But I didn't want to leave on a bad streak that I'd be likely to take with me, so I decided to hit one more bag.

I'd hit five or six balls before I noticed they had all landed within a few feet of the shag bag 165 yards away. The next three balls landed in the same spot, and I noticed a subtle change taking place in my body as a curious sense of balance rose, until I felt like I was in a flotation tank. Mentally I froze; the only thing that seemed to work was my vision. I continued to hit balls, my eyes recording the club head reaching out, turning forty-five degrees and flicking a ball from the pile into position. The club went back, returned, swept the ball away without a divot, without a sound, the crack I'd been hearing at impact all day suddenly gone along with my body. I watched the ball fly the same trajectory as the others, land in the same place, and roll up against the shag bag. I kept hitting, hitting, hitting—swinging, swinging, swinging. I don't know how many swings I made before I realized that all the balls were gone. But for a moment I couldn't stop, couldn't feel anything to stop. Then, realizing that I didn't remember hitting the last ball, or even the last fifty, I stopped, my body rushing back all at once, the ground heaving like the deck of a fishing boat in the North Sea. I began to twirl and tried to steady myself with the golf club as the ground continued to pendulum. I felt a spike of adrenaline shoot down my neck and I thought I was going to vomit as the sparks hit my eyes. I shook my head, trying to clear it. The adrenaline was in my legs then, and I leaned on the club, trembling like a newborn fawn.

I went over to the wall, leaned back against the cold stones and looked around the practice area. Damn, no witnesses. It was like shooting a hole-in-one while playing by yourself—no one would believe it. Hamish? He'd spit and say: "Och! Away ye go." I closed my eyes and tried to recapture how I felt when I was hitting those balls. But I couldn't; that part of my life was gone too, irretrievable in the void. I shivered and went to pick up the balls. No chore this time; they were all lying within ten feet of each other. I looked toward the Lomonds: the sun was surfing in the waves of pleated clouds and there were still two, maybe three hours of northern light left; time enough for a quick eighteen holes. I'd faced this decision before, and too often chosen the pub where my friends waited. Shouldering my clubs, I walked toward the first tee.

Seven Blocks North, Two Miles East

I spent my first three weeks at Thoreau trying to punch everyone who teased me about my speech impediments. Bostick, the vice-principal and disciplinarian, weary from seeing me in his office, attempted to solve my problems by sentencing me to three months of speech therapy with Miss Edwards. But first I had to get out of Miss Jenkins class. She was our fifth grade teacher. Everyone called her the Bowling Ball because she was so short and fat. My speech sessions were on Monday, Wednesday, and Friday during morning recess. The sessions lasted a half-hour. Recess only lasted fifteen minutes. That meant Miss Jenkins had to interrupt her history lesson to dismiss me.

—Okay, Tommy, she said pointing her thumb at me and jerking it toward the door.

I snapped my history book shut and slid my chair away from the desk.

—Hey Stutterpuss, Billy Haliburton called from the back of the room, learn to say your name too. It's Pisspail, in case you've forgotten.

I ignored the snickers from my classmates and headed to the cloakroom. I lingered among the coats, not wanting to pass back through the front of the classroom. I opened my lunch box and found the baggie of Oreos, put them in my coat pocket. Miss Jenkins voice bellowed at me from the classroom.

—Get your butt in gear, Wisdale.

I caught a glimpse of her jowls quivering like a beagle's and then turned away and escaped from the classroom into the empty hallway. I started up the three flights of stairs to the top of the old brick school building to get to Miss Edward's room. Fourteen stairs to the first landing. Change directions, and fourteen more to the second floor. Fourteen. Landing. Fourteen. Third floor. Fourteen. Landing. Fourteen. Fourth floor.

Eighty-four stairs in all. I'd climbed those steps many times. And not just to get to Miss Edward's room. The principal's and the vice-principal's offices were up there too.

Miss Edward's room was two doors farther down the hall from Bostick's office. Her room was like an attic crammed into a house as an afterthought, small and claustrophobic. The room was tallest at the doorway, from there the ceiling slanted at a forty-five degree angle toward the outer wall where the grilled window looked out onto the playground. Through that window I could see kids running crazily, kicking up sprays of sand, as they shifted directions, started and stopped, bobbed and weaved in a frantic game of keep away.

She probably was a new teacher, fresh out of college. Didn't yet have that condescending attitude that some of the other teachers seemed to have. She looked younger than my mom did, who was thirty then, and her most distinctive feature was long blonde hair, long enough that she could have sat on it. She never did though, flipped it over the back of the chair instead, where it hung like a cape. She had a high forehead, a touch of freckles, and blue eyes that glinted like marbles. If she had been my teacher in the eighth grade instead of the fifth, and if she hadn't been my speech teacher, I would have been in love with her; instead, going to see her was tortuous.

In the two weeks I'd been going to her I'd made good progress on my stutter, mostly because I was learning to talk slower. I hadn't conquered the lisp though.

—I hear you're getting teased a lot because you can't pronounce your last name, she said.

I nodded.

—Well let's work on that this session. Let me hear you say it.

—Withh-dale.

—Okay, keep repeating it.

—Withh-dale. Withh-dale. Withh-dale. Withh-dale. Withh-dale. Withh-dale. Thee, I said and banged my fist against the table, I can't thay it.

—Try again. Slowly this time. Really exaggerate the ess.

—Withh-dale. With-dale. With-dale. Withs-dale.

—Good! Now I want you to try hissing your ess. Like this. Wissssss-dale. Go slow and really drag the ess out. Go ahead, give it a try, just pretend you're a snake.

She looked at me intently, creases etching between her eyes.

—Withh-dale. With-sdale. With-ssdale. With-ssdale.

—Great! Keep practicing that for a few minutes.

While I continued saying my name over and over she went to a metal file cabinet and started looking through folders. She bent at the waist to look in a lower drawer and her hair slid away to reveal her skirt stretched tight. I focused on the curves for a moment and then they were gone as she shut the drawer, stood, and came back to the table with a sheet of mimeographed paper. She sat down, flipped her hair back over the chair, and handed me the sheet of paper.

—These are the words I want you to practice saying before our next session.

I examined the word list. Lots of S's.

—Say them for me. Just try to hiss.

—Hiths. Mithh. Kiths. Blithh. P-pp-pith.

I shoved the list of words across the tabletop.

—I'll never thay theethh.

—That's okay Tommy. You're just getting frustrated. She slid the word list back to me and said: I'll let you go a couple of minutes early.

I folded the paper twice and put it in my coat pocket.

—You are making great progress. I actually heard some ess's today. Before you know it you'll be hissing like a snake. Keep practicing, Tommy, and it will get better. I promise. See you next week.

I shut the door quickly and took off down the hall. As I went passed Bostick's office I could hear muffled sobs. I paused, putting my ear against the door trying to make out who'd been getting swats. The end of recess bell rang and then I heard a chair scrape the floor and I scooted off down the hall. When I got to the stairs I hopped onto the banister and slid, leaping off at the landing, my feet slapping the hard oak. Then on to the next banister, floor after floor, feeling free.

During afternoon recess I went to the swings where Stacey Tompkins and her friends played. Stacey was the smartest girl in our fifth grade class, the only one, boy or girl, who could challenge me at math. I'd watched her on the swings before, with her head thrown back and curly black tresses flying, seen her panties revealed when the swing peaked and her skirt flipped back into her lap. She reminded me of Christina from my old neighborhood. Christina and I used to play Truth or Dare and she was a dare girl all the way. One time in her garage I'd dared her to take her panties off, and she had. I wondered whether Stacey was a dare girl.

She and Ingrid Johansen sat side by side in the swings but they weren't swinging. They were looking at a piece of paper, each holding an edge, and giggling.

—God, it's a love letter, Ingrid said. Who's it from?

—Billy.

They giggled some more as I came up quietly from behind and reached between them and grabbed for the piece of paper, catching the upper edge as their swings swayed apart and the note ripped into three sections, leaving each of us holding a piece. They tumbled out of the swings shrieking. Stacey ran at me.

—Give me that.

I backed away and held the shard of paper up high as she jumped and tried to grab it.

—Tommy, give it to me.

—Make me, I said and skipped away.

She kicked sand at me.

—Oh, just keep it.

She turned sharply, looked back over her shoulder, and stuck her tongue out at me.

—And go back to where you came from, Pisspail.

—You'll be sorry you did this, Ingrid said as they walked away.

When school let out I went to the corner grocery store near where I lived and bought a bottle of Coke and shoplifted a frozen turkey pot pie. I always bought something because I figured then that they wouldn't suspect me of stealing. Crossing the street from the store, I walked through the vacant lot that had been freshly graded to build new houses. I pulled up a section of black PVC pipe that was used to enclose the electrical cables coming up out of the reddish dirt. I cut across the vacant lot and went through the woods to the cedar deadfall that I'd found a few days before. I gathered up the driest branches I could find and stacked them for a fire. I held my lighter at the base of the PVC pipe until it melted and started burning, then I put it under the branches. The branches caught fire and the gray smoke and steam mixed with the oily black smoke from the PVC pipe.

It began to rain, and with all the maple trees bare of leaves the scattered groupings of fir and cedar provided minimal cover. I decided to build a lean-to by the fire. I dragged a couple of long branches over, kicked off the branchlets, and then propped the bare branches against the downed cedar trunk so they were a few feet apart. Then I gathered Douglas fir boughs and laid them over the bare branches so they made a thick roof. I crawled underneath and leaned my back against the cedar and listened to rain spitting into the fire. I felt a sudden longing for my old neighborhood and my best friends, the Olson brothers, who'd lived across the street from me. They had a huge oak tree in their backyard and I'd been helping them build a tree-fort when we'd moved.

We only moved seven blocks north, from 85th to 92nd. But also two miles east, going from numbers—18th, 19th, and 20th— to names, Densmore, Ashworth, and Woodlawn. Far enough away that I had to go to a new school. Far enough away that I wouldn't see my friends any more, wouldn't get to help them finish building that fort. We'd moved a couple of weeks after Christmas so I'd transferred to Thoreau in mid-year and hadn't made any friends in the few weeks I'd been going there. I'd messed up with Stacey; that was for sure. I didn't think I'd be playing truth or dare with her the way I had with Christina.

I added more wood on the fire and started the pot pie cooking, the aluminum blacking up quick with soot. I opened the bottle of Coke and took a drink. Moving hadn't made sense to me. "We need to start fresh, live in a different house," my mom said after she married my new stepfather. So we moved to a duplex across the street from the junior high school where I'd go if we stayed in the neighborhood long enough. I'd gone to six schools already and wasn't even done with fifth grade. My mom was a bank teller; we moved but she didn't have to change jobs the way I had to change schools. This step-dad drove a cement truck. I hadn't had him long enough to know whether I liked him any better than my previous stepfather. He'd worked for a fencing company and built chain link and I didn't miss him one bit. I didn't know where my father was or what he did.

The pot pie was boiling so I took it off the fire and let it cool down before eating it with the fork on my Swiss army knife. The rain had softened to a sprinkle and it was starting to get dark so I put out the fire and headed for home.

At our last house I could look out my bedroom window to a backyard with a huge weeping willow that looked like an upended dirty mop. My bedroom in the duplex had a view of the parking lot. My mom's Galaxy 500 was parked between a rusted '55 Chevy with its right front wheel sitting on a cinder block and a metallic blue Mustang convertible. I was looking out the window when my stepfather drove up and parked his flatbed pick up. He opened the door and dumped his ashtray so the butts made a pile just inside the painted white line. And I had to keep my room so clean that he couldn't wipe dust on a white hankie. He shut his door and walked around to the front of the duplex.

I went and sat on the bed and looked at the bookshelf for something to read. I had the *Encyclopedia Britannica* set A-Z, a *New World Almanac*, President Kennedy's *Profiles in Courage*, biographies of Lou Gherig, Jim Thorpe, Knute Rockne, and the two Babes, Didrikson and Ruth. I didn't really feel like reading so I went through my box of records, The Beatles *Revolver*, Rolling Stones *12 x 5* and *Between the Buttons*, *The Animals*, *The Doors*, and a bunch of 45s until I found The Standell's *Dirty Water*. I put the single on the turntable of my hi-fi with the built-in plastic speakers. The record started to wobble, so I centered it and then dropped the needle onto the vinyl. I picked up my guitar and sat down cross-legged in front of the speakers and started trying to play along to the record. The guitar was a Christmas present, and after playing it for two months I had learned the sliding riff to *Dirty Water* and was trying to figure out *Hello, I Love you*. I hadn't taken any music lessons and didn't know anyone who played, but I enjoyed the challenge of trying to make the sounds I heard on the records and would play until my left hand cramped and the calluses on my fingertips frayed.

There was a knock on my door and then my mother came in. She walked over to the hi-fi and turned it down. I kept playing the riff for *Dirty Water*. She'd changed from the calf-length navy blue dress she'd worn into work at the Washington Mutual Savings Bank and was wearing hip-hugging lime green slacks and the yellow wool sweater I'd seen soaking in the sink for a couple of days. She used to have long straight black hair, but after she married my new stepfather she cut it and dyed it blonde so that she looked like Doris Day.

—Stop playing, she said and sat on the bed, I want to talk to you.

—If you didn't want me to play it you shouldn't have given it to me.

—Don't get smart with me, Tommy.

I played the riff one more time, until I saw her biting her lip, and then stopped.

—I got a telephone call at work this afternoon from your vice-principal.

—Bothtick?

—Yes. He said you didn't go back to class after recess.

I picked a few notes of *Dirty Water*, then said:

—I wathn't feeling well tho I came home early.

—He said you've been disruptive in class and getting in fights.

I looked down and fiddled with the guitar strings.

—I know it's been an adjustment for you, but I want you to try a little bit harder. Can you do that for me?

I shrugged. We sat there a moment not speaking.

—Maybe you should unpack the rest of your stuff, she said and nodded towards the closet.

I looked over at the two boxes, one full of comic books, baseball cards, and my Dodgers, Giants, and Angels pennants. The other box had a basketball, a football, baseballs, cleats, and mitts.

—Come on, she said, I'll help you put your pennants up on the wall.

Saturday morning I went across the street to the junior high and shot baskets by myself in the schoolyard. I made up a game to keep from getting bored that pitted UCLA vs. Houston. I'd shoot and pretend to alternate shots by each team, the score careening back and forth as I chased rebounds, launched off-balance jump shots, and drove in for lay-ups. I made sure UCLA always won, even if it meant missing a few easy lay-ups when it was Houston's shot. I was practicing left-handed reverse lay-ups when I heard someone bouncing a basketball toward the court, the metallic ping echoing against the concrete walls. It was Billy Haliburton dribbling a red, white, and blue ABA ball. He headed for my basket even though there were three others. I curled the ball around behind my back, cut underneath the basket, and flicked in another left-handed lay-up. Billy crossed the top of the key and with perfect Pistol Pete form shot a jumper that thumped off the wood backboard and caromed through the net-less rim.

—One-on-one? he asked.

—Yeah.

—To ten by one's, have to win by two.

—Make it, take it?

—Sure, but we use my ball, he said and whipped a quick pass towards my gut so I had to drop my ball to catch it. You start.

I went back behind the key and watched him take up a lazy stance at the free-throw line. I drove straight at him, faked right and then cut left and went up for the lay-up I'd been practicing. The ball came crashing back into my face as he blocked it from behind.

—You'll have to come up with something better than that, Wisdale.

I took the ball out from the top of the key, went straight at him again, but this time pulled back for a fade-away jump shot. His hand went up and the ball grazed off his fingertip. We raced for the rebound. I beat him to it and got off a shot that rolled around the rim and then dropped. I took it back and then drove hard left and tried a running jumper that clanged off the rim. I snagged the rebound and put it right back up, but too hard. Billy rebounded, took it back and drove straight at me. I planted, expecting him to pull up for the shot, but he lowered his shoulder into my chest and drove around me for an easy lay-up.

—Thatth charging, I said.

—Bull, you weren't set. One-all.

I crouched down and spread my arms out, ready whichever way he went. He faked right, left, right, got me leaning and then drove into me before going up for a jumper. His elbow caught me on the side of the head.

—Two-one.

—Watch the elbow, will you?

—Watch your face.

He drove slowly to the right side, I stayed with him and he turned and backed towards the basket, then banked a hook in off the backboard. Again he caught the side of my head with his elbow.

—Three-one.

I grabbed the ball and flung it at him.

—Check.

He laughed and then stood there dribbling with a slight smirk.

—You know Stacey, he said.

71

—Yeah.

—Well stay away from her.

—What?

Then he was driving to the right and I lurched over to try to steal the ball and he shoved my hand away. I swiped for the ball again, missed, and then backpedaled as he cut left. I thrust my arms up to block his shot and felt his elbow slam into my jaw and nose. I crouched, the blood streaming through my fingertips.

—Got the message yet?

I melted crayons on the steam radiator next to my desk. Only partially listening as Miss Jenkins droned on about the Whitman Massacre near Walla Walla in 1847. I peeled the wrapper from a violet Crayola and pushed the tip into the grayish cast-iron between the semi-hardened puddles of green and yellow. Stirring up a psychedelic swirl, I breathed in a whiff of hot wax. I added red and orange, blue and brown, pretending I was one of those Parisian's whose paintings we'd seen on our field trip to the Seattle Art Museum. My left shoulder pressed against the radiator, getting toasty while a turquoise crayon oozed a border around my tapestry.

—Wisdale, get away from the radiator.

—He's melting crayons, Stacey said.

—For Christ's sake, Miss Jenkins said, and waddled her way over to my desk. Give me that, she said and jerked the half-melted crayon from my hand.

Okay, Wisdale, Bostick said, drop your pants and grab your ankles.

I bent over and braced for the pain as he made a couple of practice swings.

—You've got four coming to you this time.

Whoosh, thwack!

Down I went, gritting my teeth to keep from crying out.

—Get up and grab the arms of the chair.

I pushed off my knees and stood up with my jeans and shorts tangled around my ankles and grabbed the chair. He knelt down, his face so close to mine I could see the burst capillaries on his nose and cheeks.

—That one make you cry, boy?

—No.

He laughed and resumed his position behind me.

—Try this one.

Whoosh, thwack!

I fell into the chair, squeezed my eyes shut, and willed myself not to cry. Bracing against the chair had only increased the resistance, and the paddle bit into my butt that much more. It was how I imagined being shot with buckshot felt; each place where the paddle holes hit had a sting of its own. He waited, letting the sting rise. My butt cheeks were throbbing, getting hotter, stinging like a sunburned back someone had slapped. I looked around for something else to focus on and saw that the initials AP had been scratched into the seat of the chair.

Whoosh, thwack!

He must have swung with an uppercut, the home run swing, because it lifted me off the floor.

Whoosh, thwack!

As much as I fought not to, I let out a groan. I leaned against the chair, gritting my teeth and squeezing my eyes as hard as I could. No way was I going to give him the satisfaction of seeing me cry.

—Pull your pants up and sit down.

My butt was on fire. I kept my back to him as I stood up so he wouldn't see how bad I was hurting. I bent down and grabbed my jeans with both hands and stood and yanked all in one smooth motion. I zipped and snapped, took a deep breath and exhaled slowly so that he wouldn't hear it. I turned and sat in the chair. I wish I could say I didn't give him satisfaction, wish I could say I didn't wince when I sat down.

—Do you know what I do when a boy gets twelve swats in one year? I put his name on the paddle. Is that what you want, Wisdale, your name on this paddle?

—No.

— You've got ten. Two more swats and I'll have to put your name on here.

He held up the paddle and pointed at it. The paddle was an inch thick, mahogany with a tight grain. The hitting surface was about six inches wide, a foot long, with a handle long enough that he could grip it with both hands and swing it like a baseball bat. He pointed to something written on the paddle with black ink.

—See that, that's Andy Plaskow. He pointed at some other ink. That's Mike Beardsley. Two of the biggest troublemakers this school has ever seen. You want to end up like them? JDs on their way to prison? That's where those boys are going to end up. You can bet on that. I've been vice-principal here for ten years. I've used this paddle a lot. Given hundreds of swats. And in all that time, there have been only two kids who've gotten their name on it. He slammed the paddle on the desk so hard it made me jump in the chair, come down onto my stinging rear.

—Don't you be the third, Wisdale. Now get out of here.

I leapt from the chair and headed for the door, jeans sand-papering my butt cheeks with each step.

Over the next couple of weeks I worked hard to stay out of trouble. I even backed down from several fights with Billy, enduring the humiliation of being called chicken and yellow belly. But there was only so much of that I could take before I hauled off and smacked him and we were busted for fighting. That's when Bostick added my name to the paddle with Plaskow's and Beardsley's. I wonder what Bostick thought after he put my name on his paddle. I wonder if he thought that would be it, no more swats for me after that. If he did think that, he was wrong. When word got out that I had my name on the paddle it gave me a new reputation. After months of teasing and fighting and struggling to make new friends a corner seemed to have been turned by my new notoriety and reputation. In terms of finally feeling like I belonged, getting my name on the paddle was the best thing that ever happened to me. Kids that previously had shunned me suddenly wanted to hear all about Bostick's paddle, but more importantly they wanted to hear about my exploits. I became a hero of sorts, the bad ass in the school, and I started making friends for the first time. My speech impediments even got better. I don't know if it was because of the work that I did with Miss Edwards or if it was a result of my new reputation. Of course Billy and I were still fighting. We tended to fight after school, when Bostick couldn't get to us. I still got my ass kicked just about every week. It was almost as if Billy's life wasn't on track if he wasn't kicking my ass. I was learning to fight better, could even get a few licks in, but he was bigger and stronger and the best strategy was just to give in after making a fight of it. It seemed as if every time one of my school pranks raised my stock, getting beat up by Billy would lower it, and as I came to realize that I would never kick his ass, I became more focused on eclipsing him with a grand act that would make everyone take notice, even him.

One day I was in Bartell Drugs checking out the new *Spider Man* and *Fantastic Four* comic books and at the other end of the magazine rack a couple of junior high kids were looking at car magazines and I overheard them talking about stink bombs.

—You need a ballpoint pen, one of the kids said, you know the kind that has the clicker on top. You take the pen apart and pull out the ink thing and fill the pen full of sulfur.

—Sulfur? the other kid said. Where do you get sulfur?

—Buy a chemistry set or steal it from science lab. Anyway, you fill the pen full of sulfur, okay? Then you take a safety match—

—The wood ones?

—Yeah. And you put it under the spring. That's all there is to it. Push the clicker and off it goes.

—I don't get it.

—When you push the clicker the spring compresses and scrapes the match. The match lights and the sulfur starts burning.

—And stinking.

—Cool, huh?

—So what do you do with them?

—We could drop them under the bleachers during school assembly.

A woman pushed a shopping cart passed me and the kids ducked back to their magazines and start talking about cars.

So the stink bomb caper was not an original idea of mine. We didn't have school assemblies at the elementary school, but I thought setting them off in the bathrooms would be cool. That was my original idea. I nicked a jar of sulfur from a chemistry set in the hobby store and started experimenting with different pens and matches until I found a combination that lit the match reliably. It surprised me how little sulfur it took to get that rotten egg smell. And the slow burn before the smoke started fizzing out of the pen was good too, making it easier for me to get away before any one noticed.

I started cautiously, lobbing one stink bomb into the girl's bathroom during afternoon recess. I was already back out on the playground when the fire alarm started ringing. The teachers came out of the building and gathered us into groups on the playground. After about ten minutes we were marched back into the building in single file lines based on grade starting with the kindergarten class. Bostick was waiting at the door and plucked me from the line. I could smell the reek of the sulfur as we started up the stairs to his office. He was sure I did it but couldn't prove it. He told me that if he caught me at it, I'd be expelled. But I was feeling invincible, and he was practically challenging me to do it again, so I decided to go for a more impressive display.

That first stink bomb hadn't smoked very much and I realized that I had packed the sulfur in too tight. So with the next batch of stink bombs I used less sulfur, giving it more room to burn fully. I decided to double up too, get both bathrooms with two stink bombs each. So during lunch hour a week after the first attack I was lurking around the first floor hallway waiting for the last of the stragglers to finish their lunches and head out to the playground. The boy's bathroom was empty, but a girl had just gone into the girl's bathroom, so I ducked into the recessed doorway of the boy's. After a couple of minutes the girl came out and headed down the hallway. I was just waiting for her to go out the door when Billy came in and strolled down the hall toward me. He walked around the corner, saw me and stopped:

—Hey, Wussdale, what are you doing?

—Shhh!

Then he saw the pens in my hands.

—Those stinkbombs? Man, I thought you were the one who did it. How do they work?

I peeked around the corner of the doorway, looked both ways. The hallway was empty. I turned back to Billy.

—Just click and they burn.

—Give me some, I'll do it with you.

—You crazy.

—Let me do it with you or I'll turn you in.

I looked at him and he was smirking.

—Okay, I said and handed him two pens. I held one up with my thumb poised over the clicker. Push down quick. That lights the match. You do this bathroom, I'll take the other. Just push the door open. Click and throw. Click and throw. Then down the hall and out to the playground. Got it?

—Yep. Let's do it.

I peeked around the corner again. Mr. Hansen came out of his classroom but went the other way to the stairs. Then he was gone and the hallway was empty.

—Go, I said.

I ran across the hallway, pushed the door open and tossed in the stinkbombs. I turned and Billy was already running. I sprinted after him, laughing, at least until Bostick jumped out from behind the corner by the stairwell. We hit the brakes then, sliding on the polished linoleum floor, until we stopped in front of him.

—Now here's a dynamic duo I never thought I'd see, he said and grabbed us by the collars. He spun us around and shoved us towards the bathrooms. Get your butts in there and put those stink bombs out.

As he bumped us down the hall we sniffed the first whiffs of sulfur. He pushed Billy toward the door of the girls and me toward the boys.

—Now get in there, he said. Find them and put them out in the sink.

I pushed through the door, and the bitter sulfur flooded over me, a sour yellow cloud that stung my nostrils and eyes. I started coughing and gagging. I ran to the sink and turned on the tap full bore, splashed water on my face and then scrambled on the floor for the stink bombs. One lay against the wall by the garbage can. I grabbed it and tossed it into the sink. It hissed, releasing a final yellow puff of sulfur steam. The other stink bomb continued spewing from inside a stall. I pushed the stall door inwards and then jerked back gagging as the smoke swirled about my face. I bent over coughing, then went back into the stall. The pen was down beside the toilet bowl. I picked it up, felt the burn, and dropped it into the toilet. I lurched over to the sink and thrust my hand into the cold water. The bathroom was still fogged with acrid smoke. The stink bombs had stopped smoking, but there was nowhere for the smoke to go. I opened the bathroom door and went out into the hall. Bostick was waiting.

—Nothing doing, he said. Get back in there. You made the stink, you live with it.

He pushed me back inside and shut the door. Some of the smoke had escaped out the door, but not very much and the rest was drifting up to the ceiling. I sat down on the floor next to the door and tried to breath as shallow as possible. The sulfur fumes still stunk, but it was bearable now, like the aftermath of a fireworks show. I started worrying about what Bostick would do. Probably expel us. Then I thought about facing my mom and step-dad, that was going to be a lot worse than anything Bostick would do. I imagined Billy crouched down in the other bathroom and wondered what he was thinking and if he regretted joining me.

Bostick didn't expel us. He thought that was too easy, wanted to teach us a lesson instead. He made us stay after school for what he called latrine duty, which consisted of Billy and me scrubbing the bathrooms with toothbrushes. We returned to the boy's bathroom with a janitor's mop bucket, but no mop. We had sponges for wiping and toothbrushes for scrubbing. Bostick played cheerleader.

—Come on, Wisdale, get in there. You're ignoring the piss stains.

Billy, scrubbing away in next the urinal, started laughing:

—Yeah, Pisspail, don't miss any of those piss stains.

—Shut up, Haliburton, Bostick said. You've got piss to scrub, too, so don't make me rub your nose in it.

I sawed the toothbrush back and forth in the yellowed grout between the tiles at the edge of the porcelain. My face was close enough to the pee trough that I could read the Pfister, USA label etched into the chrome drain fixture, and the lingering sulfur stench was supplanted by the odor of stale urine and the mock-mint of the hockey puck shaped disinfectant lozenge. A fly zoomed between us. Our toothbrushes scratched at the grout and the tiles. Bostick leaned against the far wall with his arms crossed.

—Future JDs, that's what you boys are. Straighten out now or I'll be reading about you in the papers for boosting cars or knocking off liquor stores. Won't surprise me a bit when you end up in jail.

We spent an hour on our hands scrubbing while Bostick lectured us; then he drove us home in his brand new olive green Chevy Impala. We sat in the front seat beside him. He had clear plastic seat covers. He didn't lecture anymore, just let the fear of parental wrath build. He turned on the radio and a Johnny Cash song was playing. Billy and I looked at each other and smirked. It started to rain, and he turned on the windshield wipers and they squeegied water off the glass, pushed it from side to side like waves working a beach as the tide turned. Our breath fogged the window. He rotated a knob on the console and the fan whooshed. He cranked Johnny Cash up a few notches, then reached up and used the back of his hand to wipe away the dew on the inside of the windshield. He could see out but we couldn't.

Bostick dropped me off first, after telling my mom what I'd done. She closed the door behind him and looked at me sadly, then jerked her thumb toward my room and launched the silent treatment she reserved for those moments of deep disappointment. Later, when my stepfather got home from work, he treated me to twenty-five lashes from his narrow black belt. His belt made Bostick's mahogany paddle feel like Nerf.

Billy lived a couple of blocks up and over from me. He told me to look for the jungle. His house was easy to find because it was the only house on the street completely obscured by the landscaping. Out-of-control vegetation is more like it. You'd think no one lived there. The three-foot-tall grass had gone to seed, blackberries and holly wrestled with cotoneaster and laurel. A monkey-puzzle tree grew right next to the house, its trunk a feast for ivy. A dirt path bordered with dandelion, plantain, chickweed, and buttercup led from the sidewalk to the front porch. A ripped and bent screen door lay off to one side of the porch next to a lawn chair with shredded webbing. The paint on the front door was chipped down to the wood.

A little orange-headed girl wearing dirty pink shorts and no shirt answered my knock and yelled for Billy. She ran off and I went inside. The living room was strewn with toys, clothes, and newspapers. It stank; a combination of wet dog fur and something cloying, reminiscent of the time we'd gone away for the weekend and had forgotten to flush the toilet. Billy came into the living room.

—Come on, let's go to my room.

We started towards the hall.

—Billy, a man yelled. Get me another beer.

—That's my Dad. Come on, you might as well meet him.

He grabbed a beer from the refrigerator in the kitchen and then we went into the family room. His dad was lying on the couch watching some western on TV. The images flicked back and forth between the cavalry on horseback and the Indians shooting at them from the rocks.

—Give me that.

Billy extended the can of Rainier toward his dad, who grabbed the can.

—Now get out of here.

I backed quickly out of the room and into the hallway. Billy followed, holding the side of his face. We went down the hall to his room. When we got inside I was surprised to see a bunk bed. Model airplanes hung on strings from the ceiling above the upper bunk: a P-51 Mustang, Spitfire, and a Fokker tri-plane. On the wall beside the lower bunk were posters of football players. There was Dick Butkus crushing a quarterback and Ben Davidson flattening a running back. Billy took off his jean jacket and threw it on top of the other clothes piled on the floor in front of the closet.

—How'd you get that jacket broken in so good?

—That old thing? It was my brother's, I got it when he outgrew it.

A small desk was against the wall under the window. Stacks of comic books covered the desk. I went over and started flipping through the comics: *Hulk, Thor, Iron Man,* and the *X-Men.*

—Those are my brother's.

—You share the room with him?

—Yeah, he goes to the junior high over by where you live.

—Which bunk is yours?

He plopped down on the lower bunk.

—This one.

—You play football?

—Linebacker on the peewee team.

—I played running back on a sweet-pea team last year. I didn't play this year because we moved.

—You should turnout for our team. We could use you; you're the fastest runner in the school, faster than any of the sixth graders.

—That's because you were chasing me.

He laughed and faked a left-right-left punch combination.

—Does your dad hit you like that a lot? I asked.

—Sheesh, that's nothing.

He looked at me as if he was deciding something.

—You want to see what else he does?

I nodded. He got up from the bunk and unbuttoned his jeans and dropped them to the floor. A black bruise almost completely covered his left thigh.

—He uses a galvanized pipe. Holds me down and hits me with it.

—Shit. Does it still hurt?

—Yeah.

He pulled up his jeans.

—Want to see my baseball cards?

—Sure.

He got down on his hands and knees and reached under the bunk bed and pulled out a shoebox. He slid a rubber band from around the box and removed the lid. The box bulged with cards. He handed me a Mickey Mantle rookie card.

—This is my best one. I traded a Sandy Koufax for it.

I looked through his collection. He had complete sets for all my favorite teams. I checked out the Giants. He had both the Willies, Mays and McCovey. He had Juan Marichel, the guy Rosburg had clubbed with the bat.

—You fight pretty good now, he said. A lot better than when you first moved here.

—I had to get better, the way you were kicking my ass all the time.

—Maybe we should quit fighting each other and go after Bostick from now on. Make him pay for putting us on latrine duty.

—I'm with you, I said and put the cards down. What do you want to do to him?

We hunkered down behind the trunk of Bostick's Impala, watching the janitor throwing bags of trash into the galvanized steel dumpster. He threw in about twenty bags and a bunch of cardboard boxes. Finally he pulled the freight door down, and Billy and I got busy draping Bostick's car with toilet paper, layering it on as if we were turning it into a giant papiermache piñata. We covered the car with six rolls of toilet paper and then took cans of shaving cream and started spraying it over the toilet paper. As the foam evaporated and melted down, the toilet paper became glued to the car. When we were done the only things missing were the tin cans and the Just Married sign.

—Let's get out of here, I said.

—Just a minute, Billy said, there's one more thing I want to do.

He pulled a potato out of his jacket pocket and crouched down by the tail pipe and started squeezing the potato into the encrusted metal. He glanced up at me, grinned with sheer pleasure, and then pounded the palm of his hand against the potato until it was crammed in tight. We ran off laughing, two young hyenas that had just pulled the lion's tail and got away.

Oxygen

The place I've picked is off Burrows Island, along Rosario Strait. It's not the ocean, but I'm sure he'd understand. He used to pass by there on his way from Fisherman's Terminal in Seattle to La Push, Neah Bay, Alaska.

—There's a lighthouse there, I say to the skipper of the island ferry, a barge shuttling around the San Juan Islands.

—I know the place, he says.

He's only a few years older than me, blond and bearded like a Viking. I'd expected someone older, someone who'd devoted a life to the sea, someone who would understand.

—Would it be possible for you to stop there, offshore, so I can—

—I get the idea.

—He was a fisherman, I say. My grandfather.

His eyes linger on the urn clutched to my abdomen.

—I'll pay.

—No, forget it, he says. I'm heading passed there anyway. You'll have to make the full trip though, out to Lopez and back. Three, four hours, depends on how long it takes to unload.

That would be just fine, thanks.

II

We were miles out, my grandfather and me, several miles beyond the horizon seen from the beach. We were in his domain, riding the heaving slate of the Pacific Ocean. Sonar revealed a school of fish. We drifted, oozed up and down the combers rolling beneath the hull. I was thirteen, scared, and out fishing with him for the first time. I stayed out of his way and watched his sure and easy movements while he dropped the poles, baited the hooks, fed out the line. Soon the bells on the end of the poles were ringing. The winch ground, reeling the line in, salmon flopping every few hooks. He lifted them off without slowing the winch, clubbed their heads, threw them into the cleaning tray. When all the lines were in we'd caught twenty fish. He gutted them with quick flicks of knife and gloved fingers, then stuffed them with ice down in the hold. When he was done he held up a small fish.

—Sea-going trout, he said. We're supposed to throw them back. But we'll have this one for lunch. He winked, waved towards the wheelhouse, Come on.

We went up the stairs into the wheelhouse, a tight curve of burnished teak. The spoked wheel was surrounded by the bank of electronic equipment he commanded: radar, sonar, loran, engine controls, UHF and VHF radios. Still holding the trout by the gills, he pushed a couple of buttons on a console and the engine started, then rose in pitch, vibrated the floorboards as he manipulated the throttle.

—We need the generator going to run the stove, he said. Come on, let's fix some lunch.

Down the stairs, down again on the vertical ladder into the galley below decks where the clatter of the churning pistons made thought difficult. Two bunks angled in a V to the bow, duffel bags on one, sleeping bag on the other. A four-burner stove and a fold-down table beside the cupboards. He took a can of chili from the cupboard, a can opener from a drawer, and handed them to me.

—You do the chili, he said, I'll do the fish.

He unclipped a pot and a pan from the hull above the stove and slapped the trout into the pan. He opened the door to the engine compartment and the churning pistons became deafening. He flipped a switch, closed the door, but not before the reek of diesel had filtered into the galley.

We cooked side by side. The heave of the hull seemed more pronounced in the dark confines of the galley, and with the roll and sway of the boat it was hard to stand in place at the stove. He lit a cigarette, began a wracking series of coughs.

—This damned sore throat!

He continued smoking, the bitter tobacco aroma mingling with the smell of chili, diesel fumes, seared fish flesh. We sat on the edge of the bunks and ate at the fold-down table. He poured himself a shot of vodka, downed it, poured another. I became queasy, found it difficult to breath because of the pervasive odor of diesel.

—I think I'll eat on deck, I said. I need fresh air.

—Getting seasick?

—It's the fumes.

I pulled myself up the ladder with one hand and balanced my plate against the sway of the boat with the other. As soon as my head was above deck I sucked in a deep briny breath and clambered the rest of the way up the ladder. I sat on the hold, breathing deep until the nausea dissipated. The deck pitched with the flex of the ocean as the boat slid down a wall of water, then up, cresting for an instant and giving me a panorama of the limitless horizon, the spread and sweep of the ocean.

He joined me on deck.

—Better?

—Yeah.

—Sea air cures all ails, he said.

He inhaled deeply on his cigarette, only to give in to the wracking cough again. I ate while he smoked.

Can't beat fishing, he said after a moment. It's a hard life, sure, but it's free, unconstrained. I've been doing it since the end of the war. Thirty years. If I couldn't fish I don't know what I'd do. Best years of my life have been spent on this boat. You should come with me more often, spend the summer fishing with me. You're old enough now.

—I'd like that, I said.

—Okay, next summer you can be my deck hand.

A crescendo of coughs took control of him, bent him double, then he arched and hawked phlegm skyward, over the deck and into the rising water.

III

From where I sit in the chair beside my grandfather I can watch as my grandmother makes the drinks; only a splash of vodka in the water. She hands them to us, leaves the room. I see his frown as he tastes, then drinks half before handing me the glass, eyes pleading. I fill it to the brim with vodka, watch the wave of pleasure flush his face as he swallows. My grandmother returns. He and I share a conspiratorial smile, and for a flickering moment I see him as he was: a big John Wayne of a man whose eyes were always aglow with mischief. Then he's gone again, sunk back inside his emaciated Fred Astaire body. I wonder where a hundred pounds goes.

We don't talk, rarely do when I visit; it's enough that I'm there. So few come by anymore, and I can't blame them really. I've had to call the paramedics before. Now the compressor sits beside him just in case. The pale green canister and hoses looking like a floor vacuum—which is what his lungs are when he can't breath, a vacuum. No, the oxygen tanks, the valves and switches, the black rubber mask, do not encourage visitors.

He reaches up with a pale bony hand and removes the ascot. My grandmother makes clucking noises and leaves the room. He takes the pack of cigarettes and lighter from his shirt pocket. I stare transfixed at the hole in his throat, the in-puckered reminder of the sore throat that wouldn't go away; like a cauterized bullet hole it doesn't bleed, yet never heals. He holds the filterless cigarette to the throat-hole, flicks flame from the lighter and inhales. Eyes closed, he exhales, smoke spewing from the throat-hole like a surfacing whale geysering water. He inhales again and I think this is perhaps why he has so few visitors. It's hard to take. He'd survived throat cancer, made it three years beyond the seven years the doctors said was evidence of a cure, only to keep doing this: smoking the most tar-laden filterless cigarettes through his throat.

The cough starts deep, twisting his frail body, and something wet hits my cheek before he gets the handkerchief to the throat-hole. He continues coughing as I feel for it on my cheek, grab it between thumb and forefinger, study it, the wet brown fleck of dried tobacco leaf. The cough subsides, but he's wheezing now, stabbing out the cigarette. As the plume of smoke rises from the ashtray he reaches towards the only electronic equipment he commands anymore, and flicks the oxygen pump to life. The black mask goes to his throat as the compressor whirs and throbs like an engine—like a muffled diesel engine: all that's lacking is the fumes. And I know that the sound is killing him ten times faster than the mutant cells devouring his lungs. I can tell by his eyes that he sees the realization in mine. He fumbles on the coffee table for the speaker. Lowering the mask, he places the speaker against his throat where his larynx used to be. He presses the button with his thumb, begins moving his lips, but the metallic vibrato voice is not human.

—Do you know why I drove the oil truck in the winter?

—To keep the money coming in.

He shakes his head.

—No, the speaker says as the oxygen pump keeps its pistoning cadence. I could have done anything.

The black mask goes over the throat-hole.

—It was the smell. The diesel smell reminded me of the boat, of fishing.

He closes his eyes, rests his head against the chair's cushion. The speaker lies dormant in his lap. Ten years of not being able to fish are deeply etched into his face, in the recessed eyes, the taut skin over cheekbones.

The mask lowers. The gasping growl of esophageal speech:

—You. Would. Have. Made. A. Good. Deck. Hand.

IV

The wake had been his idea: "I don't want a bunch of people standing around a goddamned hole in the ground crying over me. And no goddamned funeral either. Have a wake, an Irish wake. Drink and laugh and remember the good times for, Christ's sake."

So we do. In the house he shared with my grandmother for forty years, the house with the wall of photographs of family, friends, his boats, and he and I in oilskins, tangible proof of that one time I went fishing with him.

A crush of people arrive, the friends his life has touched, the immediate family, other branches of the family tree, the root stalk. I am the designated greeter, lucid, emotionless, dispensing hugs, words of condolence, then encouragement: This is a wake, I say over and over, celebrate his life, what he gave us.

The rush of arrival ends, the small house is packed. I think he would be pleased as the mood turns festive. But I need fresh air, revitalization. As I head for the backyard I hear several people saying: "Remember the time . . ." and pass the bathroom, glimpse the tub and remember the time it was filled with clams: "We have to keep them alive until we can steam them," he'd said.

I go down the stairs to the back door, and there, next to the garage door, sits the compressor, with its green canisters, with its hoses, with its switches, with its black rubber mask. I loosen my tie and step into the backyard. I take deep steaming breaths, sit at the picnic table on the patio, where seed husks litter the flagstones and the sparrows are busy at the feeder he built for them, twittering, beating wings, heaving seeds to and fro, splashing themselves in the tinfoil pan that is their bathtub. I hear the chicks squawking in the nest under the eaves. The parents appear content to frolic in the feeder atop the fence.

I study the fence he built, painted barn red, then surrealistically painted with sea images: an octopus, a mermaid, a tidal wave, a leaping salmon, a whale spewing water through its air hole. Fishnets hung with glass floats drape the top of the fence. Reminders all, but nothing I can taste, nothing I can smell.

I get up from the table, walk around the corner of the house. Over the gate the roses on the arbor are coming into bloom: pink, orange, red; but not the fragrance I crave. The small circle in the lawn is freshly edged. I get down on my knees, grasp the gray spokes of the cap with both hands, apply force, spin it free. I remove the cap from the heating oil tank, bend closer, my nose in the end of the pipe, and let the diesel fumes flood over my face, into my mouth, into my nostrils.

V

We edge around the northwest end of Burrows Island, stay inside of where the tankers and tugs buck the strait. The lighthouse beckons, a stark white sentinel against the verdant backdrop of fir, hemlock, cedar. Gulls glide in criss-cross patterns as we enter the cove where the abandoned Coast Guard station lingers. I sit on the engine compartment, the urn in my lap, the clattering throb of the engine in my ears. The salty air mingles with the diesel fumes, tastes like bilge water. I realize that my life has no such web of sensuality to miss. There is nothing I love doing so much that not being able to do it would kill me. That is the essential emptiness of my life.

—The tide's running out fast now, the skipper yells to me. So I won't be able to hold her here too long.

The pitch of the pistons rises as he throttles against the pull of the tide. My grandfather's boat made the same sound when he shifted into reverse as we docked, our one fishing trip together ended. The diesel fumes rise in thick plumes from the engine compartment, heat waves shimmering like a hologram. Holding the urn out over the warm updrafts, I raise the lid an inch or so and let the acrid dreg-gases of diesel waft over the ashes. I close the lid and move over to the side of the ferry, lean against the hull's damp planks, upend the urn. The ashes plunge under water en masse. I watch until bubbles float to the surface, burst in a spray of oxygen as the water turns a soupy gray.

Enter Wheelchair Man

Randy grips the outer wheel, elbows flared out, wrists angled back, finger-less gloves tightening on the chrome. The front wheels and the footrest bump the curb, and he pulls back and leans into the wheelie, hanging momentarily on the fulcrum of the tire's friction. Panic hits as his balance shifts and he feels himself going over backward. He jerks hard on the chrome, biceps straining, and snaps his head and shoulders forward. The footrest clanks into the concrete curb. Maryanne, already on the sidewalk and knowing better than to offer help, tries to hide her laughter behind her hand.

He pulls backward hard with his gloved hands and prepares to make another run. A quick spin forward of the chrome and he rolls towards the curb, wheelies up and over onto the sidewalk. He spins the wheels free and starts rolling fast.

—Oh, sure! *Now* you're in a hurry, she calls after him.

—The line is getting long, he says when she catches up with him. I hope we don't miss the beginning of the show.

—You could have thought of that when you were dawdling around the apartment.

—And you said there'd be no "I told you so's."

—Sor*ry*, she says as he speeds forward and joins the throng of teenagers waiting in line to enter the arena.

Randy had picked Metallica because he'd heard it would be the hottest concert of the summer. He hadn't been to a show since his accident, and Maryanne worried about how he'd feel in the huge crowd. Now that they are here, he feels excited because everyone is lit, energized, driven along by songs blaring from the PA system and the pot and booze circulating through the crowd. Black jeans and black shirts are everywhere; many of the shirts with Metallica in white letters on the front or back. Someone shouts out "Metallica rules" and the crowd erupts in cheers. The guy next to Randy hands him a bottle of Jagermeister.

—Hey, wheelchair-dude, take a hit of this.

Randy takes a drink, passes the bottle back to the guy and they exchange high-fives. Randy looks over his shoulder and sees Maryanne talking to a red-haired girl in jeans and purple halter-top. Maryanne is wearing her short black leather skirt and a black short-sleeved turtleneck. He notices the other guys checking her out as she makes her way through the crowd to him.

—Sorry for taking off like that, he says as she rests her hand on his shoulder.

—I knew you wouldn't go far, she says and holds up the tickets, I've got these.

The wheelchair seating was a small area at the front of the street-level balcony section. Ramps led down to the stage and the arena floor. Three other guys in wheelchairs are already there when Randy and Maryanne arrive. An usher sets up a folding chair for Maryanne.

—Great view, the guy next to Randy says.

—Yeah, but I wish I was down there, Randy says and leans forward to look down at the crowd shoving against the line of yellow-shirted security staff.

—Not me. Those mosh pits are crazy.

A joint passes down the line of wheelchairs. Randy takes a hit and hands it to Maryanne. The joint circulates, the cloying scent mingling with the smell of sweat and booze. A thick haze of smoke drifts like fog across the balcony. The PA system blares thrash-metal without the bass frequencies so that it's useless to talk without yelling. Randy settles into his high.

Being at the concert reminded Randy of the crowds at the football games. He hadn't been a jock, didn't hang out with that crowd. He simply loved football. And he ran the ball better than anyone else, so good they had to take him on their team, if not in their clique. Running with the football was the only time he felt free, both in control and out of control at the same time. He loved that moment of anticipation while they all waited for the snap. The quarterback calling the count, the line tensed, the wingback in motion, the defensive back tracking him on the other side of the line, the linebackers stunting, jab-stepping forward, all except the middle linebacker, crouching, hands on knees, keying on Randy. And then the snap, the line surge, the quarterback faking to the fullback, turning and pitching it to Randy who caught the ball and loped off on the hip of the pulling guard while his shadow, the middle linebacker, sprinted for the corner, all over the play. Randy flicked his eyes over the meshing lines looking for openings as his lead blockers took on the end and the linebackers. Then part of the line caved, the defensive tackle sprawling over the back of the lineman who'd cut him down, and Randy saw all he needed to see. He pushed hard on the back of the blocker he was following and cross-stepped and cut. The sprawled lineman reached a padded forearm and Randy felt the hand grabbing his thigh, the fingers clasping and he instinctively spun free of the grasp, cut quickly right, away from another lineman. Catching a glimpse on the periphery of the middle linebacker, who'd overrun the play, struggling to change directions, Randy cut hard back to the left and was momentarily free in the secondary. The cornerback and the free safety converged on him, lowered their helmets together, and there was nowhere to go but straight into them. He ducked down, legs churning, and drove his helmet into theirs. All three helmets making contact simultaneously in a crackle of plastic as the defenders were knocked backward on their butts and Randy's helmet split in half and fell away.

When he remembered that last game now, he didn't think about the three touchdowns he'd scored. The 228 yards rushing. His 77-yard punt return late in the fourth quarter that sealed the win. The celebration in the locker room. What he thought about was hitting those guys so hard that it busted his helmet in half and knocked them both out. The crowd gasped, went momentarily silent, then erupted into cheers as he lurched forward and kept running. At that moment he felt stronger than he had in his entire life, strong enough to lift the stadium over head.

He remembered that, and how later, he and Maryanne, his best friend and girl friend since ninth grade, had driven out in his Mustang to Pine Lake for a different kind of celebration. A celebration that haunted him now as much as playing football did, as much as that last concert did. They'd parked, got in the back seat, and shucked their clothes. Sometimes, if he closed his eyes, it was as if he could still feel the sensations as he'd cupped her rear and lifted her slowly, feeling that exquisite drag until he was barely still inside, and then swirled her and dropped her down so they were merged, panting.

—God, I'm so wet, she said into his ear.

—I know, I can feel you dripping on my balls.

She giggled and said: There goes the upholstery.

Later, as they'd lain cuddled across the Mustang's back seat, they had a silly conversation that he'd replayed over and over in his mind because it seemed as if it was the last time they'd had a conversation that wasn't related to his injury. He'd been telling her about a chess book he'd found in the library. The book described a world championship match between two Russian grandmasters: Karpov and Kasparov.

—Imagine a paint-off, he said.

—You mean like two impressionists trying to outdo each other?

—They'd have to be painters with different styles.

—So, she said, a cubist and an impressionist.

—That's it!

—Picasso versus Van Gogh. They're rivals and the paint's flying.

—Exactly.

—So what happened?

—Well, he said, the match was supposed to be first one to win six games wins the title. Karpov wins four of the first nine games and it seems like Kasparov is done for. But he doesn't give up, even though it seems hopeless, and he manages to draw the next eighteen games. Then he loses again. Now he's five games down. He has to win six games without losing another. He's got nothing to lose and goes all out and wins a game. They play another dozen or so draws, and then Kasporov wins two games in a row. He's only down three-five and he's got Karpov on the run. Then, get this, the match is cancelled, the results nullified!

—You're kidding?

—No. Some political mumbo-jumbo, he said. Just when Kasparov thought he had it won they took it away from him.

They were silent for awhile, Maryanne snuggled closer and lightly brushed her hand across Randy's chest.

—My niece does finger paintings, Maryanne said. She's amazing. Painting stuff that looks like Van Gogh. All bright orangey and yellowy and chartreusy. Her trees and flowers are all smeary and thick with paint. But it's not sloppy kid's painting. It's ordered, impressionist, just like Van Gogh. I'm pretty sure she's never seen any pictures of his paintings. And even if she had, to be able to do that at her age is amazing.

—How old is she?

—She's only five!

—Wow.

—She gave me some paintings for my room. I'll show them to you when you take me home.

The lights go down and the arena erupts into cheers as the band takes the stage. Randy puts his fingers to his mouth and lets out a piercing whistle as the first power chords saturate the arena. The lights come up. Blues, reds, yellows, and spotlights arching back and forth across several thousand screaming kids.

The band rips through three songs non-stop and the mosh pit is pogo-ing and slam banging. The first crowd surfers are pushed overhead, supported by outstretched hands. Randy becomes mesmerized by one girl who surfs effortlessly, zigzagging from one end of the mosh pit to the other. He's never seen anyone so relaxed, so trusting, just laid out, head back, arms and legs splayed.

He'd only crowd surfed once and it had not been effortless. It took him several attempts just to get up. The hands jabbing him sharply in the back made him jump forward and slip back down. The fear mounted, and then his feet were grabbed and he was heaved up atop the pit, again and again. But he never relaxed the way this girl did. He felt a sudden wave of self-pity as the harsh memory of his face plant in the mosh pit came crashing back. If only he could have relaxed, let the hands support him. But he couldn't let go, couldn't trust. Every time he felt himself starting to slip through the hands holding him up, every time he felt himself on the verge of falling, he began to thrash, trying to right himself. Finally, after a bunch of abortive attempts, the mosh pit gave up on him. They quit trying to hold him up as he thrashed his arms and legs about, and as everyone cleared out of the way, he'd smashed into the concrete floor of the stadium.

The separated shoulder and the broken nose caused the pain, but it was the thoracic/dorsal vertebras, the crushed ones, that left him paralyzed from the nipples down, that put him in the Providence Rehabilitation Center. Randy shared a room with Rob, who was a victim of his own drunken driving, and who talked endlessly about the time he'd been bitten in the balls by a brown recluse spider. Rob's balls had swollen up to the size of grapefruits, and now that he was paralyzed those swollen balls had come to symbolize the potency he no longer possessed. It was Rob who told Randy how lucky he was that his bladder was stuck closed. "Otherwise you'd be living with one of these," Rob said and nodded at a plastic bag full of orangish-yellow pee.

Thinking about Rob reminds Randy that he's on the clock, and he checks his watch. Close enough. He tells Maryanne that he's going to the bathroom. She starts to rise to go with him but he motions her back and rolls toward the balcony exit.

Back in Providence they told him he would lose all of his friends. And he had. All except Maryanne. He'd thought that she would leave him once she knew he was going to be in a wheelchair for the rest of his life. Eighteen is no age to hitch your wagon to a wheelchair. He frequently tested her, kept pushing her away, seeing how much she would take, but despite all his surliness, she never faltered, took all he dished out and stood by him.

Once, in the throes of a dark self-pitying mood, he'd screamed at her: Why don't you get it over with, just leave me? And she'd yelled back: Like I'm going to desert you. And he'd said: Why not, the others did? And she'd said: Don't you know me any better than that? After what I went through with my father? Sometimes her devotion made him happy, but most of the time he wished she'd given up on him and got on with her life. Most of all, he hated depending on her.

He rolls from the balcony and heads down the ramp to the main floor, passing two guys running up the ramp fresh from the pit, eyes glazed, faces bright red, jerseys drenched in sweat.

—That was off-the-hook, one says.

—Let's grab Gresch and get back down there, the other says.

He reaches the bottom of the ramp and rolls into the bathroom, into the wheelchair stall. Takes the catheter and the tube of KY jelly out of his pack, drains his bladder. No pleasure in the pissing, just the quelling of the fear that he'd forget to release the pressure he can't feel. His bladder, like his spasmy legs, continuing to function, without his control, without his sensing them. He could watch his legs twitch, knew they had a life of their own. To his stuck-shut bladder he had no access, no recourse but to drain it every four hours like the changing of the watch. Four bells, insert catheter. Eight bells. Twelve.

He rolls over to the entrance to the main floor, pauses, soaks in the thump of the drums and the bass synchronizing with the crunch of the palm-muted power chords. He looks into the seething mass of kids jumping up and down and singing along with the vocals, and with a hard shove of the chrome outer wheel, rolls himself into the fray.

At first he stays on the edge of the crowd, but he is quickly sucked in deeper as more kids push their way into the mosh pit. Then someone has a hold of the handles on his chair and is guiding him deeper into the crowd.

—I'll get you in there, wheelchair-dude, the guy yells at him, and Randy realizes it is the guy that gave him the hit of Jagermeister.

Before he knows it, he is once again right in the middle of his favorite place in the world, the nerve center of the mosh pit. He can't see the band anymore, just the kids slamming back and forth on all sides. Then the opening riff of "Enter Sandman" whips the mosh pit into a frenzy of waving arms and banging heads. *Da de duh dow dun dow. Da de duh dow dun dow. Da de duh dow dun dow. Da de duh dow dun dow.* As the riff thunders on, starts evolving aggressively, Randy realizes he is in with the crazies, but the crowd is packed in so tight there is no way for him to escape. The guy on his right is furiously air-guitaring the riff, keeping the beat by head-banging, his hair flying in all directions. The crowd surges forward and he rolls with it, then the surge reverses and the air-guitarist is knocked across Randy's wheelchair and into his lap. He shoves the guy off him as a crowd surfer comes their way, gliding over the up reached hands. Then guys are going up all around him, jack-in-the-boxes popping up as the band launches into the verse. As the song pile drives on, Randy realizes the guys around him are scheming.

—Let's put him up, one guy says.

—No way, dude, we'll never get him up, it's too heavy.

The first guy says something he can't hear to a couple of others, and then Randy hears:

—Are you game?

—Let's do it.

—Yeah, let's do it.

Then they are around him.

—We're putting you up wheelchair-dude.

—No fucking way! Randy yells. I don't want to go up.

—You're going up.

Four of them are crouching around him, searching for handholds on his chair. He tries to shove them away.

—Don't fight it, dude, you're going up.

He feels them starting to lift, and his heart is beating so wildly he thinks his chest is going to burst.

—Ready? On three. One. Two. Three!

They heave and up he goes. Randy catches a glimpse of the band as the guitar solo starts, Kirk Hammett doing deep dives on his whammy bar. Then Randy can feel the guys' arms trembling and he tilts over to the right, starts to go down. Other hands reach in to help and he's tilted over to the left, more hands and he bobs back and forth. He feels as if he is going to tip over, that he's going to crash into the cement floor again, and he starts shouting to be let down, but his shouts are drowned out by the roar of the crowd. He feels a hard push and he goes up higher, and then he is falling backwards. He looks around, frantic, sees hands reaching up to catch him, and then he's on his back, suddenly stabilized, surfing. He can hear the guys below getting ready:

—He's coming over here.

—Hold him up.

—Send him this way.

All around hands are reaching up to support him and he just lets go of the panic, throws his arms out and his head back the way the girl did, trusting the sea of hands to keep him aloft. Suddenly he's tilted up and spun around and he sees the crowd going berserk, hands upthrust, faces alight. He looks up at the balcony and sees Maryanne with her hands to her mouth, but the other wheelchair guys are cheering, their arms stretched so high in the air Randy thinks they must be standing. And then the whole crowd is singing as one, Randy included, as the band chugs into the chorus.

Spun around again, Randy sees the band powering into the outro, locked into the groove, laying down that crushing riff. The hands holding him aloft are rocking him from side to side and up and down in sync with the music, in sync with the screaming crowd. Randy sees James Hetfield close in on the microphone, still picking out the riff as the rest of the band lays off. Hetfield cycles through twice more, and then he stretches his arm out, pointing into the crowd, pointing right at Randy as the last note sustains, feeds back.

The screams of the crowd lift off, engulfing him, until he thinks his ear drums will burst, and Randy feels himself riding higher and higher on the sea of hands.

Their ground floor apartment had a concrete patio that ramped up to the road, but that was not its best feature. The lawn edged the patio and sprawled out twenty feet to the creek rumored to run with spawning salmon. The lawn was smooth and firm enough that Randy could get over to the edge of the bank and cast into the shallow gurgling pool created by the waterfall spilling over a dead-fallen big-leaf maple. The far side of the creek bank was clogged with salmonberry, bracken ferns, cedar and hemlock seedlings, and full-grown alders and maples. The near side bank was kept trimmed so the residents had access. Randy had never caught, or even seen, a salmon in the six months they'd lived in the apartment, but that didn't stop him from trying.

The sun blazed an orange-yellow patch across the lawn. Maryanne sunbathed on a blanket. She seemed smeary in the heat waves, a scene from her niece's finger paintings. She propped herself up on her elbows, smiled when she saw him looking at her, and crooked her finger at him. He reeled in the line and secured the hook in the cork grip. He lay the fishing pole down, released his brake, and maneuvered across the lawn.

—Isn't the sun great? she said and flipped her head back so that her face was turned up full into the sun. I just love it when it's hot like this.

—A nice change from the rain, he said.

—I'm not getting burned, am I? she asked and surveyed her exposed skin.

He reached over and pressed his fingers against her shoulder. The white blotches quickly flushed pink. He said: Maybe a little.

—I'm getting hungry, she said and patted her stomach with splayed fingers. I'm in the mood for steak and potatoes.

—Black Angus?

—Yeah, she said and flashed a big smile. Help me up.

He reached out and grasped her upstretched hand, pulled against the resistance as she crossed her ankles, tucked her feet under her rear, and sprang up.

Go

Mike Carter, fueled by anger and self-disgust, pushed up the dusty trail connecting the seventeenth green to the eighteenth tee. The path crested in a thick stand of hemlock and cedar and fed onto the tight mown turf. Carter took a deep breath and expelled it as a heavy sigh. He stood his clubs and looked down the fairway, hands on hips. Garth Gibbons and Tommy Oh, his main competition for the Boeing company championship, were only forty yards down the fairway and still walking toward their balls. He could see the next group ahead just on the other side of the lake. Looked like a long wait. That's fine, he thought. He needed to get himself together. Needed to stop thinking about Susan's job interview down in San Francisco and get his mind back on the golf.

His concentration had been wavering all afternoon, moving back and forth from the golf to his conversation with Susan that morning. They'd argued—and not for the first time—about her out-of-town job interview. Argued the entire 45-minute drive to the airport. They'd stood, not speaking, at gate D7 waiting for the departure of her flight to San Francisco. Finally, as the first class passengers began boarding, Carter tried to make amends.

—You'll do great, he said, you always do.

—Yep, she said.

—Have you ever *not* gotten a job you went after?

—Look, Mike, I just need to know you're up for this.

—I am, I am.

—Because there's no point in me going all out for this job if you're not willing to move.

On his drive back to their north Seattle home, Carter detoured through the Green Lake neighborhood where he grew up. He parked on the street in front of his childhood home, surprised to see it still painted the same light blue. His parents didn't live there anymore, hadn't lived there for many years, but the neighborhood still tugged at him. Within walking distance were the places he played when he was a kid: The Woodland Park Zoo, the ball fields at Lower Woodlands, the pitch and putt golf course, and Green Lake itself. Susan was from San Francisco; nothing held her in this area except him. He wondered if she would visit her childhood haunts on her trip, if she'd end up parked across from her childhood home. He knew it wasn't just the great job opportunity that drew her to San Francisco; with Alex finally off to Washington State University to study veterinary science, she felt free to think about going back home. Being in the neighborhood where he'd grown up made him understand her desire. But where would that put him? He'd have to leave his hometown so she could return to hers. How do two people work that out? What was a fair result if they both couldn't live in their hometown?

—Jesus Christ! I hate that climb, Tompkins said as he walked onto the tee. He laid his clubs down, his breathing ragged. He took off his hat and extending his arm out, wiped his forehead with his shirtsleeve. He put his hat back on and then pulled out the scorecard. You made five, right? he asked.

—Do you have to fucking remind me? Carter said.

Tompkins laughed. I had six, he said. Shit! This is no time for us to choke.

—You might be choking, Carter said, but I'm not.

—Yeah, right.

Carter wasn't choking. His three-putt on sixteen was the result of trying to ram in the long birdie putt. He wouldn't make medalist by lagging safe. The six-foot comebacker he'd hit a bit too hard and it dipped in before spinning out of the hole. He hadn't choked on seventeen either. Hit that four-iron great, straight at the pin. It just got held up in the gust. Only landed a yard short and rolled back down the bank into the water. Maybe three was the club. Didn't want to end up in the rear bunker, not with the pin on the front edge. That bunker shot back toward the lake was nasty. And with the green baked hard the three-iron never would have held. Another couple of feet and he'd have been tapping in for birdie. Bad break, that's all.

Tompkins sat on the end of his bag while Carter stared down the fairway. Tommy Oh—a summer intern—was headed to Arizona State on a golf scholarship in the fall. Gibbons had once had a great game; not that he couldn't still play on occasion. One of Carter's great satisfactions in life had come five years ago when he broke the course record that Gibbons had held for fifteen years. Gibbons' fabled 63. A record nobody had come close to. And when Carter finally broke it, he was pretty sure that all the rumors insinuating that Gibbons hadn't *really* shot that 63 in the wind and rain were true. Carter was glad that Gibbons was playing with Tommy Oh; the young kid would keep Gibbons honest. If he and Susan ended up moving to San

Francisco this might be Carter's one and only shot to win the championship. All he wanted was the chance to win the thing fair and square.

Carter was a second-generation Boeing employee. His father had started out as a wing installer building the first 747. Working as an engineer on the big jets was the only job Carter had ever wanted. He knew if they left Seattle they'd never come back. So if they went to San Francisco, what would he do? He couldn't imagine. He also couldn't imagine staying in Seattle and letting Susan go to San Francisco by herself, and she'd made it clear she was prepared to do that.

Tommy Oh had found his ball in the rough bordering the trees and was experimenting with restricted backswings. Okay, Carter thought, let's see how the young hotshot handles this one. Gibbons was still searching the reeds for his ball. Carter was pleased that someone else was having problems. Despite playing the last two holes in three over par, he was still one under for the round and four under for the 36-hole qualifier. He'd had a two-shot lead over Tompkins after yesterday's first round. Tompkins faded fast; three over on the front nine. He's out of it now after triple-bogeying seventeen. Both Tommy Oh and Gibbons had been three shots back at the start of the round. He supposed somebody else could have got hot out there. Even so, four or five under would get him medalist honors and number one seed for match play. Carter wanted that number one seeding. Partly it was ego talk. For most of the last twenty years he'd had the lowest handicap. On paper he'd always been one of the best golfers in the company but he had never proved it in the championship. Not that he'd tried and failed; he'd just never played in the event. He didn't play in the golf leagues and he rarely played in any of the company-wide events. The first few years back in Seattle after getting his engineering degree at Utah State he hadn't played because his job had kept him off the course in the summer. Later, though, it was deliberate avoidance. The handicap events were dominated by the sandbaggers; and Carter wouldn't play with them. And if he didn't play the handicap events, he couldn't play in the championship. This year was different; given the direction Susan's career was heading he'd decided to play while he still had the chance.

Up the fairway, Gibbons had found his ball. He was bent over contemplating his lie, then peered across the fairway at Tommy Oh, who was still experimenting with ways to extricate himself from the woods. Carter could see the wheels turning. Go ahead, use the hand mashie, you bastard. Gibbons glanced back at the tee and saw Carter watching him. Got you! Gibbons picked up the ball and went through the process of taking a legal drop. He laid down his driver and then faced the hole as he dropped the ball from his outstretched hand. When he was done, he looked back at the tee and flipped Carter the bird. He got the clasped forearm in return.

—I wouldn't piss him off too much, if I were you, Tompkins said. That UAL plane coming down the line is having interior fit-up problems.

Carter managed a Payloads engineering team that designed stow bins for all 767 aircraft models. Tompkins was the manufacturing engineer in charge of planning the lavatory and the galley installations. When those units changed, Carter's stowbin designs had to change too. Gibbons was the lead quality assurance inspector for stowbin final assembly, and he made the determination whether a part, assembly, or installation was tagged for rejection. Carter and Gibbons got along okay, although they locked horns every time certain installations came down the line. The mechanics had low tolerance for chronic design problems. When Gibbon's workload increased he made sure Carter's did too.

—Like that's a surprise, Carter said. I hate it when you shift that galley back into the 43 section.

—That's the customer, not me. Besides, you could always redesign it.

—Don't even get me started on that one.

The green ahead was clear and Gibbons and Tommy Oh prepared to hit their shots. Carter took out his driver. Gibbons played a weak iron shot that appeared to come up short of the green. Carter tried to push negative thoughts out of the way. Five times before he'd stood on the eighteenth tee needing just a par to tie Gibbons' course record, birdies to break it. He'd hit into the bunker, the woods, the lake—he'd blown it every way imaginable. Choked. Choked big time. Even when he finally broke the record he'd choked on this hole. A par would have given him sixty-one and beaten the record by two. He'd gone from rough to rough and made bogey.

Just then Tommy Oh hit an amazing shot from the edge of the trees. Somehow he'd managed, with a restricted backswing, to hit a low sweeping hook. Carter watched the ball run up the hill onto the green, an awesome shot.

—You're up, Tompkins said.

Teeing his ball, Carter made another run at negative thoughts. He couldn't seem to get comfortably aligned. Felt like he was aimed too far right, out into the lake. So he fidgeted around, and then he felt like he was aiming too far left, into the trees. It took him about ten seconds over the ball to fidget himself into a pretzel, no longer knowing how to set up to hit the shot, let alone take the club back. He stepped away, went behind the ball and tried to visualize the shot. Come on, Michael, quit choking! Dig deep!

And then he had the picture in his mind. Not pretty, but a shot he knew he could hit. The image became stronger and he held it, the ball starting towards the trees and then hanging there, riding the tree line, before fading back over the bunkers and catching the left side of the fairway. Carter stepped up to the ball and aimed over the bunkers. He swung quickly while the image was still vivid, tightened up his left hand on the way down so the clubface wouldn't square up. The ball screamed away. Carter held his follow through and watched as the ball got closer to the trees.

—Turn! Turn! He shouted and leaned hard to the right.

The ball started slowly fading away from the trees as it ran out of momentum. It landed in the rough and stayed there.

—At least it's dry, Tompkins said.

When the UAL plane hit final assembly Carter spent the whole day in the factory sketching out design changes and signing off the mechanics' workarounds. Gibbons was tagging everything that didn't fit perfect. Carter was pissed. He suspected that Gibbons was trying to rile him on the eve of their semi-final match. The mechanics were flipping shit, too, taunting him with hands clenched to their throats, followed by gagging sounds. On the other hand, he knew that particular stowbin design was botched. Had been from the beginning, and it was particularly annoying because United had ordered 38 airplanes with that configuration. Every ninth plane down the line and Carter and Gibbons and the mechanics were redesigning it by rejection tag.

When the last of the tags were signed off, Carter headed back to his office determined to confront his boss about a redesign. He felt he no longer had anything to lose. Susan's interview in San Francisco had gone great, she was just waiting for the offer letter. That gave him a fall back.

Peavey was in his office answering his email when Carter walked in and sat down. Peavey swiveled around, saw Carter's demeanor, and said: Let me guess, UAL.

—This is ridiculous, Carter said. Everyone knows it's a bullshit design and they keep expecting me to fix it. And when I don't it makes me look like an idiot. Why won't you just let me fix the damn thing once and for all?

—You know what I like about you, Carter? You've got passion. That tells me I made the right decision.

—What? By not approving the design change?

—The design will change all right. Just not on the scale you're thinking, Peavey said with a slight smirk. United wants to add a crew rest.

—Oh, Christ, that means a complete interior redesign.

—It gets better, Peavey said. Manufacturing will only sign-off on it if we use a design/build team.

—Great. Design by committee.

—It gets better, Peavey said. They want co-location.

—Meaning?

—We're going to move a design team out to the factory, make you all sit together.

Carter was stunned. A half-assed suggestion of his had come home to roost.

—The good news, Peavey said, is that engineering still has clout. We—*you*, Carter—are going to manage the team.

—When is this happening?

—A couple of weeks, Peavey said. It's not announced yet. I'm just giving you a heads up.

When Carter got home, Susan wasn't there yet, so he fixed himself a double scotch rocks and plopped down on the couch and put his feet up on the ottoman. Their routine since Alex had gone away to college was that whoever got home first would start something for dinner. He was more in the mood to de-combust than cook. He'd gone to Peavey half expecting to quit or get fired. Instead he was getting his dream job. Just when he thought things would simplify, that his job would blow-up, leaving them free to move to San Francisco for Susan's career, he was being promoted. Now what? She could pursue her career—although not with the company she'd interviewed with—just as well in Seattle as in San Francisco. He had no such options. Boeing designed airplanes in two places: at the Renton and Everett factories on the outskirts of Seattle. Narrow bodies to the south, wide bodies to the north. That was it. Well, maybe she wouldn't get an offer and the problem would go away. She'd come home from the interview excited but cautious. She didn't want to get her hopes up until she had the offer in writing. One thing he knew, he wasn't telling her about his promotion. The last thing he wanted was Susan thinking he was putting up a roadblock to her career.

Carter and Gibbons had a four o'clock tee time and it was still in the upper 80's with no breeze when they were clear to hit off. Carter flipped a tee for honors and it went to Gibbons.

—Luck, Carter said and extended his hand for Gibbons to shake.

—I'm gonna humiliate you, Gibbons said as he walked over to tee his ball.

The first hole went downhill, dropping about thirty yards, with the green sitting in a depression at the bottom of the hill. Not a long hole, about 400 yards from the back tee, but the only flat lie in the fairway was a stretch 75 yards or so in front of the green. The rest of the fairway sloped either left or right and ran steeply to the rough on either side. Anything going hot would bounce off the slope into the trees. There were two plays: one safe, one risky. Hit a long iron to keep it in the fairway, playing the next shot with a 7-iron from the light rough on whichever side of the fairway the ball rolled. Or go bombs away with the driver and try to reach the flat spot in front of the green.

Gibbons stung a perfect one-iron down the left center that faded back into the crown and then rolled slowly over to the left edge of the fairway. He walked over to Carter and said: Hu-mil-i-ate.

Carter pulled out his driver and made several full throttle practice swings. He teed his ball and glanced over at Gibbons, who was smiling as if he'd already won the hole. I'll show you humiliation, Carter thought. He settled into his stance and made a slow, wide backswing, keeping the clubhead out in front of his body as he turned. He parked the club on plane and in the slot at the top, shifted his left knee towards the target and snapped his hips around as hard and fast as he could. He felt the clubhead lagging behind and then the crack at impact and the club was extending and chasing after the ball and wrapping around behind him and slapping into his shoulder blades. The ball took off low, a line drive to straight away center. Shit! He crushed that one. The ball hit on the down slope, took a couple of big bounces, and rolled onto the flat where it stopped about 60 yards short of the green. Carter picked up his tee, looked at Gibbons and said: Hu-mil-i-ate that.

The match see-sawed, changing momentum on made or missed putts. Carter took an early one up lead, and then Gibbons moved to one up. They were back to all-square when they reached the par three eleventh and had to wait awhile for the group in front to finish. Gibbons paced, while Carter sat in the shade at the back of the tee. Mind free to wander, Carter started thinking about his promotion and wondered what Gibbons knew. So he went fishing.

—By the way, Carter said, I didn't appreciate all the rejection tags yesterday.

Gibbons laughed. You think that was all on your account?

—Hey, I've spent whole days in the factory signing off your tags, the majority of which required minimal changes. I kept your line moving. I didn't have to do that.

Gibbons stopped pacing and said: So when are you going to redesign the fucker and fix the problem?

Carter realized that Gibbons didn't know about the crew rest project, so he said: It's cheaper to stay with the existing design.

—That's bullshit and you know it. I've checked out the microfiche too, you know. I saw your initials. This design flaw has been around for years and we're sick of working around it.

—It's not my call.

—Yeah, right. When are you going to get some balls and buck your weasel of a boss?

They glared at each other, then Carter said: The green's clear. Just hit your goddamned shot.

They both hit lousy 6-irons. Gibbons' pull hooked left of the green. Carter's was hot and low, hit the green hard and jumped over the back into the deep rough. Gibbons hit a great chip to two feet and then tapped in for par while Carter figured out how to play his pitch. He had a decent lie and knew he could get the club on it clean. As he studied the green trying to read how fast the ball would run, he saw Gibbons standing there smirking. Fucking bastard. He was going to hole it just to wipe that smirk off Gibbons' face. Carter settled over the shot, softened his hands and flipped the ball out just over the fringe, where it bounced and started rolling, a little fast at first, then it slowed, curled around toward the hole, hit the flag, and dropped in for a birdie.

—Bastard, Gibbons said.

The match was over at that point and they both knew it. Over the remaining holes Carter played flawless, with a controlled fury. When he rolled in a long birdie putt on 15, it ended the match 4 and 3.

Carter watched as Susan opened the Fed-Ex envelope. Her hands shook as she read the offer letter.

—So? he asked.

—Six figures, she said, plus options.

He whistled. That's nearly double what you're making now.

—Check out the title, she said, pointing to the letter so he could read it too. Vice President of Product Development.

He hugged her, wrapped her tight in his arms, partly to share her joy and partly to hide his conflicted feelings.

—I want this job, she said.

In the championship match Carter played Tommy Oh. When they reached the seventeenth, the long par three over the water, Carter, thanks to a hot putter, and almost in spite of himself, was two-up. He didn't even need to take the hole for the win, a halve would be good enough. As they waited on the tee, Carter wondered what his son, Alex, would think if his parents moved from Seattle to San Francisco. How would he feel not having his childhood home—the only home he'd ever known, at least until he moved into the dorm room—to go back to? Would he still want to visit if visiting meant not going *home*? And what about the stuff in Alex's room? The posters, books, CDs, the closet full of clothes, all the belongings he hadn't taken with him to college. What to do with them? Box them up and ship them to Pullman? Or would Carter and Susan, when house hunting, need to seek a place with a spare room, a room Alex might or might not ever use?

Tommy Oh played his shot safely to the back of the green, but left himself at least a sixty-foot putt down the slope. Not a threat. Carter teed his ball and took his stance. Just what had he been trying to prove by taking these guys on now? Prove to them that he could win? That he was the best? What did that mean anyway? He waggled, swung the club back. Winning wasn't going to change a damn thing. A slight pause at the top as he focused on the back of the ball. He dropped his right shoulder and pulled the club down hard into the ground, just laid the sod over it. The divot was so deep it stayed attached, curled over like a wood shaving. A reddish-brown clump of dirt stuck to the club face. Go, he said weakly, just before the ball plopped into the middle of the pond.

Cleanliness Is Next To Emptiness

Caryn hesitated outside the last of the secure doors leading to Genomic Microchip's cleanroom. She wiped her shoes on the static mat, then swiped her card, listened for the clunk of the latch, and pushed inside. She glanced toward the cleanroom; the other technicians were in the gowning area or already through into the lab. At her locker she speed-dialed the combination, snapped the lock open. Her right calf started to tremble, and she knew she'd overdone her morning exercises, delayed until the last possible minute coming into work, and now she dreaded getting into the suit, mask, and goggles.

She slumped on the bench, still feeling guilty for baiting Josh, for starting an argument while he was half-awake. She knew she shouldn't dump the way she felt on him, knowing he'd never understand, would try to blame himself for the mess she'd made of herself. How could she reveal that she felt lost with him? Not his fault, she knew. How could it be? She didn't know herself which direction to go, just that she felt off-track. Could she redirect Josh's energy toward her instead of against? He seemed a heater with the element burnt out, his fan still churning, blowing its chill air. A loud clanging interrupted her thoughts.

Caryn spun around at the sound, but she only saw a hairnet bobbing above the partition. Then Caryn heard Lucinda:

—Where are the scissors! Who took the damn scissors!

A second hairnet appeared.

—I did, Jacqueline said. We're not using them anymore.

—What? Why not?

—Too many gowns were being cut.

—How am I supposed to get the plastic bag open?

—Use your teeth.

Another clang.

—Cut the hysterics, Lucinda, and just do it. And don't forget to tuck your hood in this time.

Caryn rubbed her knuckles harder into her calf. God, she hated this place.

The suiting-up procedure had nearly forty steps and when she'd first started the job it took a half-hour to get ready to enter the cleanroom. Now, after three years practice, she had the routine down and could get into her gear in five minutes. She'd quickly learned to save time by not wearing makeup or lipstick, which just had to be scrubbed off anyway. And keeping her hair cropped short made it easy to slip on the lint-free head cover. The Personal Hygiene section of the Cleanroom Procedures Manual, what they called the CPM, had laid down the law: "The high degree of cleanliness required necessitates the development of the following habits: bathe frequently; shampoo regularly (making sure to control dandruff); wear clean undergarments and outer garments; do not wear worn out shoes." She always showed up for work scrubbed clean and makeup free but that was still inadequate because, as the CPM pointed out: "By far the dirtiest thing in our cleanroom will be the people who use it. Even the most carefully manicured person generates a shroud of particles from their skin, hair, clothing, and breath." You had to score at least 90% on the 20-question quiz at the end of the CPM before you could work in the cleanroom. She'd been proud those first few weeks to be a 100-percenter, on the fast-track. She caressed her goldfinch pendant. Well, Dad, I still use a microscope, it's just not for biology anymore. She removed the necklace and hung it on a hook in her locker. Before closing the door she rinsed away throat particles with a squeeze-bottle of water.

In the gowning area, next to the bins filled with plastic bags of gowns, booties, gloves, hairnets, masks, and hoods, a sign said: "ATTITUDE toward cleanliness ultimately determines the success or failure of any cleanroom!" She went over to the shoe cleaner and cleaned both of her shoes and then put on the plastic shoe covers. Attitude, she thought, as she sat on the dirty side of the bench, that's what Josh would tell me to work on. She put a bootie on over the shoe cover and swung the booted foot over to the clean side of the bench. Then she booted the other shoe and swung it from clean to dirty. She put on nylon gloves and then used her teeth to rip open the plastic bag containing the gown. She wondered if Jacqueline had considered what germs might be introduced by this new procedure. She put on the gown, careful not to let it touch the floor. The CPM was quite clear: "Personnel with colds, temporary sneezing and coughing, and severe sunburn should not enter the cleanroom until they have recovered." And now we are ripping the bags open with our teeth?

She zipped the gown snug at the neck. If you had a cold you couldn't work. So she didn't shake hands, and she washed her hands after every contact with someone. She carried a small spray can of Lysol in her purse so she could spray things of hers that other people touched, such as her steering wheel, stick shift, and parking brake after taking her car into be serviced. She hadn't had a cold in three years.

She put on the latex gloves, the hairnet, and then the mask. She snugged the cloth over her mouth and nose, knotted the string tight to her nape. Affixed the goggles. She felt as though she always wore a mask, portraying things she didn't feel, while her father's voice echoed, "stiff upper lip, Caryn, stiff upper lip." The successful one her friends from school looked up to. Career. Boyfriend. Adjusted. On her way. How could she talk to them? Confess the truth about her feelings of failure? She couldn't. Not trapped behind her mask. She hated actresses, hated their accomplished mimicry, yet here she was, a player, putting on a show. You can't win any awards, Caryn, if nobody knows you're acting. So ashamed that her life was in this state. So off-track that she didn't know what to do anymore. Outwardly successful, yet, to herself, she reeked of failure. A perfume she couldn't wash off. A shame she couldn't share because she was ashamed to have such shame. Who am I to want more? To want *what*?

She put on the hood and tucked its fringe under the gown's collar and stepped into the stall. A quick flick of the toggle switch on the compressor and the air-shower thrummed to life. She stretched her arms out and up as the air first gushed, then blasted into her like a ham-handed masseuse. "What am I doing!" she shouted into her mask as the shower whooshed away her words, but not her thoughts. Everything unresolved. Nothing resolved. She pirouetted several times, then posed, one hand reverse-cupped overhead, the other descending in slow motion to press the switch down.

The sign on the wall above their microscopes said: "NEVER sneeze, cough, or spit toward your wafers, even within your mask!" So when Lucinda started sneezing, even though most of the sneezes were directed away from the wafers, Caryn knew their batch was shot. Jacqueline, as if she'd been waiting for just such an opportunity, was at their station even before Lucinda had finished her sneezing fit.

—Crispiana! Jacqueline yelled. You're fired.

—Don't you—

—No. You were warned.

Jacqueline turned on Caryn, gloved hand jabbing away.

— O'Connor, go with her. I'm calling security now, so she has five minutes to get her locker cleaned out.

Jacqueline wheeled around and stood with her hands on her hips facing the other technicians.

—What are you all staring at? Get back to it.

At the door to the locker room Caryn and Lucinda hugged through their suits.

—Hurry up, now, Caryn said, security is on its way. I'll call you later, she said as Lucinda crossed through into the locker room.

Through the Plexiglas Caryn watched Lucinda shuck off her hood and suit. Lucinda slumped onto the bench. Her thick black hair tousled, as if she'd been sitting in the back seat of a convertible. Get your stuff together and get out of there, Caryn thought. Too late. Security guards, burly ex-footballers, shoved through the locker room doors. One grabbed Lucinda between the upper arm and the armpit and yanked her from the bench and to her feet. Lucinda sagged in his grasp. The other guard shook open a black plastic garbage sack and started stuffing the contents of Lucinda's locker into the bag. Orange and yellow wind-breaker, black pumps, a couple of magazines, a paperback book, a plastic food container, and a stack of opened envelopes wrapped together with a rubber band. He heaped her belongings into the bag without regard for order or damage caused. The last item out of the locker was Lucinda's purse. He thrust the purse at her but she didn't reach for it. He tucked it into her stomach. Her hands hung limp. He grabbed her wrist, forced her fingers to grasp the strap of the purse. He flicked at the locker door, slamming it shut. Lucinda flinched. The guards half-ushered, half-dragged her out of the locker room.

When her shift ended, Caryn was the first to push out through the glass doors of the factory. She strode across the asphalt parking lot, the hot sun making each step slightly sticky, as if she were walking with sponges attached to the soles of her flats. The muggy air and the searing sun were a relief.

As she walked through the manager's parking lot with its BMWs, Mercedes, and Lincoln SUVs, she wondered how bad Lucinda had needed this job. Caryn felt a sudden stab of hatred for Jacqueline; if she'd known which car Jacqueline drove she might have keyed it. Of course, as Josh frequently pointed out to her when she vented to him after her shift, Jacqueline had pressure too. And didn't the whole company's performance depend on getting those chips out the door? Caryn tried to understand, but couldn't excuse Jacqueline's sadistic streak.

Inside her car, Caryn leaned back against the headrest and breathed deep with her eyes closed. One more day, she'd made it through another day. Now, let's get the hell out of here. She started her car as the others began streaming out of the factory doors. She backed from the stall and quickly sped towards the exit before the shift-change traffic bogged her down. She called Lucinda, but got her voice mail. She figured Lucinda was probably in a bar self-medicating. If Caryn had known where, she would have joined her.

The traffic and the car were heating up. She flicked the air conditioner on and merged into the lane for the freeway on-ramp. Up ahead the light changed and the cars stopped. She was behind a muddy red Jeep. The top was peeled back from the roll bars and scrunched in behind the spare tire and the spare gas can. A long antenna arched from the front of the Jeep to the back. Three orange pennants hung from its tip. The driver wore a canary yellow tank top, and his broad tanned shoulders pushed out on either side of the seat back. Bushy red hair. He reminded her of an older version of a young man she'd seen years ago at Dorothy Lake when she was in the Girl Scouts. A young man she hadn't thought about in years, although for years she'd fantasized about him every day, drifting off into daydreams during class or on the bus home from school, or using his image to submerge into sensual sleep.

Caryn had turned thirteen during the summer she saw her fantasy man. Her Girl Scout troop went hiking and bird watching every weekend. On the trip to Dorothy Lake they'd hiked the three miles from the trailhead and set up camp along the lakeshore. Then they were free to explore or swim. Most of the girls chose to swim. Caryn decided to go off by herself to bird watch.

The trail from the lake headed steeply up through sub-alpine fir, mountain hemlock, and vine maple toward the moraine at the base of a rocky ridge. Caryn hoped to see finches in the scrub alder along the edge of the boulder field. Just before reaching the granite scree she scared up a covey of quail and chased them down the trail. As they ran, the quail's heads moved back and forth like chickens pecking at grain. The quail zigzagged on the trail then dodged left into clumps of salal. Caryn quit chasing and followed the trail out of the woods and onto the avalanche chute with its jumble of moss and lichen stained boulders.

Eek! Eek! Caryn heard the pika's call and looked for it in the rocks. The pika's eek was intermittent and she scanned the boulders with her binoculars until she had it in the lenses. The pika sat up and let out an eek, then ducked under a rock and resurfaced a few feet away. The pika worked its way up the slope of the moraine, eeking every time it stopped. Caryn climbed over the rocks, following the eek of the pika, to the top of the ridge. From the crest she could see down to a small lake surrounded on three sides by the steep scree slides from the ridge. On the fourth side, forest edged the lake, except where a sparsely treed peninsula jutted into the water. She swept her binoculars around the peninsula. She spotted a dark brown tent partially hidden in the hemlocks. Next to the tent was a fire pit ringed with blackened stones. On top of a stump cut flat were a water bottle and a mess kit.

Suddenly the tent flap opened and a young man came out. He had long curly red hair and a bushy beard, he looked like a cross between a Viking and a mountain man. Tall, tan, and muscled, he stretched, arms oozing into flexed poses, then took off his shirt. Next he removed his hiking shorts and his underwear, dropping them in a pile by the tent. She leaned forward, pushing the binoculars tight into her eye sockets, as he ran onto the rock promontory and dove into the lake. He went in shallow and stayed under for at least ten seconds. He surfaced, sputtering like a whale, thirty yards out into the lake. He yelled "whee!" and started treading water. She could hear the splashes and his ragged breathing. He started swimming hard, elbows pistoning, stroking another fifty yards across the lake. Then he dived under, bobbed up, arched with arms out stretched, and floated on his back. He floated like that for a few minutes, staying buoyant with occasional small paddles and kicks, before leisurely swimming back to shore. He climbed out of the water, boosting himself off the rocks with his arms and leaping onto the bank. He stood up naked, his back to her, dripping water. He reached his hands up and smoothed his hair, squeezing the water out so that it streamed down his spine and flexing buttocks. Then he lay down in the sun on top of a flat shelf of granite.

Horns blaring. The stoplight had changed and the Jeep was thirty yards ahead and pulling away. She shifted into first and powered off, accelerated rapidly through the gears, trying to catch the Jeep. She closed the gap as they approached the freeway on ramp. Then the Jeep made a right turn without signaling. She was torn; freeway or follow? She was almost past the point of turning, and then decided to follow, snapping the wheel over and pushing hard on the brake pedal. She fishtailed her way around the corner.

She kept her distance as the Jeep drove toward the shopping mall. The Jeep entered the mall parking lot and headed for the main entrance. A car backed out about five spaces from the closest spot and the Jeep turned in quickly and parked. Parking karma, she thought, now where's mine? She drove by and turned down the next aisle. She looked over and saw the mountain man get out of the Jeep. He was wearing black hiking shorts and hiking boots. His legs were tanned and muscled. He started walking briskly across the parking lot. She frantically searched for a parking spot, going down the end of the aisle and up the next. Nothing. She went down the next aisle and finally found a spot near the end of the row. He was gone, already inside the mall. She sprinted, weaving back and forth between the cars, tacking diagonally toward the entrance.

Once inside, she scanned the people, seeking his red bushy hair and his canary yellow tanktop. He could be anywhere, in any of the shops. She peered into shops as she passed, but didn't see him. She reached an intersection, not sure which way to go. She looked down both directions and couldn't see him walking. She figured he wasn't a window-shopper or lingerer, he'd probably go right to the place where he wanted to buy something. But where? She went over to the informational kiosk and studied the listings of stores. Where would he go? Music stores? Sports shoes? Book stores? Then she saw it: The Walking Store. Just five shops ahead.

He was standing in front of a rack of walking shoes and talking to the salesman. Caryn glided by, not wanting to go in, but not sure what she intended to do now that she had found him. She crossed over to The Body Shop from where she could keep an eye on him. She perused the body bars: oatmeal, peppermint, green tea, chamomile, gingko, lemon, vanilla. She glanced across the way and saw he was sitting down waiting as the salesman approached carrying several shoeboxes. The strong soap aromas stung her nose so she moved away from the body bars. She picked through brushes, loofas, and sponges as the salesman fitted him with shoes. She fended off the sales clerk and glanced over to see the guy walking around the store trying out the shoes. Looking through the shampoos, she found one made from an extract of tea-tree oil, a natural anti-septic for controlling dandruff. She was tempted to try it, and then she noticed him leaving the store wearing the new shoes. His boots were laced together and hung over his shoulder.

She followed about twenty yards behind as he approached the food court. He wove his way through the crowd of tables and then went outside to the courtyard, where there was a farmer's market. Caryn went after him, leaving the air conditioning, the fluorescent lights, and the Muzak of the mall behind.

Outside, the hot muggy air was trapped under the tents, flush with the aroma of bananas and tomatoes. The stalls of fruit and vegetables stretched out for thirty yards on either side of the aisle. People crowded together, checking out the produce, bartering. The mountain man went to the fruit stand. Caryn worked her way closer as he examined apples, nectarines, watermelons. He paused over the cantaloupes, picking up several and studying them. She moved closer, stood right next to him as he sniffed and poked the cantaloupes. She was close enough to see the damp spots on his yellow tank top, close enough to smell his sweat when he raised another cantaloupe to his nose. Oh my God, she thought as he turned toward her with the cantaloupe still against his nose and smiled. He extended the cantaloupe toward her face and she leaned into it, brushing her nose and upper lip against the rough skin where his nose and mustache had been only a moment before.

—What do you think? he asked.

—Not ripe yet, she said.

Her left leg began to shake and she backed away from him, backed into another shopper. He started laughing and she turned away, began making her way through the crowd.

—Funny, he called after her, I thought you were.

Josh surprised her that evening with flowers and a card. Inside the card were tickets to a murder mystery at a local dinner theatre.

—You've been down, he said, and I wanted to do something to cheer you up.

—That's so sweet, she said as she hugged him.

When they got to the theatre the maitre d' seated them at a large center-stage table where they sat by themselves at one end with the rest of the table extending onto the set. The waiter brought an ice bucket and a bottle of Dom Perignon.

—You're outdoing yourself, Josh, Caryn said after the waiter brought an appetizer of fresh salmon.

—Tonight we celebrate the good life, he said and downed the rest of the champagne in his glass. Drink up, Caryn. Eat, drink, and be merry, for tomorrow—we'll have killer hangovers.

It was his corny old joke from their college days and she couldn't help laughing.

—There you go, he said, now you're getting the spirit. No more sad sack from you tonight, he said, and filled her glass with champagne.

The actors and actresses came on stage from the wings and, to Caryn's shock, sat down at the table with her and Josh.

—Oh, my God, she said and looked over at him.

The actress who sat next to her was a mid-40's blonde with enormous cleavage squeezed up and out of her white sequined gown. With her platinum wig and feather boa, she had Mae West covered. She raised her hand above her head and snapped her fingers several times, then called out in a loud voice: Randall, bring another bottle of champagne. These city slicker relatives do appear to be lushes.

As the audience laughed, the actress leaned close to Caryn and said into her ear:

—Just play along, honey, and I'll make sure you have the time of your life.

Next morning, Caryn started her daily workout by stretching her shoulders, back, quads, and hamstrings; then she launched into her upper body routine with the free weights. Three sets of ten, blasting biceps, triceps, forearms, shoulders, and then finishing up with some isolation work on her weak link, her rotator-cuffs. She went straight through the routine with little rest between lifts, enjoyed the burn. With her MP3 player and her book she headed out to the stationery bikes. She started up Yo-Yo-Ma playing Bach's Cello Suites, set the bike's difficulty level to seven and the timer for forty-five minutes, and then she started pedaling. She opened her book, Horgan's *The End of Science*, and started reading. He'd already dispensed with philosophy, physics, and cosmology; now it was her science's turn, biology. The section on evolutionary biology was painful, and she stared blankly at the television monitor mounted on the wall. Biology had been her first love, the career she'd envisioned for herself ever since it had been her favorite subject in sixth grade. When they had to dissect the baby pig, she had been the lead dissector, in her glory. And looking at a drop of pond water under the microscope, well, that hooked her.

She'd graduated with a degree in biology, magna cum laude. How proud her father would have been. She started pedaling faster, pushed the resistance button up a couple of notches and bore down on the pedals. How had she messed up? Where did her life start to go wrong? Sunburns. She got sick of getting sunburned. Or having to hide from the sun, of always running for the shadows. Sick of slathering herself with sunscreen, paying the price if she left any square inch of flesh bare, unprotected. She could mark key events in her life by her sunburns. The dinner-plate-sized water blister on her back at ten, when she had to sleep on her stomach for three days, the acidic pungent aroma and the sting in her skin as her mother wiped vinegar on and around the blister. The tops-of-her-feet-sunburn, the halter-top-strap-sunburn, the singed-forehead-sunburn. And the date she screwed up by falling asleep beside the pool, getting so burned that she was throwing up and had to call the boy to cancel and he had never asked her out again. After awhile it just became easier to avoid the outdoors as much as possible.

She'd taken the job at the medical lab after graduation because she had wanted to do something in bio-med after her father had died of a staph infection. He'd gone in to have a kidney stone removed, except he was also invaded by someone else's impurities. But processing urine, blood, and stool samples had not been the antidote she thought it would be. And it was that proximity to other people's waste and illnesses that drove her to quit the medical lab and seek asylum in the cleanroom. That and a documentary she saw about dust mites, the microscopic herds that grazed on the dust and skin flakes in furniture and carpets. Seeing that microscopic cataclysm of life feasting in her living room freaked her out. She went on a cleaning spree. Vacuuming, scrubbing, sterilizing. And then kept at it. That was one of the things that had attracted her to Josh in the first place; he was into cleanliness as much as she. Now, though, he'd become a fucking fanatic. She used to be one too, and that helped her get the job at the Genomic Microchips. When she interviewed they were impressed with her passion for eradicating dust, didn't even laugh when she'd said, "Dust never sleeps." They also liked that she was an only child, was comfortable working alone, which made her a great candidate for a cleanroom technician, where long hours were spent, often alone, staring into a microscope.

She'd always wanted a brother, or even a sister, but her mother always said, "I did it right the first time, so I don't need to do it again." As if that was supposed to make Caryn feel special. Being an only child had some advantages she supposed, like learning how to keep herself amused. But she also felt it had done irreparable damage to her social skills. Just at a time when she needed to be making small talk, she'd be off in her head somewhere carrying on a dialogue with herself. She'd been doing it so long now that she didn't know how to shut it off. Didn't know how to ask other people the same questions she asked herself.

Her mother was not the kind of person who ever put anything away. When she took a blouse out of the closet she dropped the hanger on the floor. She left cupboard doors open when she got out glasses and plates. Caryn could always tell when her mother had been in the kitchen; it looked like it had been ransacked by detectives seeking evidence. Her father would come home from work and spend the first half-hour rearranging the house. Shutting cabinet and closet doors, pushing in drawers, re-hanging hangers, throwing out newspapers and debris from her mother's coupon clipping, rinsing the dishes and loading the dishwasher. Caryn marveled that her father never complained about these chores. He seemed to accept that her mother would never change and peacefully cleaned up after her.

It always seemed ironic that her neatnik father had died from a staph infection. And she guessed it shouldn't surprise her that she'd be with someone who was also a neatnik. Josh. Now *that* is not ironic. She was beginning to hate his emotional sterility, the emotions neatly compartmentalized, given out in precise doses, and only when asked for or required, never freely, never unexpectedly, never ever spontaneously. Just like her father. The accountant. So good at it that he made it to controller, then CFO, before a speck of gram-positive bacteria did in his neatly controlled existence. At least Josh isn't an accountant. Not that being a statistician for an insurance company was much better. He plotted, and re-plotted, life expectancies based on mundane parameters such as only children of single parent families, or gang-members from east LA, or Korean immigrants operating convenience stores. But did he know the life expectancy of an emotionally sterile couple living together without marrying? Did he know whether they would live longer if they married or if they separated? Did he know which would live longer, fuller lives? Could his statistics tell that?

A week later Caryn was bent over her microscope, checking the integrity of a silicon wafer, when her pager started vibrating. She had her voice mail set up so that only urgent messages caused the pager to vibrate. She immediately started spinning out worst-case scenarios. It's Josh. He's been in a car accident and is in a coma on life support. Or her mother has fallen down the stairs and broken her hip. She checked the pager. She didn't recognize the number. She shut down the scope, left the cleanroom, and went into the gowning area and removed her gear and put it into the receptacle. From the phone in the locker room she called the number. The phone rang a couple of times and then a young woman said:

—Human Resources, this is Mary. How may I help you?

—This is Caryn O'Connor in Fab1. You sent me an urgent page.

—Oh yeah! Didn't you work with Lucinda Crispiana?

—Until she got fired last week.

—Have you heard from her since then?

—No. I've called her several times but all I've gotten is her voice mail.

Caryn glanced toward the cleanroom, apprehensive that Jacqueline would begin wondering where she was.

—Is anything wrong? Caryn asked.

—Her brother called us. The family is worried because they haven't been able to reach her and she didn't return their calls. So her brother called us, wondering if anything had happened. Apparently she hadn't told them about losing her job.

—Oh, Caryn said, wrapping the excess phone cord around her wrist like a rope. I don't know what tell you. I really didn't know her that well.

—I understand.

—She kept to herself.

—Her brother said that you were the only person at work that she ever mentioned. So he wanted me to check with you. Can I give you his number so you can call him if you hear from her?

—Sure.

After the call, Caryn sat down on the bench wondering what might be wrong with Lucinda. She had a dark vision of Lucinda sitting alone in her apartment with the shades drawn and a blanket wrapped around her, or worse, lying in a bathtub with her wrists slit, arms dangling over the edge of the porcelain. She fought those off and instead imagined Lucinda packing up her car and leaving town without a word to anyone.

—O'Connor, what are you doing?

Caryn looked up and Jacqueline stood there scowling with her hands on her hips.

—I had an urgent page that I had to call back.

—Looks like your call's over. So get a move on.

Jacqueline turned and started walking back to the gowning area. Caryn stayed put on the bench.

—The call was about Lucinda. No one has heard from her since you fired her.

Jacqueline walked back over to the bench.

—What does that have to do with you getting back to work, O'Connor? Do you want me to write you up? Don't think I won't do it.

—Don't you have any compassion? Caryn said, incredulous. Do you even care that someone you fired has disappeared?

—That's her problem. Mine is the production schedule.

—What in the hell happened to you? Caryn said. You used to care about your team. I used to *like* you.

They stared at each other for a moment and Caryn watched the uncaring glaze fall across Jacqueline's eyes. She stood up, and as she did, Jacqueline smirked, and that was it.

— I quit, Caryn said.

—Fine then, Jacqueline said, appearing as equally pleased with that result as any other. Finish out your shift and then turn in your two weeks notice.

—No, Caryn said, I mean I quit *now*.

—Be a quitter, then, Jacqueline said and stuck out her hand. Give me your badge.

Caryn unclipped her badge and tossed it to Jacqueline.

—I have to call security, Jacqueline said. But I'm guessing you'll be out of here before they arrive.

—Don't bet against it.

By the time Caryn arrived at her apartment, the giddiness she had felt as she left the factory had dissipated and she was slip-sliding toward the ache of uncertainty. Josh was on his knees, wearing bright yellow rubber gloves up to his elbows and scrubbing the kitchen floor. There were spray bottles of bleach and Lysol on the counter along with sponges and brushes.

—My, aren't we industrious, she said as she took the jug of purified water out of the refrigerator.

—I hate this floor, he said, it's impossible to keep clean.

She drank from the jug while he scrubbed. She considered ways to tell him that she'd quit her job. She thought about his probable responses and decided that she didn't really want to discuss it. She put the water back in the refrigerator, grabbed an orange, and started peeling. The peels piled up on the counter and juice dripped on the floor.

—Whoops, she said.

Josh peered at her from over his shoulder.

—Sorry, she said.

She definitely did not want to talk to him about her job.

—Okay, then, she said. I'll leave you to it. I'm going to check on Lucinda.

He resumed scrubbing, working his way along the edge of molding by the stove.

—How long will you be gone?

—I don't know. Why?

—I'm going for a run after I finish here.

On the drive over to Lucinda's apartment complex Caryn tried calling. The phone just rang and rang. She didn't know who else she could talk to, anyone else who might understand. Certainly not Josh, her friends, or her mother. Didn't need any of those predictable conversations. The last thing she wanted was to get into one of those arguments where she had to defend her decision. Whose life was it anyway? Why couldn't her friends have her best interests in mind? They claimed they did, but everything always revolved around preserving the relationship. Of course it was okay for *them* to change. Why did she always have to be the one that stayed the same? Why did she have to be the stable one? She was sick of playing that role, sick of playing along with everyone else's scripts.

She parked in the visitor parking spot and went to the manager's office to find out which apartment was Lucinda's. The name plate on the manager's desk said Beverly and she sat there under a pile of teased henna hair sorting through keys which were strewn all over the desktop.

—I'm here to see a friend, Lucinda Crispiana. What unit is she in?

Beverly didn't look up from the keys.

—Bill collector?

—No, we used to work together and I hadn't heard from her.

—Well, she moved out without giving notice. Stiffed me a month's rent, too.

—Did she leave a forwarding address?

—Nope.

During the drive back to her apartment Caryn felt the sharp sting of envy toward Lucinda; that she could just pack-up and go. Meanwhile, despite quitting her job, Caryn still felt trapped, desperate to get unstuck. Josh wasn't home, but he'd left every square inch spotless. She was really getting sick of Mr. Spic-n-Span. She stalked around the living room. Then, noticing the magazines neatly stacked on the coffee table, she shoved them and they slid onto the floor. That was a spirit lifter. She went to the bookshelf and pulled out all the books from the bookshelf and threw them onto the floor. Ha, take that.

Caryn stepped into the kitchen. The orange peels were nothing. She'd show him a mess. Mr. Anti-septic had no fucking idea what a mess

117

was. She opened the lower cabinet and yanked out the garbage pail and dumped its contents. Coffee grounds, orange peels, rotting lettuce, and left over spaghetti sauce splattered on the linoleum and the cabinets. She kicked it around, splashing a bag of decomposing cucumbers onto the wall.

She went into the bedroom and yanked clothes out of the closet and pulled out drawers and dumped them upside down, spilling the clothes in a heap. Out of steam, she sat amid the pile of clothes. What was keeping her stuck here? She didn't see how the pain could be worse anywhere else. But even if it could be worse, she couldn't stay, not now. She couldn't live this sanitized life any longer.

Caryn stopped at a sporting goods store in a strip mall. She grabbed a shopping cart and went to the camping section. First she picked out a backpack; then she started filling the cart with other camping gear. Sleeping bag, folding air mattress, compass, gas stove, gas cartridges, water pouches, flashlight, batteries, vest, gloves, hat, fork, knife, freeze dried spaghetti, stroganoff with rice, beef almondine, energy bars and gorp. Then she went over to the case where they kept the expensive field glasses. She asked the clerk for the smallest, most high-powered binoculars.

Through the binoculars she surveyed the store. She looked down the aisle. The pale beige tile was littered with dust, sand, grit, crumbs, and stains from spilled food. She sharpened the focus on a line of ants and followed them to a pulverized Cheeto partly ground into the floor. She saw enough debris to bring a whole semiconductor plant to a grinding halt.

—I'll take these, she said and handed the binoculars to the clerk.

Delisted

The all-employee meeting had been scheduled on short notice. Conversation buzzed anxiously among the employees as they boarded the rented buses. Some employees were optimistic because software downloads from the media website were way up. Other employees were alarmed by the arrival of a huge truckload of cardboard moving boxes. Martin paused in front of the elevators and looked down the hall where the guards from the private security firm were taking up their positions. Two plain-clothes secret-service types statued in front of his office door, and several uniformed guards, guns and nightsticks visible on their belts, were cordoning off the executive wing. The elevator doors opened and Martin stepped in. He jabbed the button and waited. His Director of People Development talked to the head of security. He only picked up snatches of the conversation as the elevator doors closed, the words "protect ourselves" and "psycho." Had it really come to that?

2

Martin's company had kicked into high-gear twelve months previously at a Four Seasons ballroom jammed with over 200 employees who'd been hitting the no host bar for a couple of hours. They'd been celebrating their company's IPO. Martin jumped on top of the grand piano with microphone in hand and began exhorting the crowd.

—Which company raised the most venture capital money last year? he yelled.

—FutureNow! FutureNow! the crowd chanted.

—Which company is the media darling?

—FutureNow! FutureNow! the crowd chanted.

—That's right, people, Martin yelled, *you're* the future now!

As the crowd whooped and cheered, hugged and danced, Martin felt exhilarated; his perma-grin, in place all day, unerasable now that his dream of taking the company public was a reality. Two years! He'd caught the internet rocket all right. From thirty maxed-out credit cards to a billion dollar market cap. Crazy! The crowd started chanting his name and the adulation was cedar shakes thrown onto his fire. Now he had a success that would show all those doubters back home. They'd be talking in the coffee shops about his latest appearance on CNBC, or gawking over his *Wall Street Journal* interview. They'd be bragging about him at their cocktail parties, telling their I-knew-him-when stories. Those hometown doubters would look at him differently now—every last one of them wishing they'd invested in the company when they'd had the chance. So he was a baked-out ski bum who'd amount to nothing, was he? Martin threw an uppercut and grasped his upthrust forearm. Take that!

3

Six months later, Martin, his chief financial officer, his vice-president of business development, and his vice-president of sales hunkered around the star-fish shaped speaker phone in the middle of the conference room's table. At the white-board, diagramming the licensing scenarios, was his chief technology officer. A web of green, blue, and yellow lines connected up clusters of network clouds, database servers, and IP addresses. On the other end of the conference call was the chief information officer for one of the big integrated oil companies. Landing this contract would give Martin the high profile customer he needed to expand the business exponentially.

The negotiations had stalled on the question of licensed users. Martin wanted the whole enterprise—125,000 users—booked up front so he could announce a huge deal. The CIO wanted to start small—500 users at the headquarters office—but he was willing to initiate a development project to customize the software and then roll it out to the rest of the employees next year. For Martin, the trade off was a big pile of upfront license revenue and a splashy announcement that might induce other customers to buy, versus a small amount of services revenue and the potential for a licensing windfall in the coming year if the development project went well. Before the conference call, Martin and his CFO had been through the numbers—they needed the cash flow, *now*.

—I know you want that press release, the CIO said, but for my budgeting purposes I'd rather spend the money on services this year. Work with me on this, Martin.

—Look, Stewartson, let me sweeten the pot. Do the whole deal now—pay up front for the next year's projected licensed users—and we'll throw in a year's worth of customizations at no cost.

The chief technical officer wrote on the white board in big green block letters: DON'T DO IT. But Martin ignored the note and spent ten minutes haranguing the CIO until finally the words he was waiting for came through the speaker phone:

—Okay, Martin. You win. We'll do it your way. But you better deliver on those customizations.

After Martin had clicked off the call, the CFO raised his hand and exchanged high-fives with Martin.

4

I'm not sure I like this PR campaign, Martin said. It's too *soft*. It makes me look like I'm selling toilet paper, like I'm desperate for business.

—We think you need to lighten up, said his public relations representative. You have the reputation for negotiating like an IRA terrorist. You say you are for interoperabilty and flexibility, but then you badger everyone into long-term exclusive contracts. No one believes you'll give up your weapons.

Martin started laughing.

—Look, he said, what else can they do to compete with me? They can't say I haven't built a good product. They can't say that I'm a moron. The best way to compete with me is to pitch the image that I'm an aggressive bully, that I'm an asshole. They've got nothing else on me. I'm a winner. Stick with that, the rest is just noise.

5

We've got a killer road trip planned, his software development manager said. We fly into Denver, grab the rental, and then jam west on I-70. We're hitting Breckenridge, Arapahoe, and Copper Mountain before some full-on partying in Vail. The weather forecast has a fresh dump of powder on the way.

—Sounds like a great trip, Martin said.

—Why don't you come with us? It would be like old times. Remember Whistler?

Martin smiled briefly as he remembered that wild trip and the ground-floor condo with a dry sauna inside and an outdoor hot tub on a deck that you could ski right up onto.

121

—Sounds great, Martin said. But I don't think I can break away this week. Contract negotiations.

—Too bad, we're planning some major thrashing. If you change your mind and want to fly in for the weekend, we'll be at Breck Saturday and Sunday. Just page me and I'll hold a room at the condo for you.

The manager left and Martin swiveled his chair around and stared out the window across Elliott Bay to the snowy peaks of the Olympic Mountains. Skiing road trips. Those were the days all right. He was lucky if he skied a couple of times a year now. Once it had been seven days a week in season. His first ever job was working the ski lifts at Steven's Pass when he was a sophomore in high school. The job only paid minimum wage, barely enough to cover the cost of the gasoline to drive back and forth to Seattle. But it made him feel as if he was pulling one over on the world, particularly those shmucks he went to school with who worked the fast food restaurants. Minimum wage and what? Greasy burgers? Come on. Martin skied for free and got meals and equipment at cost. Best of all he got to play, inserting occasional work stints in between bouts of skiing. Now he was a workaholic just like the rest of his family.

The brother managed a grocery store now. Back then Martin thought the brother's life was a joke because he never did anything for fun. Just like the parents, all he did was work. Paper routes, mowing lawns, saving money. Everyone said the brother had his shit together and that he would go places. Martin was the ski bum, the one the parents worried about. They never worried about the brother—he was just like them. They worried that Martin wouldn't amount to much, chastened him to be more like the brother, particularly after the brother got the job at the grocery store. First he was a boxboy, then, when he started college, he shifted to nights where he stocked shelves and mopped floors; even then, everyone said he had management potential. Martin thought his brother had no life: school, homework, dinner, nap, and then off to the store for the graveyard shift. Martin on the other hand was home from school by noon and heading for the slopes. He'd ski for several hours and then work the lifts from seven until they closed. He was determined not to be like the brother. At first, anyway. Later, after he decided to go to college, he changed tacks and went all out to eclipse the brother's success. No kids, no tract house, no weekends spent at the home improvement store or working on the house for Martin, that was the brother's life. Martin was going big-time. Let those old-economy CEO's take the ski vacations; he'd ski once he owned the resort.

6

The bandwidth negotiations were breaking down because their ISP wasn't convinced that Martin would switch to a competitor.

—I just don't see how you can do it, the lead negotiator said and leaned back in his chair and looked around the room at the half-dozen people from each team. Our terms are fair. It will cost you more to switch. Not to mention the downtime.

Concealed by the tabletop, Martin used his pager to signal his secretary to make the call. Ten seconds later the phone in the conference room was ringing. Looking at the caller ID on the phone's display, he said: It's the wife, let me put her on the speaker-phone.

—What's up? he said.

—Hi honey, is lasagna okay for dinner?

—Lasagna? Fuck lasagna. Goddammit, I said I wanted pizza.

He hung up the call with a jab of his index finger and then leaned forward on his elbows.

—Where were we? Oh yeah, you were just about to tell me how you are going to lower your rates so I won't switch to your competitor.

7

The status meeting with his department heads was full of slippage; the sales director reported slipping sales and the development director had slipping software schedules.

—Somebody cheer me up, Martin said. How about you, Marketing, what do you have? You're usually the chipper ones.

The Marketing Director stood up and began passing out slick four-color brochures.

—We've just launched the new campaign, she said. These are the product brochures that we've sent to every company in the Fortune 1000.

The conference room buzzed with admiration as the brochures circulated around the table. Martin flipped through the pages, quickly seeing the public relations firm's influence.

—What the fuck is this shit? Martin screamed and threw the product brochure across the conference table at the Marketing Director. You actually sent shit like this to prospective customers? How could you do something so fucking stupid?

Around the table no one said a word as Martin's glare tracked from one to the other; they just stared down at whatever was in front of them.

8

Why are you telling me this? Martin asked his Administrative Assistant.
—Because no one else will, she said. They're all afraid of you.
—You've got to be kidding!
—No, I'm not.

This struck him as ludicrous. He'd built the business for them, provided their livelihood. Now he was protecting it. Someone had to make the tough decisions—why would they begrudge him that?

—I think you should consider an executive coach, she said.
—What for? It's not like I'm training for the Olympics.
—I'm *serious*, Martin. You need some objective advice to help you through this rough patch.

Martin didn't see how a bunch of rah-rah, psycho-babble was going to help him through anything.

—I know you're' skeptical, his Assistant said, but give it a try. What do you have to lose?

9

The Executive Coach followed Martin into his office.
—Look at this view! she said, admiring the mid-winter sun setting behind the Olympic Mountains. I'd never get anything done if I worked out of an office like this. How do you do it? she asked as they settled into chairs.

—Can't afford not to, Martin said. It's the most expensive office space on the west coast.

—Really? she said, eyebrows arching. If you can afford this, then I'm not charging you enough.

When Martin didn't laugh with her, she removed a brochure from her briefcase and handed it across the desk to Martin.

—Here's my client list. As you can see I've coached executives at all the top companies in Silicon Valley, as well as here in the northwest.

—You're selling a seller, Martin said, tossing the brochure aside. So cut the spiel. What are you going to do for *me*?

—What's your worst result? the Coach asked.
—Going bankrupt.
—Okay. Let's get that into a problem statement. Identify causes, consequences, and then an action plan.

Ten minutes later they'd boiled the problem down to two action strategies.

—That's it, the Coach said, that's your plan.

—Repair customer relationships? Martin said.

—Show them you are working for *them*, the Coach said.

—Raise new cash? Martin said.

—Sweet talk the street, the Coach said.

10

While waiting in O'Hare for his connecting flight to New York for the analysts meeting and his appearance on the Finance Network's Internet Crossfire show, Martin picked up a ski magazine in the bookshop—a special new gear issue. He sat in the VIP lounge reading about all the new skis. He hadn't bought skis in years; still had straight skis in fact. He'd entirely missed the sidecut revolution. And now they were making twin-tips, swallow-tails, mid-fats, and big-mountain skis.

The new-schoolers, rather than conceding the slopes to the snow-boarders, were revitalizing skiing by taking their skis into the half-pipe and throwing board tricks from their skis. He remembered that crazy time when he and all the other ski-instructors at Alpental had spent a week building a 150-foot long berm so they could attempt a world record for simultaneous back-flips. After three attempts they set the record with fifty-five skiers landing the jumps. Tame stuff compared to the extreme skiers and the stunts he saw depicted in the magazine. He'd skied off rock faces in his teens, but nothing like the cornices, couloirs, and avalanche chutes the skiers did nowadays. It made him wonder what he'd be doing now if he'd stuck with ski instructing, if he hadn't switched directions by going to college and doing the MBA thing. Probably own a ski-school. Probably live in Vail or Aspen or Park City. Or maybe he'd just be a ski-bum using big-mountain skis to slash down the verticals at Jackson Hole.

He missed the freedom he'd once felt when skiing. Freedom from having to depend on anyone else. How he got down the mountain was totally under his control. He could go as fast or as slow as he wanted. He could take risks without seeking anyone's approval or asking anyone's help. And what was he doing now? Going off to sweet talk the street.

11

They sat in director's chairs in front of the Internet Crossfire logo on the Finance Network's set; the Host and the Internet Analyst on one side, Martin across from them. They each had a camera aimed at them. Martin was burning up under the lights. After the introductions and a few softball questions about the company's earnings report, which had been released after the market closed the night before, things started to get dicey.

—So, the Host said, now that your stock price is plummeting, and so much of your employee's compensation is tied up in stock options, are you worried about having to increase salaries to compensate for all the out of the money stock options?

—I'm confident that business is improving and that that improvement will eventually be reflected in the stock price, Martin said.

—Are you considering repricing the options? the Host asked.

—Not at this time.

—Wouldn't that be dilutive to the shareholders? the Internet Analyst said.

—We're not considering a repricing at this time. I'm confident that business will improve and that that will be reflected in the stock price down the road.

—If that's so, the Internet Analyst said, then maybe you'd like to comment on a report that hit the wires just a bit ago: Inside Trader is reporting that a week ago you filed to sell 200,000 shares.

In the moments that it took Martin to remember to breathe he could see the Host and the Internet Analyst smirking. Martin gulped and searched for something intelligent to say.

—Does that filing indicate your lack of confidence in the company's prospects? the Internet Analyst asked.

—No, no, no, no, no, Martin said. Not at all. Just routine selling to diversify my portfolio.

—So there's no truth to the rumor that you were hit with a margin call?

—Well, yes, after the release of the earnings warning three weeks ago I did have to cover some positions.

—According to my sources, the Internet Analyst said, your company is facing a cash squeeze and you had been borrowing against your stock holdings to finance operations. Then, when the stock started declining you had to sell more shares to meet the margin calls. Isn't that, in fact, what is going on?

12

As soon as the flight attendant announced that the use of electronic devices was permitted, Martin reclined the leather seat a bit and removed the laptop computer from his briefcase. After the operating system had booted up he snapped one end of the cable into the modem card and the other end into the data port on the air phone. Once connected to the company server he started downloading email. His mailbox was crammed. Half a dozen reporters seeking comments for their stories: *The Wall Street Journal, The Industry Standard*, CNBC, CNN. There were a couple of emails from members of the board of directors. He opened one with the subject line, "What the…" it went on to say "…fuck got into you, Martin? The stock is getting hammered in after hours trading."

He ran a quick quote check on the E*TRADE site. Sure enough, the price was down 18 points since the close. He saw an email from his PR firm titled "Damage Control." And half the development team had sent him email complaining about the stock price. Then he saw the one he'd been dreading. The message was titled "Here it is" and had a 10-megabit video file attached. The distribution list was to everyone in his company.

He double-clicked and the file started streaming into the video player. It was his interview on the Internet Crossfire show. He clicked the sound down to zero so no one else would hear. He knew what was said, anyway, and he felt a scalding blush as he remembered, and then nausea as he watched and saw that he'd had a sheen of sweat on his forehead. He was shocked to see himself biting his lip while he listened to the questions. And then the gulping, bobbing Adam's apple. The frantic looks away from the camera at the monitor. He had no conception of himself that included looking that bad and he was mortified that everyone in his company had seen him that way.

Seeing the disastrous interview on video made it worse, something he couldn't escape, something that could—and would—be replayed over and over. A piercing pain stabbed behind his right eye. He stopped the movie, disconnected from the server, and put his computer away. He leaned back in the seat and closed his eyes for a moment. Did they have barf bags in first class? He yanked at the seatback pouch. Laminated safety card. Napkins. *Fortune ASAP* magazine. He removed the folded up white paper bag and slumped back into the seat clutching the bag to his chest. The progression was laid out in front of him like a row of dominoes: cut business development, cut product development, cut the sales staff, down they go one after the other. The only question was how long he could hold out before tipping that first one. There'd be a few defenders who'd say that it was just bad timing, that the market had turned south at the wrong time. But Martin knew better. That was the worst part; he'd brought it on himself.

He looked around at the family occupying the other seven seats in first class. In the seat next to him was a young boy, probably five- or six-years-old, already asleep. Sleeping with his mouth closed and without snoring, his blonde hair curling around his neck. The two teenage girls across the aisle were buoyant over some magazine, absolutely carefree. Earth-mom, fecund again, contentedly smiling beside her ten-year-old son who dueled a video game with assured thumbs. And dad, probably one of

Martin's would-be customers, clearly awash in cash and in-the-money stock, lounging in his pre-washed denim and Mariners baseball cap, the baby asleep in his lap. Everything was in sync; the family purring like a perfectly tuned engine. Maybe a family needn't be a prison, maybe he and the wife should have had kids. A groan popped from Martin's lips as if he were a vacuum-sealed lid. Fat chance.

He tried to remember the last time that he and the wife had taken a vacation together. She'd had her spa visits to Palm Springs with her friends. And he'd played golf with customers at conferences. But he didn't think they'd been anywhere together since he'd started working on the business plan. Four years. He doubted whether she'd go anywhere with him once the death spiral began. No. She'd demand a divorce, demand the house, demand the cars, demand whatever was left after bankruptcy. She'd find another husband, a rich husband, become someone else's arm candy as quick as quick can. Well what did he expect from a trophy wife? He picked her from among the other sorority girls he dated because she was studying interior decorating. Her ambition was to someday have her house featured in *Seattle House and Garden* magazine. Not a client's house, *her* house. He'd grown up with second-hand furniture and clutter. He'd been certain that she'd create a home with impeccable style, something that would show everyone that he'd made it. So he'd chosen her the same way he'd chosen his car, his house, his secretary, perhaps even his company. Trophies all. Eye-candy to show-off. The trophies symbolized that he'd made it. Proved he could hunt with the big dogs and not get munched. Except now he felt as if he were a little dog on its back with a junkyard dog's jaws closing in on his jugular.

13

Martin paced around his office while the lead investment banker who'd underwritten his IPO talked down Martin's expectations for a secondary offering.

—Try again in the spring, said the voice in the speaker-phone, after interest rates are cut.

—That might be too late, Martin said.

—Hang in there.

—Easy for you to say as you hand me the noose.

—Give me a break, Martin. In this market, and with your burn rate, there's nothing I can do.

—Fuck the burn rate! My job's to build the business. Your job's to raise the cash so I can do that.

—Martin, the banker said, we can't ride you all the way down. Cut costs. Stay alive. Then we'll see what we can do when the market improves.

—Do you know what you are saying?

—Sorry, the Banker said. Gotta go.

Martin yanked the phone off his desk and slammed it against the far wall.

—Fuck! Fuck! Fuck! he screamed, punctuating each expletive by banging his forehead on the door.

14

Martin and the Venture Capitalist were discussing strategy over drinks.

—You're golden now, the Venture Capitalist said.

—Yeah, right, Martin said. The share price is on its way to zero and the NASDAQ is itching to delist us.

—Nothing you can do about it now, that die is cast. But don't underestimate the value of having managed a company into the ground.

Martin sputtered a mouthful of scotch onto the bar.

—I'm serious, the Venture Capitalist said. You are more valuable now that you've got a failure under your belt.

—How's that? Martin asked.

—You screwed up. Made mistakes. But you've got your lessons learned, right?

Martin sucked on an ice cube.

—Look at it from my point of view, the Venture Capitalist said. The easy money is washed out. So it's blood from a turnip time. Rookies get nothing now. I'll be putting my money on guys that went down swinging and have something to prove. Guys that won't make the same mistakes twice. Guys like *you*.

They sipped their drinks and Martin began to realize that he wasn't going to get the money he needed to stay solvent.

—So what are you saying? he asked.

—Liquidate, the Venture Capitalist said. Shut it down before you burn through any more cash. Sell what you can and get out.

—Just like that?

—You know what they say about dead horses, don't you?

—Shit! Martin said. He caught the bartender's eye and used two fingers to signal another round.

—Not to worry, my friend, the Venture Capitalist said. I've already got another horse for you to ride. Great business plan, but management has no clue how to grow the business. I'll push the CEO out and put you in.

15

Martin heard the wheels turning on the cable and tucked his chin against his chest as the chair-lift bounced over the tower at the crest of the ridge. The trees had been cleared from the slopes here and the wind sweeping across the mountaintop started the chair swaying. A burst of snowflakes blew down the back of his parka. He hunched down lower, turtled as much as he could, trying to protect both the front and the back of his neck from the blowing snow. He swung his skis back and forth, getting the blood circulating. The arch of his left instep started to cramp so he stopped swinging the skis and huddled in his parka as the chair headed across the ridge toward the final tower and the exit ramp. The snow fell intermittently, the light flakes slanting with the gusts.

Exhausted from a full night of skiing, he knew that packing his gear and heading to the slopes after the NASDAQ call was the best thing he could have done. It still pissed him off that the delisting notification came only a few days after his funding attempts fell through. The bankers no longer returned his calls, but apparently the lines of communication between the bankers and the exchange were wide open. The NASDAQ had an appeal process, but with the stock below a buck for more than three months, and being shut off from additional funding, there wasn't much point. Delisting from the exchange would start the death spiral.

As his chair approached the tower he wished this wasn't the last run, wished that the lifts weren't shutting down for the night. He loved night skiing, loved skiing fast with only partial visibility, especially on nights like this when the moon played peek-a-boo with the snow flurries. He thought about his teenage years when he'd flirted with being a ski-bum and how he'd come to give that life up. College, MBA, starting FutureNow, it seemed a lifetime away from working the lifts, serving on the ski-patrol, and ski instructing at Alpental. He'd gotten tired of living in the van parked in the ski resort's parking lot. He loved the skiing, but not the "bum" part of the lifestyle. When he looked around at those who had been living that way for years he didn't see much of a life. A few were making it big as extreme skiers for the movies, but the most successful at maintaining a skiing lifestyle were the people who ran the small businesses: the ski rental shops, the clothing stores, the ski schools. Who looked up to a ski-bum anyway? Only other ski-bum wannabes. Everyone else sneered—especially the parents. Oh, with one breath they might say how great it was to be out skiing all day—but with the next breath they're saying he's a bum and couldn't make it anywhere else. Then the brother graduated and landed the assistant manager's job at the grocery store. Another success that rankled Martin. He decided to go to college, to learn enough to give himself a shot at one of those ski resort businesses. Show those skeptics.

He didn't know it when he signed up for that first computer science class, but he was about to get hooked. Microsoft was the hometown rage then and he was lucky enough to land an internship in the product group that was trying to build the next generation online bulletin board. Tired of paying Compuserve to host their online customer support service, Microsoft had set up the product group to put Compuserve out of business. But despite that mission, Microsoft had missed the coming of the internet. Martin didn't. First time he used the nascent web browser, even though the pre-release code was buggy, and there was less than a dozen web sites to surf, he knew that bulletin board services were dinosaurs. He wrote the FutureNow business plan while working on his MBA.

The internet business had appealed to him for the same reasons he'd loved skiing. None of the technology had ever been done before so it was a chance to establish a new set of rules, a chance to achieve success without depending on anyone else. And despite the long hours he worked, he still felt as if he were playing because he wasn't settling down into the routines and ruts that signaled the drudgery of work. There was the heady aura of adventure and risk. The adrenaline flowed just as it did when he laid the first tracks on a slope of fresh powder.

He stood up and skied down the ramp as the chair continued on overhead. He carved hard left at the bottom of the ramp and cruised off across the ridge. The flurries had let up and the moon glowed behind a thin gauze of fast moving clouds. With the moonlight rising he decided to head for the back bowl, away from the lighted runs. He left the ridge behind and skied toward a brightly lit chute. The slope was narrow and steep and full of sharply etched and chopped off moguls. He skied down into the funnel of trees and started slashing through the moguls. On top of one bump, sliding off into the trough. Then fighting off the groove, before going up and over a teardrop mogul that compressed his knees into chest. He opened up, sliced right, left, right, compressed, popped and caught air, compressed, left, right, left, then blasted out of the bottom of the mogul field and onto a knoll with his legs burning and his breath ragged.

The lighted runs headed left; the trail to the back bowl went right. He chose the trail with a whoop and let his skis track the grooves in the twisting white ribbon. Into near darkness as the trail cut deeper into the grove of trees he opened his eyes as wide as he could searching for grey light. A brief glimpse of stars and he picked up speed, felt the branches whipping against his parka, caught a whiff of the fir's pungent breathing, and he shot out of the trees and onto the steep slope above the bowl.

He carved hard left, then right, to cut his speed, and then skied across the slope to the edge of the trees and slowed to a stop. He let his breath calm and his eyes adjust to the light. The moon was out of the clouds but most of the bowl was still deep in the shadows. He couldn't see a clear path. The upper edges of the bowl were a light ashen grey, but as the bowl deepened in the middle, the snow looked like charcoal. The outlet was down there somewhere, a gap in the trees that pushed up onto the old downhill racecourse that led back to the lighted slopes and the lodge. Memories of all the runs he'd made down that racecourse were on him like flurries. That seemed like the last time he'd done anything for himself. He was doing everything for everybody else now. Trying to please customers, employees, shareholders, the Board of Directors, the bankers, the venture capitalists, the public relations firm, the reporters, the executive coach, the wife—trying to please everybody but himself. He looked up at the moon and the wisps of clouds blowing past, then made a sharp turn down the fall line and took off.

Within ten seconds he was at-the-edge-of-control speed, his jacket snapping in the slipstream. He could feel the burn on his cheeks, the snot streaming out of his nose. His skis rang sharp, a discordant metallic hiss. The snow was crusted over powder, a foot deep, criss-crossed with a few tracks, but little skied. He couldn't see the bumps and holes well enough to navigate and decided to ski straight through. Relaxing his legs, he let the skis run free into the dark of the bowl's basin. He spotted the gap in the trees off to the left and started carving that way and headed up the other side of the bowl and out through the notch onto the downhill track. He slid hard on the packed trail, his edges chattering, and then was into his tuck, just like old times when he'd raced his friends down the mountain to the lodge. The course was dark, a ten-yard-wide track kept packed by the snow-cats, and he skied it from memory, tight in his tuck on the straight-aways, trying to keep his skies flat on the turns, going faster and faster towards the fall-off and the big air. A hot sear burned across the top of his thighs and for an instant he thought he was crazy, and then he was airborne, momentarily weightless, sailing, unable to see the landing area until an instant before he hit. He fell back on his skis, his butt bouncing on the tails, and he fought to get up, wobbling from ski to ski. A tip caught and he went twisting into a slo-motion veer before cart-wheeling several times and sliding face first to a stop in a spray of snow.

Ski-less, he rolled over onto his back and sucked several deep breaths. Other than his breathing it was eerily silent without the scrape and whoosh of his skies. His face tingled, became wet as the snow melted. He could smell his own sweat as the salty steam wafted up from beneath his collar. Clouds bunched up in front of the moon and he watched bursts of white filaments followed by thick clots of grey until the moon was gone. He turned his head and saw the luminescence of a light pole. Crystalline flakes sparkled around the corona of light and he thought they might be pieces of him blown free in the fall. He stared at the crystals until a flurry blew them away in a swirl of snow. It had been an awesome run, pure instinctual abandon, and a long, long time since he'd felt so loose. He wondered if skiing like that could be taught. That's the kind of ski-instructor he'd wanted to be, someone who could get you out of yourself, out of everything that was holding you down. He shivered from deep in his back, where it lay against the snow, then got up and searched for his skis.

16

In the Red Lion Inn conference room Martin was wrapping up his delivery of the bad news. Into the silence of his trailing words, all the faces gazed back at him. The stone-faced executives. The jumpy-eyed and lip-biting managers who still had to deal one-on-one with laid-off employees. The majority of faces were disbelieving, stunned, in shock. Martin saw a few smirks, too; cynics settling for the I-told-you-so pleasure. And he saw some fear—the mortgage-and-kids-in-school crowd. Martin couldn't begin to imagine what expression was on his face. Although this was the climactic high-stress moment for those receiving the news, all he felt was relief. After months of fighting to save the company, months of too little sleep and too much booze, he could finally let go.

—What about an acquisition? someone called out.

Martin took a deep breath, let it out through puffed cheeks.

—Unfortunately, he said, the vultures are already circling. No one will buy us now—they'd rather pick through the pieces.

17

As they considered offers for the marketing department's database and the other intellectual property—the patents, the specifications, and the code base—Martin could see that his CFO was in his element. For him, the asset sell-off was the culmination of the ultimate resume-building experience. Bringing out the IPO was only useful if he went to another startup, not likely in this market. But the CFO was headed into the auto industry.

—Periodic downsizing, restructurings, layoffs, and asset sales—it's all just part of the cycle for those guys, the CFO said. They do that shit every year for some part of their business. This is exactly the kind of experience I need. You'll see, Martin, this experience is worth its weight in gold. Real gold, not that fool's gold we were playing with here.

Martin knew the CFO was right; it was all just a game. And Martin also knew that he'd been good at it, could play the game with the best of them. But his concern at that moment, however, was to raise enough money to cover the final payroll run.

18

Martin felt suddenly claustrophobic in the crush of the press conference. Where he once loved the flash of the lights, the microphones thrust at him, the shouted questions from the reporters, he now felt besieged. He used to love being the center of attention, and it hadn't mattered whether that attention was adulation or animosity. Now, if he'd had a machine gun, no one would have been safe. But he didn't. So he bolted. Pushed his way through the arms and shoulders, growled at the faces shoved too close to his. Bulled his way through the garlic breath and stale sweat, away from the barks and shrieks and guffaws. He shoved with his elbows, hips, and knees, cleared a path for himself, until, finally, he popped out of the crowd and onto the sidewalk, feeling as if he'd slashed his way through a bramble-choked path.

He walked backwards down the sidewalk, staring back at the thick pack of reporters and camera crews, some still filming him as he made his getaway. But he hadn't gotten away, he saw that now. He didn't know where he'd gotten to. He felt a continuous and rising stab of panic and started running, arms pistoning hard until he was careening down the sidewalk in a full sprint, screaming at people to get out of his way.

19

The only assets left for sale were arrayed on the warehouse floor: computers, routers, disk drives, software, desks, file cabinets and chairs, plus boxes full of office supplies. All up for auction now. Among the crowd—who had paid $500 apiece for the opportunity to bid on the startup's remains—were several former employees looking to buy their old computers back on the cheap.

20

Two years later Martin was in the meat department at his local grocery store sorting through the selection of rib-eye steaks when he spotted Conor Matthews, his former software development manager, walking toward him. Martin dropped his head and turned away, hoping Conor hadn't recognized him. Suddenly he was awash in a flood tide of fear and embarrassment, tinged with an equally sudden anger at himself. He should have felt proud. He'd done a 180, backtracked, started over. His pride at turning his life around was rudely shoved aside by anxiety. He didn't want to talk to Conor—or anyone else from his former company, or from his former life for that matter. He knew it was absurd, bordering on irrationality, but he didn't want any of them to know what he was doing now, didn't want them to know that he'd dropped out of high-tech and become a ski-instructor.

—Martin. Is that you?

—Conor, hi.

They shook hands.

—Wow. It's good to see you, Conor said. Where'd you land? You just disappeared—we all kept expecting to hear about that next IPO.

—Where are you working these days? Martin answered.

—I'm over at Metaware.

—How's that going for you?

—Great. They promoted me to Director of Development. Threw a bunch more stock options my way. Got me involved in strategic planning. So things are going great. Business is booming. I'm hiring like crazy—can't find enough developers. We just landed a new software development project with a big oil company.

—Really.

—You know the guy, too.

—Not Stewartson?

—The very same, Conor said. Shit, that was one of our biggest debacles at FutureNow, wasn't it? Man, you got some bad advice on that deal. Those licensing terms hosed us big time.

—Lots of lessons for you there, Martin said.

—Yep. But we got the bastard good this time. Sucked him in with low up front costs and bare bones functionality. Then we're going to dangle new features in front of him and make him pay over and over.

They slipped into an awkward silence, gazing around at the other shoppers. Martin wondered whether Conor was getting a dig in, or if he was just full of himself.

—So, Martin, what are *you* up to?

—Just kicking back, Martin said.

—Ah, keeping a low profile. Company in the quiet period?

—Something like that. How's Cary and the kids?

They talked for a bit longer about Conor's family, and then they parted, with Conor handing his business card over to Martin with a suggestion to get together for a beer sometime. Martin figured that would never happen and he guessed that Conor thought so too.

He pushed his cart absent-mindedly through the aisles, catching a glimpse of Conor at the checkout counter. Perhaps he should have been friendlier. He felt crappy about being evasive. But, really, what business was it of Conor's what he was doing now? Did Conor really need to know that

Martin was divorced and bankrupt and working again as a ski instructor as if the preceding ten years had never existed? He was in a quiet period all right. After he'd turned down offers to assume the top spot at two different startup companies, people stopped calling. He wasn't in anyone's Rolodex anymore. Wasn't in anyone's email address book. Wasn't on headhunter's mailing lists. And reporters no longer called him when they needed a quote about the state of ecommerce. About the only list he was on anymore was an ignominious one: Harvard Business School's case studies of failed businesses. The wife bailed about the time that article came out. Turned out she was a trophy collector too, and being with him was no longer good for her image.

He stopped his cart in the magazine aisle and perused the covers, then picked out one with the headline teaser: "Out of the ashes—the internet fights back!" He flipped through the pages unable to focus. Success or failure, which was it? And how did you decide such questions? Whose success was greater: A champion athlete with a room full of trophies and a pile of million-dollar endorsements? An Oscar-winning actor making fifteen million per movie? An emergency room doctor who saved half-a-dozen lives every night? Was anyone who didn't achieve such accomplishments a failure? Who was it better to be: a CEO or a ski instructor? And from whose perspective was the question decided? Was he a success because he thought so, even when no one else did? Was he a success when others thought so, even if he felt himself to be a failure? What made the difference? What made one perspective right and the other wrong? What made one life meaningful and another a black hole of doubt?

One thing he knew: he'd had a once in a lifetime experience. There will only be one time in history when the internet would emerge from the private back-channel networks of the defense department and the research universities and explode into mass consciousness. And he'd been there, right in the thick of it, one of the entrepreneurs making it happen. Just because he got bucked from that horse didn't mean he had to get back on another. Or did it? A part of him felt that he knew the difference between success and failure. When he led a group of hot-shots on a moonlight schuss through the back bowl he knew that his CEO life, despite all its successes, had failed him. But now, after listening to all of Conor's successes, it seemed ludicrous to think that his internet career was a failure. The uncertainty made his head spin. The venture capitalist community considered the failure of his company a kind of success, a necessary steppingstone in his career. You're golden, they said. Why on earth would you give that up to become a ski instructor? To follow some adolescent dream? Another set of eyes through which he was now a failure.

Martin tossed the magazine onto the bottom shelf and looked at the explosion of magazine covers devoted to a hundred different lifestyles.

Golfers, musicians, actors, doctors, skiers, CEOs, their eyes implored him from the magazine covers. So many options. Having options was supposed to be a good thing—it meant you weren't trapped. So why did he feel trapped? Trapped by all of these options. Just pick one for Christ's sake! *Any* one. And give it all you've got. What did it matter which path he took to success? Wasn't success, in any of its forms, success? But it did matter. It mattered a lot. In fact, it was everything. Or was it? He didn't know anymore. Shit! He used to be so sure of himself. So sure that he possessed all the answers. That he was master of his destiny. Where did that certainty go?

Eiderdown

L̲ori accompanied Kevin when he went shopping for a new sleeping bag
at the recreational equipment co-op. She couldn't help shopping for
herself, however, and paused him to sort through a rack of fleece
sweatshirts. Finding one she liked, she handed Kevin her purse and snuggled
her left arm into the sleeve and pulled up the zipper. She pirouetted in front
of Kevin and cycled through several poses as if in a catalog shoot.

—Is it me? she asked him.

—Makes your boobs look bigger, he said.

She tugged the zipper down slowly while arching her shoulders. A
quick shimmy unlocked his eyes, brought on the blush. She laughed and said:
Go do your sleeping bag thing while I pay for this.

Standing in line at the checkout, Lori felt amused—so Kevin *was*
interested. That could change everything between them. They'd met a few
months before at the VertZone, an indoor climbing wall, where they
attended the same rock climbing class every Wednesday night for eight
weeks. Exiting a relationship, Lori used the class as an outlet for her pent up
anger and frustration while she kept up her no-advances defense. Although
he never expressed his motives in those terms, Lori knew Kevin had also
ended a relationship recently. She glanced over at the sleeping bag area and
saw Kevin talking with a green-vested sales guy. Kevin was tall, basketball
tall, and skinny. A bit too skinny, really, from all the biking, hiking, and
running he did. Not her type at all. She usually went for broad shoulders,
mounded pecs, and pumped biceps. But he did look good in shorts, and
she'd seen other women checking him out. Still, he hadn't come on to her.
They'd started hanging out after class, pints at the brewpub across the street,
and occasional shopping excursions for climbing gear. She had fun hanging
out with him, but now she wondered—stay friends? Or become lovers?

The fleece sweatshirt paid for, Lori went over to where Kevin was deciding between two sleeping bags. One was mummy style, the other square bottomed.

—They're both eiderdown, the sales guy said, our warmest winter bag.

—So which style do you recommend?

—The mummy's smaller and lighter, if weight's a factor. The square bottom is roomier, and traps more air, so it's warmer too.

Kevin pondered the differences. The sales guy looked at Lori then turned back to Kevin. Another thing about this square bottom one, he said, pausing to look again at Lori. You could buy two and zip them together.

—Oh, no, Lori said, shaking her head. We're just friends.

The sales guy nodded and smirked.

Kevin pointed at the square bottomed bag: I'll take that one.

—Good choice, the sales guy said, and looked again at Lori. You'll love the eiderdown.

Back in the checkout line, Lori had an idea. Are you doing anything this weekend? she asked.

—Nothing planned if that's what you mean, Kevin said.

—We should go backpacking, she said. Do an overnighter. You know, break in your new sleeping bag. She saw his look and lightly slapped his arm with the back of her hand. Not that way! As friends, silly. I can use your old sleeping bag.

He didn't say anything and she could see him considering the idea. She wondered what he was thinking. They'd never spent more than a half-day together before and she hoped she hadn't scared him off with her comment. It will be great, she said. We can get steaks and marshmallows to roast over the fire. Come on, it will be fun.

—Denny Creek would be okay, he finally said. Still freezing at night, though.

—Then you'll find out if all this money you're spending is worth it.

After a five-mile hike Lori and Kevin set up camp along the eastern shore of Pratt Lake, which was nestled between scree strewn slopes. They'd passed three or four groups of hikers heading down the trail as they'd been heading up, but found themselves alone at the lake. Pikas eeked their calls from the rocks. A woodpecker's work echoed from the standing dead wood down where the creek flowed out through thickets at the north end of the lake. Songbirds, expecting scraps, sang out and frittered around the outskirts of their campsite.

Kevin removed the tent gear from stuff sacks and arranged them in a row: plastic ground sheet, tent, rain-fly, poles, and aluminum stakes. He spread the ground sheet and quickly staked the tent's four corners through the ground sheet's eyelets.

—This is a two-person tent? Lori said.

—Wait till I get the poles up—it's a dome.

—What can I do to help? Lori asked as he assembled the poles by stretching the elastic connector-cord and snapping the sections together.

—Nothing.

He slid the poles through the sleeves so they crossed over the top of the tent, then bent and fastened the ends until the tent raised itself on the poles' arches. He shook out the rain-fly as if it were a bed sheet and draped it over the poles. Half-a-dozen strings with loops at their ends hung from the rain-fly. Kevin started staking a corner. Lori grabbed a stake, hooked the string loop, and pulled the fly taut and then pushed the stake into the ground. She stood and smiled at Kevin but he was already working another corner. She grabbed another stake and went to the opposite corner. She squatted and tugged on the string, pulling into the tension until it suddenly released and she fell back on her butt dragging the fly off the tent. Kevin laughed as she stood and brushed off her jeans. He started restaking the fly. She picked up a stake to try again.

—Look, he said. I'm used to doing this myself.

—*Excuse* me, she said and flung down the stake.

—It'll be easier if I—

—Fine.

—You can gather firewood.

—I'd rather do the hunting, Lori said.

He looked up from the other side of the tent: What?

—I said, have fun.

She headed into the bush and started picking up twigs and small branches. He'll probably want to start the fire too, she muttered to herself.

White smoke drifted off into the branches of the mountain hemlocks, sub-alpine firs, and vine maples, the fringe of trees that separated their campsite from the lichen-covered boulders at the base of the ridge. She'd gathered some slightly damp wood and it hissed in the crackling fire. As darkness edged in, Lori was disappointed to see clouds were bunching up against the Cascade crest just to the east; she'd been hoping for a starry night, maybe even to sleep out instead of inside the tent. Ever since that eighth-grade field trip to Yellowstone, her idea of ultimate romance included a mountain man, animal passion, the ground under her back, and the stars overhead. No four-poster with a frilly canopy for her. She wanted to meld with man and earth and feel herself hurtling through the Milky Way.

Lori watched Kevin searing the steak he'd cut into strips and skewered on a stick. The aroma of sizzling fat and meat made her ravenous.

She devoured the kebab he handed her, savored the charcoal-crusted meat. Then they roasted marshmallows, laughing so hard as the gooey cream puffs burst into flame, that they ended up torching more than they eat. Later, as they drank tea spiked with 151-rum and told ghost stories, Lori was pleased with herself for suggesting the trip. She wasn't sure what might happen, but she was anxious whether the campfire would spark Kevin's amorous feelings. He wasn't the mountain man of her dreams, but she wondered if he could make her howl with the wolves. So she was disappointed when the light sprinkle turned to cold rain and then thick snow. Kevin went off to pee in the bushes. When he returned they put out the fire.

—That's that, he said stirring a stick around in the wet ashes. Time to try out the eiderdown.

—Speak for yourself, she said.

—Sorry.

She took toilet paper from her pack and then realized what she'd left at home. She felt her cheeks flushing as she turned to Kevin. I need your plastic shovel, she said.

—Huh? Oh, too bad. He handed her the shovel. Do you have a flashlight, he said.

—Yes, she said and flashed it at him. Any suggestions on where?

He pointed at the trail heading away from the lake. Go up to where the switchback's start. That's far enough from the water and the brush is not as thick in there.

When she returned to the tent, Kevin was already in his sleeping bag. He shined the flashlight on her and said: Where does a bear—

—Shut up, she said.

She took off her parka and unzipped her fleece sweatshirt. He kept the flashlight on her.

—Do you mind?

—Sorry, he said and turned off the light. I thought you'd want to see what you were doing.

—No. *You* wanted to see what I'm doing. Look away.

She unzipped her jeans and then laid back on the sleeping bag to slide the jeans off. She turned her back to him and took off her turtleneck shirt, removed her bra, and then put the shirt back on. She slid into the sleeping bag and plumped the parka into a pillow.

Kevin unzipped the flap of the tent above where their heads were so they could look at the snow falling.

—Nothing to worry about, Kevin said. It's wet snow.

—Darn, I was hoping we'd get snowed in, Lori said.

—Not in this place.

The wind shifted around, and a chilling breeze started blowing into the tent. Kevin zipped the flap. Side by side in the dark, scrunched down inside their separate sleeping bags, they listened to the snowflakes blowing against the side of the tent's rain-fly. Now what? This was not what Lori had in mind. She wished she knew what Kevin was thinking. Whether he wanted to kiss her, whether he desired her, whether he'd fantasized—as she had—about making love out in the wilderness. Part of her just wanted to blurt out: So, do you want to do it or not? The other part of her didn't want to take the risk.

She drifted off to sleep and woke some time later chilled and shivering. For several minutes she thought about getting up and putting on her jeans and her parka. Then she started thinking how if she and Kevin were in bed and she was cold she could just snuggle up to him. They'd never been in bed before, hardly even hugged, in fact. But she was freezing in the cheap summer bag while he was toasty in his eiderdown. She decided to take a chance and nudged him: Kevin, you awake?

He groaned.

—This sleeping bag is worthless, Lori said.

Kevin wriggled his bag over against hers. Scoot up close, he said.

What? Was he clueless? Was she going to have to ask? She waited a few moments. Apparently she would. I'm really cold, she said. Do you have room for me in your bag?

She waited again as several seconds passed and she desperately wished she knew what was going on inside that head of his. Did he think she was making a pass at him? Maybe he didn't want her in there with him?

—Well, he said finally, as if at the end of some weighty thought process, it might be a tight fit, but there's only one way to find out.

She heard the zipper on his sleeping bag going down. Lori unzipped her bag and crawled out. She slid her feet into his bag, kicked him in the knee, apologized, scrunched in some more, bumping him all the way down until she felt her feet at the bottom of the sleeping bag.

—You're naked, Lori said.

—I always sleep that way.

—You might have said something.

—Sorry.

They squiggled around, breathing hard, until they were spooned with her back to him.

—Is that okay? Lori asked.

—If I can close the zipper, Kevin said.

He reached his arm over her and started tugging the zipper, which seemed stuck. He jiggled it back and forth, finally pulling it free and zipping them in. Then he tightened the drawstring snug around their necks and shifted his arm down until it hung across Lori's waist.

—Better? he asked.

—Yes, thanks.

Lori felt awkward then and wondered what she had been thinking to want this because they'd never been that close before and they'd only been friends and there they were spooned together and breathing hard. Kevin's face rested on her neck and his breath warmed her skin. She could feel his heart beating against her back. Her shivers subsided as the heat radiated from his body into hers.

And then it started. The erection. First she felt a slight pressure moving on her panties, although the rest of his body was still, and then she could feel his erection growing and pushing against the cleft of her buttocks. Oh my god, she thought. What now? She could hardly breathe. Were they going to do it? She felt herself flushing, getting wet. What would his next move be? Kiss her neck? Caress her breasts? Reach his hand down? What did she want him to do? She wasn't sure. She waited. Nothing. Don't just lie there, Kevin, she thought, do *something*. She waited. Tried to keep her breathing under control as the seconds passed. Kevin's erection kept getting harder. Yet he acted like nothing was happening. Maybe he was waiting for her to react. Should she be the one to do something? Wriggle back against him, let him know she was okay with going further? Maybe she should make a joke to lighten the tension? Except she couldn't think of anything funny to say. She'd suggested getting into his sleeping bag hadn't she? How much more of a signal did he need? Then, after a minute or so, he blurted out: Sorry.

She waited, but that was all he said. *Sorry*. Not, sorry I couldn't help myself because you turn me on so much. Not, sorry I've been fantasizing about this ever since you asked me to go hiking. Just *sorry*. She bit her tongue, afraid to say anything, afraid it would betray her hurt.

—It's involuntary, he added.

As if *that* was supposed to make her feel better. He popped wood and still didn't want to make love to her. Jerk. What could he possibly be thinking? She couldn't imagine. God, what had she done this time? Stop it! Whatever you're doing, Lori, just stop it! She clamped down the tears and let him lie there with his hard-on and his pounding heart.

The next morning Lori and Kevin hiked out through a light snow flurry that turned to a misty rain and finally, at the lower elevations, a fog that seeped through cedars and hemlock, dripping from needles and branches, its own kind of rain. By the time they reached the car park at the trailhead, they were wet and cranky. Lori drove back to Seattle while Kevin slept with the seat reclined and his head against the doorframe. She kept the radio's volume a notch louder than his snores. The fog disappeared as they neared the city.

She dropped Kevin at his apartment and headed home. Walking into her apartment she tried to banish the misadventure with Kevin from her mind. She checked her phone messages. Just one, a chatty meandering from her mother. She showered, made coffee, toasted some bagels. She browsed the paper for a while, but couldn't concentrate. She checked her e-mail. Nothing but spam. She felt desolate; her apartment becoming the last place she wanted to hang out. She wanted to be someplace crowded with people, but people that she didn't have to interact with. Outside the afternoon had turned bright and sunny so Lori decided to go roller-skating at Green Lake. She changed into shorts, a bikini top, and her new zip-up fleece sweatshirt.

Driving to the lake she nearly rear-ended a bright yellow Volkswagen convertible that cut in front of her. The car had two bumper stickers, one read "Naughty Girl," the other "Tease." Lori pulled around the car to get a look at the driver. First she saw the blonde hair, then the girl bobbing her head and singing along to the radio. Twenty at most, only a few years younger than herself. Why the advertisement? Lori wondered. Just whom was she trying to attract with those bumper stickers anyway?

At the lake Lori put on her skates and glided out onto the asphalt path, which was divided by a painted teal stripe. Walkers, runners, and couples with baby strollers crowded the inward, lakeside, while skaters and bike-riders zipped along on the outward side. She slipped in between a couple of bicyclists. She skated slowly at first, easing her way around the beginners with their clonking half-walking half-skating locomotion. When she felt in a good rhythm she leaned over and picked up the pace, her arms swinging freely as she pushed with her thighs and glutes. She struggled to keep the previous night's debacle out of her thoughts—she'd already thought about it the whole drive back to Seattle. What more was there to process? Anyway, whose fault was it? His, of course. *Involuntary*. What a jerk. No, chicken was more like it. Still, what had happened with Jesse? And Carlos? Shit, Lori, just stop it and move forward.

A loop around the lake was nearly three miles and as she approached the place where she started by the old bathhouse theatre, the hiking caught up with her and she felt the burn in her legs. She eased off, stood up and coasted for a bit, feeling hot and sweaty. She unzipped the fleece sweatshirt and tied it around her waist. The moisture that had beaded on her bare stomach wicked away as she glided along the path.

The guys skating passed her looked over their shoulders at her now. She started tentatively, smiling at the good-looking ones, amused by how easily the exposed flesh of her back worked as an advertisement. A cute guy in short-shorts and no shirt returned her smile. Okay, she thought, here goes.

—Nice butt! she called out.

He laughed, slowed down, turned and skated backwards, keeping her pace just in front.

—Show me yours, he said.

Lori did a slow pirouette, then glided with her back to him. She reached down for the sweatshirt and flipped up the flap of fleece.

The Bridge Back to Home

The events that precipitated my return to Boston involved acts of cowardice I can scarcely admit to myself. I had just turned twenty that summer and left Boston for Craigspittle, a small Scottish village on the cusp of the highlands, from where I hoped to escape my family's traditional occupation. A year later, my decision to return home was made while standing on an old stone bridge. The same bridge the men of Craigspittle—who also were facing an uncertain future—had marched over in 1314 as they left town to join Robert The Bruce at the Battle of Bannockburn.

I had gone for a Sunday morning walk in the village and that was when I saw Shona—my girlfriend's sister—on the bridge. Her hands were thrust deep into the pockets of her ankle length coat and she was leaning over the stone wall.

I called out to her as I approached and she gave a start, then quickly turned away as I stopped beside her. I sensed something was wrong and asked: You all right?

She was silent for a moment and kept her face hidden with her hair. Then, pulling the hair away from her face with a hand, she turned towards me and holding her head up defiantly, said:

—See for yerself.

Her right eye was ugly black and swollen shut. A coarse nausea turned my stomach.

—When did he do this to you, Shona?

—Last night.

I leaned against the wall, the chill in the cold stones spreading from palms into body, and looked into the black waters of the burn.

—Have you been to the police yet? I asked.

—God nay! He'd kill me then, surely. Besides, the police wouldna' do anythin'.

—What about your father?

—Och away! she said, and spat into the burn. They're two of a kind.

—Someone ought to string him up by the balls, I said, and I've a mind to—

—Nay! she said, grabbing my arm and digging her fingers in fiercely. You'll do nothin'. Nothin' ye hear. It'll only make things worse.

I started to protest but she was insistent.

—Promise me ye'll stay oot of it. Promise! she said again, squeezing my arm until it hurt.

—I promise.

We stood there, silent in the mist, watching the water race past the bridge on its way to the sea.

The week before, on Halloween, I had gone down to the 'Spittle Inn pub right after the five P.M. opening. I'd barely seated myself at the bar before the publican started needling me.

—Aye, yer almost a Scot noo yerself, Jim said, setting down a nip and a pint. How will ye be able to go back to America like this, have ye asked yerself that, laddie?

—Maybe I won't go back, I said, and tossed back the whiskey, which I chased with a swallow of ale.

—Och aye, wouldna' that be a switch noo, Jim said and got me another nip.

—Don't bet I won't.

—I didna say that, Yank. Besides, there's been some talk amongst the lads, ken, wondering if yer going to settle doon here.

—Yeah, well, Megan has her sights set on America.

—Aye, Jim said and laughed, ye right kent that lassies intentions.

The heavy pine door swung open, letting in swirling snowflakes as it slammed against the paneled walls of the pub. Jock and Paddy, my best friends in the village, rushed in followed by Shona and her husband Grant. They sat at the bar, Jock and Paddy on one side of me, with Grant and Shona on the other. I'd never cared much for Grant, who always seemed surly, even when he wasn't drinking. I liked Shona though, and not just because she was Megan's sister. She worked in the grocery store where I did my shopping and I always enjoyed talking to her while she rang up my purchases.

Jim set down a round of drinks for everyone. For a while they drank and made small talk. Then Grant said to me:

—So ye'll be bringing your wifey to the bonfire tonight, eh Yank?

—Yes. And she's not my wife.

—I telt ye he wis under the thumb, Jock said.

148

—I don't think so, I said.

—Och away! Shona said, Megan'll have ye married and raising bairns by this time next year.

—And lovin' it too, Paddy said.

They made fun of my embarrassment for a bit, then Grant downed the last of his pint and said, Drink up, it's time to go.

Jock and Paddy downed their pints, then Jock said:

—Ye coming with us Yank?

—Well—

—Course not, Paddy interrupted, he's got to pick up the wife.

They laughed and headed for the door. Shona was still trying to finish her pint.

—Shona, come on! Grant said.

—I'm hurrying.

—No fast enough, Grant said and grabbed Shona's arm and pulled her off the bar stool. She let go of the pint glass and beer sloshed onto the bar.

—Let go, she said, you're hurting me.

He raised his arm as if to backhand her. She ducked and he started laughing and pulled her towards the door.

Shona gave me a scared look over her shoulder and said: We'll see ye at the bonfire, then?

—Right, I said. See you later.

Jim wiped the mess on the bar and after Grant and Shona had gone out the door he said: He's a right bastard that one.

What enthralled me most about living in a small Scottish village was the remnants of paganism that still existed. The Halloween bonfire, with its origins in the Druidic *bone*fire, was one such tradition I'd looked forward to, even if its pagan overtones had long since been purged.

The bonfire was to be lit in the village's sacred place—also long-since profaned—which was known simply as "The Den." Located a quarter mile outside the village proper, The Den was a thickly wooded ravine cleaved from the moors by the Craigleigh Burn. Its history was shrouded in mystery, but my friends, ripe with drink before other fires, had boasted of the sacrifices made there in less civilized times, sacrifices both animal and human.

There were about thirty of us around the fire that Halloween night, mostly couples in their late teens and early twenties, but because the lads in the village outnumbered the lasses, there were half a dozen lone males there as well.

Megan was short and buxom, with a curly mass of raven-black hair that she usually left uncombed and strewn wildly about her heart-shaped face. She specialized in direct, unsettling gazes, although if she was of a mind to, her dark brown eyes could be shyly seductive. Her nose was a wee upturned thing sprinkled with freckles and if she liked you she would wrinkle it up and treat you to a broad smile that dimpled her plump cheeks. She liked to talk and I loved listening to her throaty lilt. She was half-past eighteen with a maturity tempered by a wicked black sense of humor. We'd been going around together more or less regularly for a couple of months, often enough to be attached—not as often as she wanted, but as often as I was willing to risk. In my book we weren't even going steady, but according to the village gossip we were practically engaged.

Megan and I arrived at the party after the lighting of the fire, but in time for the supper of mince pies and haggis. Bottles of whisky passed freely back and forth among those circled about the fire. After the meal we were for dancing and singing. First the traditional, with Davie Pride's pipes bleating eerily about The Den as we sang "O' Flower of Scotland." That soon degenerated to rock 'n' roll blaring from someone's boom box as the flames threw our shadows against the stark night-white of the birches. Following a rowdily sung chorus of Wishbone Ash's "Phoenix," we gave the night back its silence and sat drinking and talking and laughing, midnight having come and gone and taken with it the Hallow's Eve.

Megan and I were sitting on a log near the fire, roasting marshmallows on a stick, when the scream pierced the night. And in the silence that followed, Grant's voice, sharp, brutal, could be clearly heard:

—Ah'll treat ye howe'er I want, ye stoopit boot!

I looked up and saw them on the fringe of the fire's light: Shona twisting and flailing, Grant with a handful of her long blond hair.

—Nay mare! Nay mare! she screamed hysterically, canny ye na' le' me alane!

In response, he yelled out obscenities and split the night with a vicious slap. Although Jock and Paddy were only ten feet away they did nothing to stop him, and as his arm reared back for the next blow I leapt up and rushed at him. But I was too far away and before I could get there he'd slapped her twice more, knocking her to the ground, and as she rolled away from him, screaming, he kicked her repeatedly. I took him down with a diving tackle, but before I could hit him with my fists Jock and Paddy pulled me off. I fought to free myself, yelling that I was going to kill the bastard, but they held me fast, arms pinned behind my back. Grant glared at me, eyes feral in the glow of the fire.

—Just stay oot of this Yank! he said. She's my wifey nay yers.

—If you think I'm going to do nothing while you beat her you're crazy.

—Aye, ye aye tried to stop me did ye na', he said, and let loose a sadistic laugh as I struggled to get at him.

Shona lay fetal on the ground, whimpering, and Grant grabbed her under the arm and jerked her to her feet and half-dragged half-carried her across the bridge and down the path out of The Den. Jock and Paddy let me go then, and I turned on them, livid.

—Why in the hell did you stop me!

—Och! She's nay worth the bother, Paddy said.

—The hell she isn't! He can't go around beating her like that and get away with it, and if you're not going to do anything about, I will.

—I wouldna' if I was ye, Jock said. He'll just come after ye sometime when yer back is toorned.

—Besides, Paddy added with a laugh, she likes it ye ken, makes her feel loved.

—Bullshit!

—They've been like this fer years, Jock said handing me a bottle of whisky. Just forget aboot it laddie. Yer in Scotland noo na' the wild west.

I took the bottle from him and threw it as hard as I could into the night. It ricocheted about in the branches for several seconds, then broke against something solid. Jock looked wistfully towards the sound of the smashed bottle and said:

—'Tis a pity.

—Get stuffed! I told him and turned away.

Everyone looked at me as if I were a lunatic. Everyone except Megan. She was still sitting on the log, hunched over with her face buried in her hands. I went to her then, sat down beside her and put my arm around her.

—Thanks, she whispered.

—I can't believe this, I said.

That Sunday morning on the bridge, after Shona walked home, I leaned against the damp stone wall of the bridge and contemplated an uncertain future. Even though I'd heard the jokes in the pub about Grant giving Shona "the boot," that didn't prepare me for what I'd witnessed at the bonfire, nor to see the aftermath of a another of Grant's beatings a week later. And the realization that everyone was acting as if the whole episode were normal only increased my sense of isolation. Of one thing I was certain: I wouldn't be marrying Megan and settling down in Craigspittle to raise bairns. Grant as my brother-in-law? While he beat Shona over and over again? That I couldn't do.

So I returned to my rented cottage and made ready to leave. After bagging stuff for the garbage, I prepared some boxes for mailing, which I took to the post office the next morning on my way to empty out my bank account. Afterwards, traveling with just my backpack, I drove to a used car lot in Edinburgh and sold the car for enough to buy a one-way plane ticket. I didn't give notice to my landlord or my boss at the golf course where I worked. I didn't say goodbye to my friends in the village. I just left. By Tuesday I was back home in Boston without ever having seen Megan again.

I still cringe at my cowardice. The way I snuck out of town. But what else could I have done? I couldn't have dumped Megan and remained living in the village. Craigspittle was just too small—they never would have treated me the same after that. And despite the razzing to the contrary, everyone knew I'd return to America anyway; it was just a matter of when. So who could fault me leaving?

How incredibly naïve I was, you must think?

I'm a cop now—fourth-generation Boston PD—and I've served in the domestic violence unit for twelve years and seen worse beatings than Shona received—worse than you can imagine. I don't run anymore. But back in Craigspittle? What can I say? It wasn't my time or place. It wasn't my home.

Gas Money

Radcliffe sat at the picnic table stabbing the middle finger of his left hand at the portable typewriter—tatch tatch tick titch tatch brrring tatch titch tatch—imprinting words one letter at a time on the stock-white page, words which he hoped would create the illusion that he was still in business. He spat the husk of a sunflower seed towards the grass overrun with lawn daisies, buttercups, and dandelions. He flicked the carriage return, ratcheted the paper up a line, blew into the notch where the keys struck the page, and began again his one finger assault—tatch tatch tatch.

He felt confident about this proposal. He'd surveyed the bank's landscaping, prepared a thorough analysis of the maintenance tasks needed to clean up the mess winter and some low-ball bidder's shoddy work had made of the grounds. Of all the businesses he'd scoped, the YourStreet Bank branch in Ballard was his best shot—a clear case of neglect. Then he felt a spike of fear because he needed this contract so badly. After purchasing the post office box and filling the truck with gas, he only had two hundred seventy six dollars left. He'd quit smoking a month ago and that had saved him, what? At least eight bucks a day. Drinking, too. How much saved there? Who knows. When he'd been flush with cash he'd never kept track. But a lot, way more than he spent on smokes.

Food, gas, postage, and phone calls. Those were his expenses. He could skimp on food spending—the orchard in the park had been a fortuitous find—but not gas for the truck. Gasoline was his lifeline and he couldn't afford to run out—he needed the mobility. If he didn't park somewhere different each night he risked being rousted by the police, or worse, having the truck impounded. He'd be played out then, left with no choice but to join the line at the downtown homeless shelter. He couldn't skimp on stamps either; he needed to keep sending those proposals out until he got a bite. The proposals made that first professional impression on paper, paved the way for his follow-up phone call, let him save the in-person pitch for closing the deal.

A Seattle parks department truck parked in a nearby stall. Radcliffe watched as the stocky black guy with a watch cap pulled down over his eyebrows removed the Weedeater from the truck's bed and slung the strap over his shoulder. The motor started on the first pull, which launched a couple of crows from the branch of an alder. The guy revved the motor, cut the choke, and started in on the tall grass around the parking curbs: zzzzrrrrzzzzzsssszzzz. Bits of grass flew up into the blue-black two-cycle exhaust.

Discipline and focus, Radcliffe said to himself, discipline and focus—tatch tick tatch brrring. But parking curbs done, Weedeater guy began on the picnic tables, trimming along the edges of the concrete slabs. When he was three tables away, and moving closer, Radcliffe jumped up and yelled at the guy, Hey! he said. Hey! Hey! Until the guy cut the power on the Weedeater to an idle and yelled back, What?

—I'm trying to work here, Radcliffe said.

The guy cocked his head, mouthed something Radcliffe didn't hear, then yelled, And what the fuck you think I'm doin' here? He cranked the throttle and kept trimming, staring at Radcliffe, daring him to take the confrontation further.

—Fuck you too, Radcliffe muttered.

He left his stuff on the picnic table and walked the hundred yards to the Honey Bucket. Nearly gagging on the fetid smell as he pulled the plastic door open, he stepped up and in and locked the door. The smell was worse in the semi-dark and heat of the loo; an aerosol of shit. The paper seat cover dispenser was empty. He studied the toilet seat—a few pee stains, but nothing fresh. He looked into the hole: shit, toilet paper, a bag of tortilla chips. He fought another gag. The swelling and pain in his abdomen intensified. At least the toilet paper was plentiful. He felt the loose end of a roll: raspy.

He unhooked the straps and lowered his overalls to the floor. He sat, wincing as his butt cheeks touched the cool plastic. The Weedeater, buzzing away at grass, seemed to be coming closer. A beetle the size of a quarter crawled under the door jam and across the floor towards his boot. How they loved the stink. Radcliffe read the history of cleanings and inspections posted on the door. The Honey Bucket's last cleaning had occurred two weeks previously and based on its documented 10-day cycle it was overdue for another. That explained the mounting pile of shit beneath him. The zzzzrrrrzzzzzsssszzzz of the Weedeater was right outside, spraying grass and pebbles and twig shrapnel against the side of the Honey Bucket.

That's deliberate, Radcliffe thought, the bastard was trying to annoy him. Can't even take a dump in peace. The Weedeater moved off and

Radcliffe bent over from a sharp cramp, his head down close to his boots and overall straps—he shouldn't have eaten so many of the apples and plums from the orchard. Intense pain as the first blast of diarrhea let loose. At least with the deep hole there was no splash back. He stayed bent over, took a sewery breath, unable to distinguish his smell from the mess below, and thought *bootstraps*. That's what he had to do, pick himself up by them. Another wave of gassy cramps before the next salvo exited.

He had returned to Carkeek Park because it was a place where he felt safe. As a kid he'd played on its beach and in its woods. He tried to catch salmon from Piper's Creek with stick, line, hook, and worms. He'd skimboarded when the tide drew down from the rocky beach to the muddy sand of the tidal flats. Played Frisbee and catch at those fried chicken, potato salad, corn on the cob, and watermelon picnics. Hunted under decaying logs for salamanders and skinks and tree frogs to take home to his terrarium. Put pennies on the rails for the train wheels to smash. Now he sought refuge in the park after dragging his tail home to Seattle to—Radcliffe started laughing with the thought—to get his shit together.

The cramps subsided and as he wiped himself he wondered where to wash his hands. No choice but the creek. He hoped the salmon would forgive him. He fastened the overalls and unlocked the door and stepped out. Took a huge gulp of fresh air and then blushed as he saw a woman waiting with a little girl in hand. The woman blushed too; she must have heard him grunting.

—How is it? she asked. I mean, is it clean?

Radcliffe looked at the girl squeezing her legs, shrugged, and said, Only if you can't wait.

Radcliffe hadn't dug cattail tubers since he was a kid, and back then he and his buddies had thought they were "roughing it," but there he was, digging in the mud along the edge of the pond created by Piper Creek's runoff. The pond water was scummy, clotted with kelp-colored algae blooms and he was uncertain the tubers were safe to eat. He'd watched the duck family—two adults and seven peach-fuzzy ducklings—feeding in the pond for several hours and he figured if they could survive the pond scum so could he. In the willow trees behind him the crows jumped from branch to branch, cawing, waiting for a chance to scavenge a stray duckling. The parental ducks seemed oblivious to the possibility, and equally oblivious to him. Ankle deep in the pond's muck with the slippery goo squeezed between his toes, Radcliffe wondered if maybe he shouldn't prey on the ducks himself. A well-aimed rock could do the deed—it wasn't as if the ducks were quick moving targets. Although not an ethical move he could explain, he wasn't ready, just yet anyway, to leap into that class of predator.

—Hey Mister, whatcha doing?

Radcliffe looked up, and two young boys, not quite ten he'd guess, in cutoff jeans and tank tops, were standing in the reeds behind him. They carried plastic buckets. I'm digging cattail tubers, Radcliffe said.

—What for? one of the boys asked.

—I'm going to eat them.

That got the boys excited and Radcliffe pointed out the best parts of the tubers for eating, and described how to clean them. He handed over a couple of tubers.

Radcliffe said, Have your mom wrap 'em in foil and bake 'em like a potato.

—She'll freak, one of the boys said.

—Thanks Mister, the other boy said.

—What do you have in your buckets? Radcliffe asked.

—Frog eggs, one of the boys said.

Radcliffe looked in the bucket. Thousands of eggs, looking like miniature eyeballs, floated in the pond water. That'll be a lot of tadpoles, he said. But he doubted whether a single one would see maturity.

Two weeks later Radcliffe was first in line waiting for the post office to open. The responses to his proposals had begun arriving over the past few days, so he started his day by checking the post-office box. Behind him in line was a man and a boy/girl—Radcliffe wasn't sure which—who, judging by the asymmetrical facial features and the lumpiness over the right eye, was retarded. Radcliffe made eye contact and the boy/girl said, You smell.

—Shhh, the man said. Be polite, please.

—Stinkee-poo, the boy/girl said.

—Sorry, the man said without embarrassment.

—Stinkee-poo.

—Jerry, stop that.

—He's a stinkee-poo.

Radcliffe couldn't help but laugh as Jerry pinched his nostrils closed and turned away.

A postal worker unlocked the doors. Radcliffe went to his box and sifted through the few letters, saw the YourStreet Bank logo, and ripped the envelope open. He scanned the letter; it was signed by a Mr. Brad Owens, Assistant Branch Manager, and requested that Radcliffe call for an appointment to discuss his landscape maintenance proposal.

—Yes! Radcliffe said out loud.

Behind him, Jerry said, You're a stinkee-poo.

Brown or black? Radcliffe slid a hangar along the rack to get a better look at the jackets. The brown was subdued; the black seemed too much the power-suit. He bent over and sniffed. The brown smelled of cigarettes and vacuum cleaner dust. The black of mothballs. Well, what did he expect from a thrift store? He fingered a tweed jacket, and then a tan corduroy—less businessy jackets those, more the landscaper image; just because he was meeting with bankers didn't mean they expected him to look like one too.

—What's the occasion?

Radcliffe turned, then looked down at a frizzy orange-haired woman. She was barely five-feet tall, even with the hair. He guessed she was in her seventies. She smelled of coconuts and watermelon and menthol. Excuse me? he said.

—You're deep in thought over those jackets, she said. Figured it must be for something special.

The name tag on her store smock read Mabel. Radcliffe hesitated, slid his finger up and down the ridges of the corduroy jacket's sleeve. I need to make a good first impression, he said.

—Okay, Mabel said. Man or woman?

—Man.

—This a family thing? Mabel asked. The father of some gal you're sweet on?

—No, no, Radcliffe said. Kind of a job interview.

—Oh, she said, and scanned the rack. So something confident, but not flashy. There we go, she said pulling out a dark grey jacket and handing it to Radcliffe. What are you? A forty-two? Radcliffe shrugged, and she said, Well, try it on then.

Radcliffe put on the jacket, which was a skosh tight in the back, but seemed to fit otherwise.

—Hard to tell with those overalls, Mabel said. I'm guessing you need slacks and a shirt?

—Shoes, too, Radcliffe said.

—We got it all, she said and spread wide her arms to include the whole store.

—I can only spend thirty-dollars on the lot, he said.

Mabel frowned, said, Oh boy. Then, brightening to the challenge, she grabbed Radcliffe's arm, Come with me, she said. We have a bunch of stuff in back that just came in. I'll fix you up.

Radcliffe gave the dollar to the clerk, who said, Have a good swim, and handed back a towel and a locker key. Although he nodded, Radcliffe hadn't come to the afternoon session at the YMCA to swim. He needed a shower. In the locker room he undressed and immersed himself in a spray as hot as he could stand, hoping to scald his pores clean. After his muscles relaxed he lathered up with soap and shampoo from the wall-mounted dispensers. The soap was turquoise and mediciney smelling and stung his eyes when he washed his face.

Out of the water, Radcliffe toweled aggressively, seeking to rub off any residue the rinse missed. Then, still naked, he took his underwear to the sink, which he filled with hot water and soap, and started scrubbing.

The poolside locker room door opened and three teenage boys came in laughing. Water dripped from their hair and knee-length swim trunks. They headed for the showers, but as Radcliffe continued his scrubbing, he heard one of the boy's say, Look at those zits.

—His back's fucking covered with them, another boy said.

—So's his fat ass, the first boy said.

Radcliffe kept scrubbing, didn't make eye contact with them in the mirror. He couldn't afford a scene.

—Look at him, a third boy said. Scrubbing the skid-marks from his drawers.

One of them farted loudly and they broke into high-pitched laughter. Someone said, Let's get out of here.

After they'd left, Radcliffe turned sideways and looked over his shoulder, trying to see his back in the mirror. The red bumps looked like chicken pox. A few had fresh bloody crusts, their heads broken when he'd toweled dry. He looked away, disgusted with himself. Turning the tap on full, he rinsed the underwear in icy water, then he twisted the fabric until his hands and forearms cramped and no water was left to wring out. He thumped the button on the hand dryer with his fist, shook out the shorts, and thrust them under the hot forced air.

Radcliffe sat in the bank's lobby waiting for his meeting with Mr. Owens. He still felt uncomfortable in the clothes Mabel had picked out for him. He'd studied his image in the mirror enough to see, and know, he looked presentable, but the clothes weren't, after all, *his*. He hadn't lived in the clothes and he hadn't earned the right to wear them without feeling self-conscious. He watched Owens—an early thirties MBA type who definitely had lived in his pin-striped suit, white shirt, and plum-colored tie—talking on the phone, comfortably leaned back with his straight black hair pressed into the burgundy leather headrest of his executive chair, free hand alternately waving and chopping, occasionally resting palm down on the desk top. As he watched Owens, Radcliffe modified and rehearsed his strategy. He'd play to the guy's ego, make Owens feel as if he'd out-negotiated Radcliffe; not give him too good a deal though—that'd just make Owens suspicious—but good enough to make him feel superior and in control of the transaction.

Strategy in mind, Radcliffe felt confident he could pull the interview off and make the sale, when a tall, broad-shouldered woman in a navy blue suit with gold buttons walked up and extended her hand, Mr. Radcliffe, she said, I'm Gina Karlsson, the branch manager. Radcliffe stood, shook hands. Sorry to keep you waiting, she said.

As they walked to her desk, Radcliffe looked over at the gesticulating Owens. I talked with Mr. Owens on the phone, Radcliffe said, so I expected to meet with him.

—Brad screens all the business proposals for me, she said as she rounded the corner of her desk and sat down.

Radcliffe sat in the black vinyl chair she gestured to and tried to get a read on her. No family pictures on her glass-topped desk. Just a few neat stacks of paper and file folders. A bank-logoed coffee cup sat on a felt-bottomed coaster.

—I won't take too much of your time today, she said and opened a folder. Radcliffe recognized his proposal, which now had parts highlighted in yellow and notes written in the margins. As I'm sure Brad told you, she said, we were quite impressed with your proposal.

Radcliffe, trying to maintain a confident demeanor, said, I try to focus on projects where I can bring an immediate benefit.

—Good, she said. Let's go over a few things.

Radcliffe's confidence grew as they worked through safe territory: the benefits of replacing damaged plants rather than pruning; his estimates for the number of yards of bark; how much fertilizer and herbicides were needed for the planting beds. He'd produced a weekly schedule of maintenance lasting through the summer and tapering off to once-a-month in late fall. He'd expected some resistance there, but Karlsson flipped through that part of the proposal without comment. She studied the last page, the cost summary, then looked up and held the gaze. References? she said.

Even though he'd been expecting the question, her directness caught him off guard, left him no room to maneuver. He felt his carefully constructed façade cracking and peeling as if it were old plaster. He could have handled Owens in this situation; needling him, turning it into a matter of respect and honor, shifting the onus back to Owens' ego, his ability to judge character for himself. *References, Brad? You don't need no stinking references.* Radcliffe knew that wasn't going to work with Gina Karlsson—she'd see right through him. As Radcliffe hesitated, she closed the folder.

—Is that a problem? she asked.

Radcliffe tried to recover, It's just that I've recently moved to Seattle from Los Angeles. I've no local references.

—That's okay, she said. I don't have time to visit your job sites anyway. I *do* need to talk to a previous client, however. Another bank would be ideal.

No way Radcliffe could meet that request. He'd left too many jobs unfinished in California. Still, even with his image and reputation in tatters, he'd had what it took to get in the door. Given the chance, he knew he could do the job. And, at this point, what more did he have to lose? He decided, for once, just to be honest.

—Look, he said. I don't have any references, okay? The truth is I made a huge mess of my life in Los Angeles. But Seattle is my hometown— I was born right down the street in Ballard Hospital—and I came here to get my life back on track. Radcliffe paused, saw Karlsson's widened eyes and her mouth hanging open, then added, I'm making a fresh start.

Karlsson leaned back in her chair, rested her elbows on the armrests, and steepled her fingers. She glanced briefly toward the security guard. Radcliffe tried to gauge what to say next, knowing that begging for a chance would fail—the condition of the bank's landscaping showed him that she'd been burned before, just the way he'd burned all those people in LA.

His wallet contained one hundred and eighty three dollars. How long could he make that last? He couldn't ask Karlsson for an advance on work—that was the classic fly-by-night move—his only play was to offer to do the work first, allow her to pay for performance. But how long could he hold on without getting paid? One month? Two? What to cut? Postage and phone calls, for sure. And he could cancel the post-office box now. He'd be down to just food and gas. The occasional shower at the YMCA. Right then, however, he needed to convince her to trust him. Needed her to give him a chance to prove himself. What could he say? How many months work in advance would persuade her? Food he could find. Gas money? Without that he couldn't survive.

Fresh Sludge

Allison, legal aide, reads the accusing email and shouts at the computer's monitor, Son-of-a bitch. You're not blaming me.

She clicks on files, opening them into a word processor. She selects lengthy passages of text and launches print jobs. The laser printer beside her desk churns out page after page. Every forty minutes or so she loads another two hundred pages into the paper tray. She keeps printing all night long.

2

Max, security guard, is on his rounds. The three AM loop. Starting on the ground floor he works his way higher; two three four five six seven, topping out on eight. Padding down carpeted halls. Checking doors when the lights are on. Locking them if they're not. He prowls the halls; minimum wage protection against what? Corporate espionage? Papers spread out on a desk and the click-whir of a spy-cam's shutter? He's there to guard against employees showing up at night and filling the back of a pickup truck with computers.

Two months into the gig before he gets his first action. Floor four. 3:17 AM he'll later write in his logbook. He hears the music as soon as he comes through the stairwell door. All the offices are dark. Halfway down the inside hall the grunge throb of Alice In Chains oscillates between F and F#, then up to C before descending chromatically with root-fifth sludge. The distorted bass, descending in sync with the guitar, pulses the walls. Allison types frenetically on the computer's keyboard. Max stops in front of the office, peers through his reflection in the glass, peers into the office lit by the glow from the computer's monitor. He walks away from the office without saying anything, without being seen.

3

Five-thirty AM and the fourth floor reeks of microwave popcorn. Max cruises past Allison's empty office, the grunge rock still throbbing from her stereo, and heads for the kitchen. Max stops in the kitchen's doorway. She's sitting cross-legged on the counter stuffing a handful of popcorn into her mouth. She wipes her lips with the back of her hand, chews and swallows.

—Caught me, she says.

—Doing what? Says Max.

—You security guys are so sly, she says and offers him popcorn.

—Max, he says and waves off the popcorn.

—Max? she says, chewing with her mouth full.

—You know. Like Headroom. Max Headroom.

—Not Maxwell Smart? She says, taking off a shoe and holding it up to her ear.

—That's good. But no.

—How about Maximus? Gluteus Maximus, she says. Bet the kids called you that in school.

—Not to my face.

—I can see that, she says, and raises the popcorn container to her mouth and pours in some popped kernels. Chewing with her mouth open again, she says, I'm Allison.

Max leans against the doorframe, hands in his trouser pockets. Says nothing.

—I've seen you watching me, she says.

—My job is to be aware.

—Not like that. Peeping over the top of cubicle walls.

—I'm suspicious by nature, Max says.

—A voyeur is more like it, she says.

—I'm paid to watch.

She laughs, says, There's a switch. Voyeurs usually pay to see the show.

—What makes you such an expert?

—I'm an exhibitionist by nature.

—Then you shouldn't mind me watching you.

—I never said I did.

4

First date. Max and Allison at the Seattle Center's Experience Music Project museum. Cocooned inside headphones, they spend hours not talking. Moving from exhibit to exhibit, pointing the wireless handsets at displays to download music samples and narration by luminaries and curators. They lose themselves in the history of guitars exhibit, the history of northwest rock-n-roll exhibit, and the Jimi Hendrix exhibit. In the music lab they play digital guitars. Exiting the lab, Allison says to Max, You never told me you played.

—You never asked.

—You let me go on and on about my band without saying a word.

—You didn't pause for breath, Max says.

—No excuses.

—An Alice song, Max says, and starts humming the rhythm. My band used to cover that one.

—You can crawl back under your rock any time, Allison says.

5

His three AM rounds interrupted, Max sits on the edge of Allison's desk juggling three of her blue and green earth-emblazoned squeeze balls.

—It's not like that at all, she says.

—So you only want me to turn my back, pretend I didn't see anything?

—Well aren't there video cameras?

Max stops juggling, says, You want me to edit you out of the security video?

Her smile says yes. Max shakes his head in disbelief and starts juggling again.

—Don't you keep a log?

—You want me falsify my reports, too?

—Don't look at me like I'm doing something wrong, Allison says and jabs a pointed finger at Max. I'm the one that's getting screwed here. Are you helping me or what?

6

Allison flips through the *New Orleans Weekly* until she reaches the music section. She reads the ads, scans the list of upcoming acts. After the third time through the section she begins circling prospects with a chartreuse highlighter. On a legal pad she lists nightclubs. At the top of the page she writes "THE TOUR."

7

Allison and Max follow her boss and his secretary to the University of Washington Arboretum. Follow them to where they lay out the blanket among the witch hazels. From a nearby hill, Allison peers through the camera's telephoto lens.

—You sure know where to go to see a show, Max says.

—This is the same place he used to bring me, Allison says while she snaps photos.

—Ah, Max says. He has a track record.

—Broken record is more like it.

—Stuck in a rut.

—Maybe these pictures will get him unstuck, Allison says as she winds the camera.

8

They rendezvous in the strip-mall parking lot. Max leans against his car, arms crossed, as Allison approaches carrying the envelope containing freshly printed photographs.

—We've got them, she says.

—So how much does blackmail cost?

—Eleven-eighty-three.

—Cheaper than a lap dance, Max says.

Allison turns and leans back to buff his crotch.

9

Reaching the end of the pier, Allison and Max pause their walk to watch the Bainbridge Island ferry dock. They lean their elbows on the plank railing as the seagulls swirl above the prop wash.

—So that's your plan, Max says, take the act on the road?

—What's holding you here? Allison asks.

—No one's asked me to leave, Max says.

—You'd go?

—You asking?

10

Allison skips around the office then stops in front of Max and holds up the pages from the patent application. Shoot me with these, she says.

—Your Oswald photo, Max says as he triggers the shutter, winds the film.

—Zoom on this, she says, and rattles the page.

Max, in a crouch, moves closer, continuing to tighten the focus of the lens until the text in the frame is readable. Good, she says, when he takes the picture. Let's do this stack.

—I like the way you cover your ass, baby, Max says.

—Make sure you cover yours, she says.

11

Six piles in a neat row on the avocado-colored Formica tabletop. Allison's studio apartment. She works the piles. Gathering into a stack the one-page band biography; the page of concocted reviews; the 8 x 10 glossy band photo with the band's name on the bottom border—Fresh Sludge; the demo CD; and the business card, all of which she stuffs into a manila envelope. She licks the flap, seals the envelope, and hands it to Max. Hunched over the table Max starts writing the next address from the list of nightclubs. Allison hands him another envelope. Writing again, Max asks, Shouldn't we get an agent?

—I know the circuit and the bars I want to play, Allison says and licks another flap.

—It would be—

—I'm through getting ripped off, she says and drops the envelope onto the table. Okay?

—It's just—

—My way, she says and stares him down, then jerks her thumb toward the door.

12

Max riffs through the blues scale, bending in and out patterns, works his way up the neck—B minor, A minor, G, then a quick spray of open E notes on the bottom end. Allison growls out the next verse.

Thought I had me a good man
The kind that'd see me through thick and thin

Thought I had me a good man
But he turned around and did me in.

They're sitting cross-legged, facing each other on the king-size bed. Allison strums through the verse, B, A, G. Max accompanies her by playing a bass line, picking out the root notes of the chords as she changes. She shifts to the chorus, hostile now, and Max doubles her an octave lower.

Gave 'em one last chance
Ain't trusting nobody no more
Three strikes they're out
Ain't trusting nobody no more
Through getting fucked with
Ain't trusting nobody no more.

13

Max, brow knitted, is carefully carving paper dolls with dull scissors. Push, squeeze, and pry open. Up the leg. Turn and cut an edge for the body. Push squeeze, and carefully rotate in the armpit. Open, push, squeeze, and crunch crunch crunch around to create a head. Max only hears the scissors crunch in between the chewing sound the shredder makes as it eats through another of the documents Allison has fed it.

They sit at the kitchen table in Max's apartment. The table top is covered with a dozen stacks, each a foot or more high, of manuscript pages, or, in the terminology of Allison's non-disclosure agreement—*intellectual property*. Allison is bent over the shredder, a stack of paper in her lap, feeding the whirring tines. Her foot taps out a 6/8 beat.

A note, attached to the refrigerator with a Dominoes Delivers magnet, reminds them to *MAIL THE PHOTOS!!!$$$*.

14

Allison and Max stroll into the hotel's twelfth-story cocktail lounge at a quarter past six. The bartender washes glasses in the sink behind the bar. Aside from him they have the place to themselves. They sit at a table against the far wall, away from the river view. Get a round of drinks going.

—Gather stats, Allison says to Max.

—Ten-four, he says and leaves the table.

Allison removes a sheet of paper from her purse, unfolds it and smoothes it out on the tabletop. Max, who had been walking around the cocktail lounge, begins making deliberate strides across the dance floor, cutting the room into paced-off angles. Allison charts his course, sketching lines on her paper. Max returns to the table, reports: Sixteen. Twenty-two. Eight. Call it five. Then thirty.

—The bar?

Max walks over to the bar's corner, steps it off, and reports back: Twenty by eight.

—DJ Console?

Max eyeballs it: Six and three.

—Count?

—Twenty-five bar stools. Eight booths. That's thirty-two. A dozen tables. Two to four. Call it thirty-six.

—How many standing?

Max surveys, calculates, rubs his goatee stubble: Two to three deep. Say half of them with seats, but getting drinks. So at least another thirty.

Allison points at the placard over the door frame which reads— Max. Capacity 80. She says, the take is better than that.

15

Down the corridor from the nightclub's restrooms, down where the yellow and black checkerboard tiles stopped at the door with the faux-bronze Manager nameplate, Alison and Max pause. Rivulets of dried glue streak the wood beneath the label.

—You sure about this strategy? Max asks.

Behind them the bug-light incinerates a moth and Allison wrinkles her nose.

—Act like the heavy.

—You kidding? Max says. Anyone can see it's you.

—Bitch, she says, and raps a triplet on the nameplate with her knuckles.

16

Allison shoves the curtains open as Max brings their luggage into the hotel room.

—We have a view of the river, she says.

Max dives onto the bed and bounces its springs. Carving a course up the channel's middle are five rusted barges heaped with sawdust. A tug pushes the barges. On the tug's deck, leaning against the superstructure, is one of the crew.

—Max. Look. Allison says. He's got binoculars.

—Who does? says Max, still bouncing the box springs.

—That guy on the tugboat.

Max joins Allison at the window. Where is he? Max asks.

—There, Allison says and jabs her index finger against the window. He's by the door at the front of the boat.

—Think he sees us? Max says.

—I bet he's scanning the hotel rooms for boink action.

—Probably peeps his way up the river.

—Let's give him a show, Allison says, and pulls off her t-shirt and flounces her tits in front of the window.

—Whoa, Max says.

Allison unzips her jeans and pushes them down to her ankles, steps out and kicks them across the room. She flings her panties at Max, and hops onto the small table, spreads her legs.

—Saddle up, Bucko, she says.

17

With their take they go to another city. Get a high floor at another hotel. Another room with a view of a river.

18

Allison is riding Max hard, hard enough that he starts worrying about breakage. She's shoving down on him and grunting. He arches up to stay inside of her on the upstroke, grabs her ass cheeks so he won't lose contact. She slams down harder, tries to drive him through the bed. Her grunts turn to an anguished howl and she beats her fists against his chest. Allison collapses onto Max's chest, sobbing and calling him a son-of-a-bitch. Max gasps for breath, amid aftershocks, every nerve and synapse still firing. When her sobbing subsides, he says, What in the hell was that?

—Mad sex, she says.

—What?

—I promised myself I wouldn't fall in love, you fucker.

19

Allison is sitting in a metal-backed chair at the makeup counter having eye shadow applied by a green-aproned specialist.

—The funny thing about makeup, Allison says, is that no matter how much you put on, you still look like the same person.

—So why the clown face? Max says.

—Disguise is a form of flattery.

—What about these dark circles? Max says as he bends over the counter and peers into the circular mirror. These bags? What can be done about them?

20

Halfway through the first set Allison knows she can do this—three sets a night on her own with no one to blame but herself. The crowd in the bar has quieted, listening just to her now, as she plays a song they haven't heard before, one of her originals. She leans forward on the stool until her lips nearly kiss the microphone. Eyes closed, her voice tumbles deep into its lowest register as she sings harmony to the guitar's melody. She loses herself for a while in that chorus, before shifting to the turnaround and finger picking the notes, heading towards the outro where Max used to play that slinky solo. Instead, Allison holds a unison bend, lets it moan, then cycles three times through a little riff and hits the closing G-minor, which she leaves out there, ringing, until the sustain fades into the amplifier's hollow hum.

Risk Factors

From: greggd@shoptildrop.com
Date: March 15, 2001
To: brittf@jdfandj.com
Subject: Re:ShopTilDrop.com 10-K filing

Britt,

Congratulations on your appointment as Lead Counsel
for the Chapter 11 bankruptcy preparations. Find
enclosed my draft of the 10-K statement. As you know,
most of the document is boilerplate, so I'm only
including the sections where we have significant risk
by not disclosing the facts. You'll find my comments
in brackets. Because this is my last filing as
Corporate Counsel, and likely my last legal filing
period—except for the deal I'll cut to keep my own ass
out of jail—I hope you'll appreciate (and benefit
from) the candor.
Best of luck,
Gregg

ITEM 1. BUSINESS [The difficulties start right here, Britt—it's an oxymoron. Those ultimate bull-shitters, the Wall Street analysts, get their jibes in *now* by asking what idiot wrote the original business plan (as if they didn't *know* what the fuck was going on). That question entirely misses the fucking point. It never was *meant* to be a "business." Right from the start it was a get rich quick scheme. The *founders,* CEO Larry-boy, CFO Grisscoe, and COO Jenks—more about those miserable fucks later—had no long-term plan to build a business. Their short-term goal was to capitalize on the internet gold rush by getting venture capitalists to fund their bright idea (which they knew hadn't a chance in hell of succeeding). The medium-term plan was the initial public offering.

Even after the venture capitalists took their cut, the founders stood to make hundreds of millions of dollars each. Post IPO they only had one goal: prime the media pump and fuel the hype. Keep that stock price climbing until the lockout provision—which prevented them from selling shares for six-months after the IPO—expired and they could sell their stock and cash in. Beyond that, the only plan they had was to sell the company before it became common knowledge that the business plan was a not so fragrant, steaming pile of bullshit.]

Cautionary Statement Regarding Forward-Looking Statements

This Annual Report on Form 10-K contains forward-looking statements. These statements relate to our, and in some cases our customers' or partners', future plans, objectives, expectations, intentions and financial performance, and the assumptions that underlie these statements. In some cases, you can identify forward-looking statements because they use terms such as "anticipates," "believes," "continue," "could," "estimates," "expects," "intends," "may," "plans," "potential," "predicts," "should," "will" ["we" "may" "lie" "cheat" "and" "steal" "you" "blind"] or the negative of those terms or other comparable words. These statements involve known and unknown risks, uncertainties and other factors that may cause industry trends or our actual results, level of activity, performance or achievements to be materially different from any future results, levels of activity, performance or achievements expressed or implied by these statements. [I don't know about you, Britt, but part of what attracted me to corporate law in the first place was the chance to craft such cover-your-ass masterpieces as this paragraph. Were you one of those kids, like me, who had an excuse for anything that went wrong? Or who always managed to shift the blame onto your brothers and sisters, friends and classmates? Shit, is that where all this duplicity starts? Back there in home-sweet-home? Dad cheating on mom. Mom cheating on dad. Jason, the oldest—the "good" kid among us—stealing fivers and tenners from the envelope with "emergency" written on it that was taped to the underside of the kitchen junk drawer. Don't think I've forgotten Allison. The baby. The bitch. The one who taught me the true meaning of manipulation. And that's just my fucking family! Then we go to school and mix it up with all the other twisted fucks, until the best of the lying, cheating, stealing, manipulating bunch of us end up in law school—where we're taught how to get away with it for a living. Let's face it, Britt, besides corporate law, the only other place we belong is congress. You have your *accusers*, your Cardinal Richelieu's—"Give me six lines written by any man and I will find within them something with which to hang him"—and your excusers, your Bill Clinton's—"It depends on what your definition of is *is*." Yep, that's our peer group.] These factors include those listed under this heading and the headings "Risk Factors," "Management's Discussion and Analysis of Financial Condition and Results of Operations" and elsewhere in this Annual Report on Form 10-K. In addition, these forward-looking statements include, but are not limited to, statements regarding the following:

. the anticipated increases in our operating expenditures, including in research and development, sales and marketing and general and administrative expenses [Or, how management will finally disclose all the costs kept off the balance sheet in prior quarters.];

. the anticipated cost of our revenues [Or, how that revenue per subscriber number will plummet once the divisor is changed from the number of people accessing the website (60,000 per day), to the number of customers who actually finalize purchases (100) because our heavily marked up Coach, Prada, and Louis Vutton accessories can't compete with the outlet malls, even after we implemented Jenks "free shipping" brainstorm. Now there's a fucking scam for you. Do those 100 people a day who actually buy something think they're getting a deal with free shipping? Have they never compared prices? The only thing that's free about that shipping is the lie it's based upon.];

. the anticipated increase in our capital expenditures and lease commitments [Or, that undisclosed balloon-payment coming due on our office space. Not to mention the hush-money paid to the property manager. I can't believe that fucking Larry-boy thinks that no one will turn on the fan, or that none of this shit will hit the fan, or that if it does hit the fan, that none of it will stick to him. Well, Britt, guess what? I just turned on the fan.];

. the anticipated amortization of deferred compensation [Or, how management gets rich by unloading stock options and double shafts the stockholders with both diluted holdings and lowered stock price.];

. the adequacy of our capital resources to fund our operations [Or, how long the CFO can keep the shell-game of shifting capital from one limited partnership to another, because once all the shells are turned over at the same time it will be clear that all the capital is in fact gone. A prediction: that sneaky fuck Grisscoe will be the *one* to get away with it.]; and

.   the ability of our ShopTilDrop(TM) technology to
increase the efficiency in which we manage our
customers' Internet shopping experience [Or, can the foreign-exchange calculating algorithms be tweaked so that they fleece customers on every transaction. Oh, Canada!];

Although we believe that expectations reflected in the
forward-looking statements are reasonable, we cannot
guarantee future results, levels of activity,
performance or achievements. We will not update any of
the forward-looking statements after the date of this
Annual Report on Form 10-K to conform these statements
to actual results or changes in our expectations,
except as required by law. You should not place undue
reliance on these forward-looking statements, which
apply only as of the date of this Annual Report on
Form 10-K. [In other words, our statements in this filing are not worth the paper they are printed on.]

Recent Sales of Unregistered Securities
During the fiscal year ended January 31, 2001, we
issued and sold the following unregistered securities:
From May 15, 2000 to May 18, 2000, we issued and sold
5,664,125 shares of Series C preferred stock to a
total of 25 investors, which consisted of 10 venture
capital investors, seven investors who are key
employees or directors, or that are trusts affiliated
with key employees or directors, and ten other
individual investors, for an aggregate purchase price
of $115,000,835.69. All shares of our Series C
preferred stock converted into common stock upon the
completion of our initial public offering. [On its surface, there's nothing untoward in this sale, it's the standard way management and early investors get rich off an IPO. But by falsifying the business plan, the IPO prospectus, and the subsequent financial statements until the lock-up period against selling shares had expired, which allowed these early investors— and the trust funds of management's families—to subsequently sell those shares at the height of the stock market bubble, while public shareholders continued to buy the stock based on management's ebullient, but false, public comments, we hold these sales of unregistered securities to be fraudulent.]

On September 7, 2001, we issued and sold 129,550
shares of common stock to three consultants who
performed recruiting services for us for an aggregate
purchase price of $893,806.00. [Oh this is a good one, Britt. Who were the three consultants, you might ask? Would it surprise you to learn that they were the three teenage sons of the

ShopTilDrop's CFO's sister-in-law? Would it surprise you to learn that their "consulting firm" was a wholly owned subsidiary of a wholly owned subsidiary of a limited partnership of which Grisscoe, said CFO (Sick-fuck Officer), was the managing partner? I know what you would say, and you would be right, I violated no statutes by handling all of the legal and regulatory filings for those businesses. And that attorney-client privileges prevented me from disclosing the conversations I had with Grisscoe, conversations in which it was discussed that the sole purpose of issuing these shares to what I now know to be sham consultants from sham subsidiaries, was, in fact, to siphon equity out of the company. Legally, not guilty, we might agree. But, had I crossed the ethical line at that point? Aren't questionable legal maneuvers what corporate law is all about? Wasn't that what I was supposed to be doing? Ask yourself that one, Britt, and consider your answer carefully, because it is a precipice with a slippery slope on the other side, a precipice with no safe perch in the middle, a precipice you are about to find yourself sliding down one side or the other. Which side will it be, dear Britt? Which side of the slope will you slide down?]

The sales of the above securities were deemed to be exempt from registration [and thus not disclosed to potential shareholders until after the fact] under the Securities Act in reliance on Section 4(2) of the Securities Act, or Rule 506 under Regulation D promulgated thereunder, or Rule 701 promulgated under Section 3(b) of the Securities Act, as transactions by an issuer not involving a public offering or transactions pursuant to compensatory benefit plans and contracts relating to compensation as provided under Rule 701. The recipients of securities in each of these transactions represented their intention to acquire the securities for investment only and not with view to or for sale [Which is bullshit because most of these shares were unloaded as the public bid the stock up—and that was *exactly* the plan.] in connection with any distribution [Again, distribution of wealth from the capital markets and the investing public to the pockets of those initial thirty investors, was the sole purpose of this company from day one.] thereof and appropriate legends were affixed to the share certificates and instruments issued in such transactions. All recipients had adequate access, through their relationship with us, to information about us. [And, us, in this instance, were liars.]

Risk Factors

Set forth below and elsewhere in this Annual Report on Form 10-K and in other documents we file with the Securities and Exchange Commission, are risks and uncertainties that could cause actual results to differ materially [More bullshit—these guys had absolutely no intention of ever putting in writing the real risks to investor's capital. And they certainly won't do so now as bankruptcy approaches because stating those risks would bring in the SEC and the Justice Department with a criminal fraud investigation. At first, I didn't know that non-disclosure was part of the game. I wasn't one of the founders, after all. Early on they used the venture capitalist's lawyers, but post-IPO, when the rock show started, it was time to bring in their own boy. Me. Me? When this whole internet craziness took off I was a foot soldier among an army of lawyers with a giant consumer products company. I'd applied for a few positions, but nothing got me stoked until I talked to the boys at ShopTilDrop. The chance to be a one-man legal department with a hot internet-IPO? Just as the bubble was inflating? What do you think? That was an opportunity I had to hang-ten *all* over.

They kept me out of the loop at first. Kept me on routine stuff like employment contracts, non-competes, and license agreements. I subbed out the specialty work like patents and intellectual property. They didn't put me on the inside until that first 10-Q filing, and then only after trashing my first draft, which basically reiterated the risks documented in the IPO prospectus, plus added several new sections based on recent company activities I felt needed to be disclosed. The first test of whether I was with them or not came in that meeting up in Larry-boy's office. He was sitting in a leather chair that must have set the company back five grand. Flanking his hulking cherry wood desk were Grisscoe and Jenks. So there they were, the three founders, or as they like to refer to themselves, *The Three Musketeers*. All former consultants at one of the big-five accounting firms, where, presumably, they cooked up this scheme. Of course, at that point, I still thought the business was legit.

I took the chair across from Larry-boy, and he started right in, telling me how, this being the first public filing an all, we needed to put a good spin on it, "We don't want to spook Wall Street," he said. To which Jenks, the consummate shill, added in his lilting TV preacher voice, "Don't want to give anybody an excuse to dump the stock." This was punctuated with a fake smile that should have hurt his face. Larry-boy laughed and said, "Nobody gets to dump the stock before we do." Grisscoe looked concerned. "Kidding aside, Gregg," he said, "we need you to smooth this Risk Factors section over. Cover our asses, but put a good spin on it." He handed me a copy of the filing. "I've marked some sections you should cut." I flipped through the pages. He'd crossed out all of the new sections I'd added. "None of that is material for the next couple of quarters, right?" Grisscoe said and looked at Jenks. "Nope," Jenks said. "So there's no reason to disclose it now." I glanced at Larry-boy and he shot me a lop-sided grin—the left-side turned up and the right-side turned down—that I would later recognize as his my-way-or-else look. "Think you can handle that, Gregg? Do what you do best? Put that spit and polish on it?" I guess I hesitated a bit, weighing the legalities, because Grisscoe said, "We need to know you're with us, Gregg—part of the team." I looked at Jenks. "Well," I said, "if they're not material…" He shook his head, gave me the fake smile. "And Gregg," Larry-boy said, "in appreciation for your creativity on this matter, we're kicking in another fifty-thousand options to your compensation package." And just like that I'd stepped out onto the slippery slope.] from the results contemplated by the forward-looking statements contained in this Annual Report on Form 10-K.

Our financial results may fluctuate significantly, which could cause our stock price to decline.
Our revenue and operating results could vary significantly from period to period. These fluctuations could cause our stock price to fluctuate significantly or decline. Important factors that could cause our quarterly results to fluctuate materially include:

[Okay, Britt, what were these guys thinking? Did they just think it was okay to rip everyone off? Did they think that was better than running a legitimate business? Or is criminality just part of human DNA? Do we always choose the path of least resistance? Or is it just the miserable scum-bag fucks that go into business? So, here I am, one of them, one of the miserable fucks. Don't think it makes me feel better to admit that, because it gets worse. Time to jettison the boilerplate and start disclosing what was really going on. In no particular order, here are the risks—risks I deliberately left out of all the previous SEC filings—that should have been disclosed to investors:

We will acquire the most expensive office space on the west coast.
After the IPO closes we will move our offices from the warehouse in the Tukwila furniture district to the Carillon Point Marina in Kirkland. Our executive team will occupy the fifth floor and enjoy stunning views of Lake Washington, the Seattle skyline, and the

snow capped Olympic Mountains. This move alone will increase our burn rate from $125,000 a month to over three million. **At least once a month we will charter jets and fly employees, selected customers, and Wall Street analysts and investment bankers to Las Vegas.** Their three-days of debauchery in sin-city will, of course, be on us. And all of the expenses will be written off as operating costs, the costs of doing business, which they are, because without such payola, we have no business. These junkets, of course, will not supplant the weekly Friday night champagne and caviar parties we'll sponsor at corporate headquarters, the lawn along the lakeshore being particularly well suited to entertaining.

At this point, Britt, I must confess my own personal failing, the moment when I slid so far down the slippery slope, of which I am just now reaching the bottom, that I could no longer pull myself back up. It happened the first time I went with Jenks, Grisscoe, and Larry-boy on a Vegas junket. We stayed in high-rollers' suites at the Bellagio. The arrival party was in Larry-boy's suite. Polished granite and marble everywhere. Catered spread with lobster, salmon, prime rib, king crab, and caviar. Ice and fruit sculptures decorated the table. A row of single malt scotches on the bar: Lagavulin, Laphroaig, Talisker, and some special issue 40-year old Macallans that I knew went for at least $5,000 per bottle. The women were catered, too. Grisscoe brought in eight showgirl-esque call girls, saying, "Gentlemen, just what the doctor ordered—one for each arm; or wherever else you choose to put them." The scotch wasn't the only thing costing five large each.

I pulled Grisscoe aside. "You never said anything about this," I told him. "What?" he said. "Having a hard time choosing? Don't worry, you'll get to dip your wick in each one before this trip is over." "No, it's not that," I said. "I'm not sure about this whole thing." "Whoa, whoa!" Grisscoe said and with a sharp grip on my arm and another on the tendons between my neck and shoulder, steered me into a corner away from the action. "Look, bucko, you're either one of the Musketeers or you're not. No dabbling. You can go back to your suite and say goodbye to the inner circle, or you can partake in this." He spread his arm, palm extended, with a flourish that swept the room. My eyes locked on Larry-boy, leaning back on a leather sofa with his pants around his ankles and getting a blowjob from one of the call girls. "You only get to make this decision once," Grisscoe said. "Understand?"

At first I hesitated, and not just because I'm a married man, although you might think that would be enough, but because I recognized, in the immortal words of another corporate titan, that I was at an "inflection point." I could say no and find myself quickly shunted out of the action—not just the blowjobs, but the business—or I could go along with what Larry-boy and the others were doing and enjoy the ride (pun intended). I chose to go all the way with the liars. I chose the fantasy made reality Grisscoe was offering: a chance to be D'Artangnan, the fourth Musketeer. Rationalizing, at the time, that I could always opt out anytime I wanted. Which, of course, I never did.

So I took a petite and busty blonde named April back to my suite—along with a bottle of Laphroaig to flatten my inhibitions. April took care of the foreplay. "We need to get you loosened up, Gregg," she said, leading me by the hand into the bedroom. "Get on there," she said, and pushed me onto the bed. I kicked off my shoes and tried to act eager, although at that point I was actually scared shitless. She poured the scotch and brought the drinks over. "Here's to getting off," she said as we clinked glasses. The sea-weedy and mediciney scotch burned hot in my throat. Just what I needed to take the edge off.

April stood at the foot of the bed with her hands on her hips and bent forward slightly so that the scoop of her loose black dress showed most of her breasts. The spaghetti straps barely clung to the edge of her shoulders, seemingly held on only by the friction of her freckles. Her smile was gleeful. "Don't worry about getting it up, honey," she said, "I'll make sure you're ready." "It's not that," I said. "It's just that you look a lot like my wife." She clapped her hands together several times and laughed. "So that's why you picked me", she said. "I love it." "No, no—" I tried to say because that wasn't what I'd been thinking, but April wasn't buying it. "Come on, honey," she said, "I hear it all the time. God, you married guys are so predictable. You all want me to do the nasty stuff your wives won't."

Would it surprise you, Britt, that I went limp at that moment? It wasn't just the guilt I felt for cheating on my wife with a call girl who looked like her, although I did feel shitty, at least momentarily, about that. No, the worst part was having April reveal my infantile psychology. At least it didn't seem to bother her as she slid the straps from her shoulders and let the dress fall to her hips. Both her nipples were pierced and I was surprised that her breasts weren't fake. "What do you want to do first?" she said. "Tit fuck me?" She cupped her breasts, pushed them up and together. "Now that you mention it," I said, the blood moving to right places again. She laughed and shimmied out of the dress. "Does your wife do anal?" She turned around and spread her ass cheeks. "Is that what you want to do, Gregg? Fuck me in the ass?" "Maybe," I said. April laughed again. "Or do you want to get kinky?" She went to the dresser and pulled a strap-on dildo from her purse. "Maybe you want me to fuck *you* in the ass," she said and held the dildo in place and thrust her hips to make the black cock-shaped dildo bob up and down. I felt a tinge of fear and thought, Gregg, what are you getting yourself into? Then I looked at April, with her tits and her cock, and felt a surge of desire. But April said, "Maybe later, I can see you need a few more scotches in you before you're ready for this."

She tossed the dildo on the dresser and took something else from her purse, but kept it hidden behind her back as she came to the bed and quickly straddled me. She did a bump and grind on my crotch. I breathed deep and her smells were in my head: a spicy perfume, vanilla and cinnamon, a hint of sweat, and a heavy dose of pheromones. "See," she said, "I told you I'd get you ready." That gleeful smile again. "Bet your wife doesn't have one of these." She stuck out her tongue, clicked the stud against her teeth. "No, she doesn't," I said. "That excites you, doesn't it?" She thrust her tongue out. "Blow jobs are my specialty. You know why?" I shook my head. "Because of these." She brought her hand from behind her back and held up what looked like marbles connected with string. She swung them like a pendulum over my face. "Anal beads," she said, then flashed her pierced tongue again. "They go in your ass and then I pull them out one at a time as you're coming." She put the beads in her mouth and pulled them out plop plop plop to demonstrate. Saliva dripped from the beads and landed on my shirt. "Makes you shoot like crazy."

At that point I was having difficulty breathing. April scooted back and undid my belt. "Don't worry, Gregg, no one's ever complained." She tugged on my zipper. "And I guarantee you won't be the first."

But I was disclosing risks, wasn't I, Britt?

We will use all means at our disposal to hype the stock price. We will pay business journalists to write articles hyping our company. We will pay people to log-on to message boards at investor web sites and hype the stock. We will issue a steady stream of press releases so that there is always a buzz about the company. We will ensure that our investment bankers keep the pressure on their firm's analysts to maintain strong-buy ratings. **We will twist the arms of investment bankers seeking our business**. Bribing them, essentially, by offering them our business only if their stock analysts write glowing investment reports and maintain strong buy ratings on our stock.

We will falsify the quarterly statement we file with the Securities and Exchange Commission, thereby committing fraud.

Which is the crux for me personally, Britt, because although management signed off on those 10-Q filings, what's their defense going to be? They *relied* on legal counsel. *My* legal counsel. And what's my defense? Management told me what to put in the filings. Like that will fly. Ultimately, there's no way for me to weasel out from under my complicity. I knew I was preparing false documents with the *intent*—there, I said it, Britt, the prosecutor's favorite word—to deceive investors. Of course, those SEC filings were piddlely-ass fraud compared to this next one.

We will artificially increase our revenues by entering "roundtrip" sales agreements with other retailers.

After the IPO was completed most of my time as corporate counsel was spent negotiating and drafting those sales agreements. And that was the point when I knew I had crossed the ethical line. I could rationalize away the perks I'd received, after all, there should be some compensation for the sixteen hour days I was working. And I could even rationalize away the carefully worded cover-your-ass regulatory filings because any investor, at least one not also caught up in the speculative greed, should have been scared off by those cryptic filings. But when I put those sales agreements together with other retailers, I knowingly participated in defrauding investors. Those agreements created no shareholder value. In fact, they actually cost us money because our partners netted the proceeds of the sale whereas all we got out of the deal was the ability to report higher revenues. The sole purpose of those agreements was to generate bogus revenue and thus create the illusion for wall street-analysts and investors that our sales were rising quarter over quarter. Why? Because we had no choice. Once it became clear that we weren't going to meet our sales or earnings forecasts we had to do something to keep the stock from tanking. Just keep the sham going for a couple of more quarters, get passed the various lock-up periods for selling shares, and then we could dump our stock and nothing else would matter.

Well, Britt, I suppose you are wondering what the fuck I was thinking. Didn't I have any check on my conscience? Didn't I consider myself a liar, a cheater, and a thief? I'm ashamed to say that I didn't think much about it at the time. I mean, I knew what I was doing was *illegal*—I had no illusions about that—but it's not like anyone else in business is a choir-boy either. Besides, someone was going to do the job so it might as well have been me. Now? I hang my head and say that it involved not the least bit of soul searching. Although, late in the game, I did tell myself, just six more months, then I'd sell my stock and be set for life. That was the extent of my concern. I wish I could say that I went through a moral struggle and was simply too weak to resist. But that would just be another lie. I got sucked in by the euphoria of greed and power. I felt omnipotent and it was the greatest feeling I've ever had. Of course, now that that veil of omnipotence has been ripped away, it doesn't feel anywhere near as good as April's anal beads did. So, as I stare at the computer screen writing this, what I can say is that I'm a man who ruined more lives than he helped. And how am I supposed to forgive myself for that?]

Due to these risks and other factors, period-to-period comparisons of our operating results may not be meaningful. You should not rely on our results for any one period as an indication of our future performance. In future periods, our operating results may fall below the expectations of public market analysts or investors. If this occurs, the market price of our common stock would likely decline. [The truest words in this whole fucking filing. But what it should have said was "invest at your peril, because you will be wiped out."]

Our stock price may be particularly volatile and could decline substantially.

The market price of our common stock could be subject to significant fluctuations and may decline. The market for technology stocks, particularly following an initial public offering, has been extremely volatile and frequently reaches levels that bear no relationship to the past or present operating performance of those companies. In addition, as an early stage company, small delays in customer bookings, installations or revenue could result in material variations in our quarterly results and quarter-to-quarter growth in the foreseeable future. This could result in greater volatility in our stock price. These fluctuations could also lead to costly class action litigation that could significantly harm our business and operating results. [I take full credit for inserting this paragraph when the wheels started coming off. The last sentence of which is a cover-your-ass masterpiece, a sure-fire litigation killer—as long as the fraud isn't uncovered—because no investor can claim, after reading this paragraph, that they weren't warned. I mean I'm practically forecasting the fucking shareholder lawsuits.

At that point I knew it was over. Gregg, buddy, I said to myself the day everything blew up, the day before we announced ShopTilDrop was going into bankruptcy, how'd you get yourself into this shit-storm? And you know what? I fucking let it happen.]

P.S. Realistically, there's no way I'm not going to jail—all I can do is cut a deal, manipulate the system for a shorter sentence. If I had any guts I'd leak this to the press myself—instead, I'm passing it on to you, giving you the chance to be the hero.

Oh, and Britt, should you choose to stay on the slippery slope, to shit-can these disclosures, I know where plenty of other bodies are buried. Regardless of whatever else you might think of me, when it comes to saving my ass, I'm one highly motivated motherfucker.

Winter of Different Directions

Skip Krylewski learned of his former teammate Cleve Jimson's death from a sports-page headline: AMATEUR CHAMP DIES IN HEAD-ON. Skip's first thought while reading the article was, shit, he didn't even know Jimson was back in town. Then he thought, well, that saves a bunch of them boys on tour a career of losing. And wasn't a dead Jimson a bogey off Skip's back? Ah, Jessica. Maybe he'd be playing in that game again. Well, he'd see her at the funeral, wouldn't he?

The previous winter, Skip and his former teammates all went in different directions. Jimson teed it up in Florida on the Spacecoast mini-tour. Paul Grasso tried the Asian tour. Down in the southwest, playing the Phoenix-Palm Springs circuit, was Ricky Simmonds. Skip, who had played fourth when they won the three consecutive NAIA championships, stayed in Seattle, where he worked on the greens crew at Broadmoor Golf Club. The only tour Skip played was the West Seattle Municipal Men's club. He shot in the 60's frequently enough that, despite a stroke average of 76, he assumed that the only thing between him and the tour of his choice was two months of dedicated practice. What did Jimson have that Skip didn't, anyway? Maybe it wasn't just the effortless talent backed up with hours of practice. Maybe it was the misdiagnosed astigmatism in Skip's left eye; that genetic glitch which caused him to aim habitually left and then loop the club back down the line.

Jimson's funeral was at Sheridan Memorial Park, that swampy cemetery kitty-corner across the highway from the Déjà Vu strip club, which was convenient, because after they planted Jimson, many of the boys crossed the five lanes on the diagonal, going from gate to gate, so to speak. Throughout the service Skip focused on Jessica Jaynes, Jimson's girlfriend, whose black dress had more lace than a negligee. Jessica sat in the front pew with the

Jimson clan. Skip, a bit steamed that his ex-teammates hadn't shown, sat a few rows back, next to Buck Johnson, his former golf coach.

Skip noticed a small diamond sparkling in the side of Jessica's left nostril. He wondered if she had a pierced tongue, too. Her brownish-blonde hair was pulled back behind her ears into a ponytail. She had long ears with prominent lobes and tall curves that swept forward on top. Her eyes, spread wide beneath a high forehead, were deep set and turned slightly to the sides. Skip figured she must have incredible peripheral vision. Those eyes were grey, somewhere between pewter and cooling charcoal. As he studied her, he hoped she would look over, but she remained fixated on the preacher at the rostrum. He liked the way her cheekbones and jaw line angled downward with a tautness of carved marble. She had a long nose, sharp at the tip, which pointed down, and there was a bump in the bridge, as if it had been broken. Her chin, the roundest feature of her face, was nicely cleft. The small mouth fit symmetrically with the narrowing jaw, and the full lips tapered to sharp expressive corners that Skip could see allowed her to frown without moving the rest of her mouth.

As the preacher droned on, it occurred to Skip that now that Jimson was dead, he wished he'd known Jimson better. But the truth was, despite playing on the college golf team with him for three years, Skip didn't know Jimson at all. Oh, he knew the usual things you learn playing golf with someone every day. He knew that Jimson was often bored with his talent. That he'd start rounds lazily; inexplicably hitting his tee shot on the first hole out-of-bounds, or go four over par in the first six holes; only to wake up to the challenge and go on a birdie barrage to finish under par. Skip knew Jimson didn't choke. He could play abysmal at times—but never when it counted. Skip knew, too, that Jimson had the killer instinct; that Jimson liked nothing better than burying you with birdies when you were struggling. And Skip knew it was stupid to tell Jimson to lay up, that he couldn't carry that pond; stupid to say you can't clear those trees; stupid to say you'll never make that downhill double-breaking putt; and stupider still to put your money where your mouth was.

Skip offered his condolences to the Jimson clan in the receiving line, and then had the pleasure of Jessica's lingering hug and the musk of her perfume, a blend of gardenias and opiates that put the hunger in him.

—It's not fair, Jessica said.

Damn right, Skip thought. Nobody should have that much talent and Jessica, too.

—He carried them for three years, and they didn't even bother to show up.

Skip realized she was talking about Paul and Ricky, two and three on the team. Guess they're still competing, he said.

—Thanks for coming, she said. You were his favorite, the one Cleve felt most comfortable with. She hugged him again, whispered into his ear, Stick around until this line is done, okay?

Soft spikes are great in Arizona, I'll give you that, Buck Johnson said, exhaling smoke with each word. Up here it rains ten fucking months out of the year. They're useless as tits on a boar.

—Think on the positive, Bucko, Gordon Grayson, the Mountlake Golf Club pro, said. Your kids learn balance. He made a pass at an imaginary ball to emphasize his point.

Skip looked up the hill toward Jimson's grave. Overhead, wisps of cirrus clouds streaked the sky. The maple leaves were toasted brown like newspaper heated to the cusp of flame. A pile of wet black loam was piled on a blue tarp beside the grave. Under the maple tree, a yellow backhoe lurked.

—You've been spending too much time with the geezers, Gordo. These punks are swinging so hard they'll need three-inch spikes to keep from falling on their asses.

—All you need is a fresh crop of sweet swingers, Gordon said. Bring Skip-ski back to teach them how it's done. Gordon winked at Skip.

—What you shoot yesterday, Skip-ski? Buck said. Seventy-eight?

—With two double-bogeys, Skip said.

Buck snorted. And three three-putts.

—You never could putt, Gordon said. I keep telling you to switch to the long putter. Fix you right up.

—There's another piece of equipment that should be banned, Buck said and launched into another of his tirades.

Jessica and Jimson's sister, Claire, came out of the funeral home and into the parking lot. Jessica looked around, saw Skip, and nodded toward his car. Skip walked over and waited for her.

—You want to go for a drink? he said when she got into the passenger seat.

—Unh-uh, she said shaking her head. Motel-Six.

Jessica's kayak drifted away from the dock while she buttoned the collar of her coat with both hands, the paddle balanced on the hull. The attendant helped Skip fasten the spray skirt.

—Are you sure I don't need to know how to do the—what's it called, you know, if I tip over?

—Eskimo roll, the attendant said.

—How many times do I have to tell you? Jessica said. You're not going to flip over. Unless you do something stupid. Tell him, Jessica said and paddled back away from the dock.

—She's right, the attendant said. This isn't white-water kayaking. It's like a canoe. Just stay centered and you'll be fine. Have fun, the attendant said, and gave Skip's kayak a shove.

Skip took several minutes to figure out how to coordinate the rudder pedals and the double-bladed paddle. Jessica waited for him at the mouth of the marina.

—Don't dig the blade in so deep. Start shallow and pull back, okay? She demonstrated. Got it?

—I think so.

She pointed her paddle across the lake towards the houseboats a half-mile away on the east shore. We'll go over there. Try to keep up, okay? And then she was off, paddling smoothly.

Skip worked hard to catch her. Ten sweaty minutes later he joined her on the other side of the lake. The sun glinted off her mirrored sunglasses. He let the breeze drift his kayak into hers, and she leaned over and kissed him quick.

—See, that wasn't so bad, she said.

—I'm getting the hang of it.

She turned and looked toward a channel flanked by houseboats. Back behind there is the NOAA dock, she said. That's the big weather ship.

Beyond the houseboats Skip could see masts with radar gear.

—Cleve loved exploring that place when we came here, she said. Come on, I'll show you.

—Look, Skip said. A sea-plane.

He craned his neck as the sea-plane passed a hundred feet overhead, cut its throttle, and glided in for a landing. When he turned to Jessica, she was gone, a wake disappearing behind the houseboats.

Skip followed Jessica into her garage.

—I don't know what's wrong with it, she said. The lights started getting dim and now it won't start.

Skip got in the car and tried the key. The starter turned over a couple of times, and then started clicking. He popped the hood, spotted the frayed alternator belt. Here's the problem, he said.

—Can you fix it?

—Well, like I said when you called, I don't know that much about cars.

—That's okay, she said. I'll just call the auto club and they'll come and take care of it.

—Not so fast, Jess. I think I can handle this one. Let me go to the store and pick you up a new belt. They're a piece of cake to install.

—Thanks, she said, and kissed him on the cheek.

Skip didn't know the first thing about replacing the alternator belt, but the guy in the auto parts store assured him that it was, in fact, a piece of cake, the simple matter of loosening one bolt. Two beers later, bloody knuckles on both hands, and grease stains on his shirt and jeans, he had the alternator belt tight, the car started with jumper cables, and the battery finally charging.

—My hero, Jessica said as she hugged him. Come with me, she said, and grabbed him by the belt, it's time for your reward.

Skip walked down the pathway from Jessica's apartment, cut across the lawn, then headed into the alley between buildings. When he reached the chain link fence he followed alongside, sticking to the narrow strip of crushed rock and avoiding the mud and sloppy leaves between the fence and the trees. He peered towards the apartment building trying to find which of the windows was Jessica's bedroom. Most of the ground floor lights were off and some of the windows were in inky shadows. He saw a silhouette moving behind a curtained window, shifting and swaying as if in time to music. Was that Jessica? Or someone else? He watched and waited until the window darkened, never sure whose shadow he had seen.

Skip hated putt-putt golf. Just what he needed, take the worst part of his game and run it through an obstacle course. Not what he had in mind when he suggested to Jessica that they go golfing, but she'd insisted on playing putt-putt. After watching her laughing and running around like a kid, he was glad he'd agreed.

—This is my favorite hole, she said as they waited on the seventh tee.

One of those risk-reward teasers. Steeply downhill, with two choices: A curving rollercoaster ramp or a skip-jump into a funnel. The ramp got you safely down to the lower level, but with virtually no chance of getting close to the hole. The funnel all but guaranteed a hole-in-one, if you could land the ball in the funnel.

—The secret to this one, Jessica said, is to stay close to the left board and ride the whopdeedo's down.

Skip made clucking noises, bahck, bahck, bahck. She putted her ball down the left board just like she said, and they watched as it slowly climbed over the last bump and then caromed off the lower boards and stopped eight feet from the hole. Jessica stuck her tongue out at Skip.

—That's the chicken-shit way to play it, he said. You're going down right here. He took aim at the funnel.

—That's the sucker play.

Skip hit the putt up the ramp, but he didn't hit it hard enough and the ball stalled a foot short of the lip and then rolled back to his feet.

—Told you, Jessica said. It's the sucker play.

—Oh, yeah? Watch this.

—I'm watching.

He hit the putt harder, too hard. The ball left the ramp and arced over the top of the funnel, bounced high in the air. Jessica started laughing. Some kids jumped out of the way as the ball came down on the stairs, kept bouncing until it went over the fence, and finally bounded out into the parking lot. Skip took off down the stairs to retrieve the ball.

B uck's pickup truck stopped in front of the maintenance shed and Skip set his golf bag in the bed and got into the cab. They drove off with Buck two-handing the steering wheel as he weaved around potholes in the gravel road. A cigarette was squeezed between Buck's right index and middle fingers and the smoke swirled with each turn of the wheel. The road left a grove of trees and turned to pavement as it neared the exit gate.

—How're you and that new head greenskeeper getting along? Buck said as he merged into traffic.

—He's divided the course into grids and has me on a ten-day rotating cycle, Skip said. Insecticide, fungicide, fertilizer. Looks like I'm going to be spending the rest of my career spraying. Every tenth day a grid gets blasted with the next chemical brew.

—He sure has yellowed those greens.

—That's the sulfur. He says the sour soil kills the *poa* and allows the bent grass to flourish.

—What an eejit, Buck said. *Poa*'s all the grass those greens got. Your face wasn't that bumpy as a freshman.

—No wonder I can't make any putts.

—Excuses, excuses, Buck said, exhaling smoke with the words. When are you going to see that problem for what it is?

—Which is what? Skip said, and flipped down the sun visor to shield his eyes from the glare.

S kip was practicing twenty-footers in the hardwood floor hallway between his living room and bedroom when the phone rang. Jessica, he said when he saw the caller ID display. He'd told her to call him any time she needed to talk. Still, getting called at three AM was not exactly what Skip had in mind. The phone rang twice more while he turned down the volume on the stereo.

—Did I wake you? Jessica said when he picked up the portable.

—Yes, Skip said as pulled another beer from the refrigerator.

—I'm sorry, she said, it's just—I needed someone to talk to.

Skip sat down in the hallway, leaned back against the wall and drank from his beer. As Jessica droned on he stared down the hallway at the electronic putt-returner and the half-dozen golf balls clustered back left. Grip? Alignment? The stroke? Must be in the takeaway. Buck was wrong, it wasn't all in his head. He moved the beer bottle back and forth like a putter. Definitely the takeaway.

—Skip? Jessica said.

—What?

—You'll be there for me, right?

—Anytime you need me.

—Thanks, Skip-ski. I don't know what I'd do without you.

He hung up the phone, cranked the volume on the stereo, took a long swig from his beer, and went back to practicing putting in the hallway. Well, well, well, he said out loud. May never have Jimson's golf game, but something else of his is almost mine.

Skip headed down the darkened street away from Jessica's apartment, moving along the sidewalk from splotches of light cast by streetlights, to the shadows thrown by coniferous trees. He walked fast, tennis shoes slapping the pavement with each step. Cleve this and Cleve that, he said out loud. Who does she think she is anyway? What about me? It would have been better if Jimson were still alive. At least then Skip could hope for a spectacular failure in Jimson's future. A Greg Norman-esque collapse at the Masters, say. Or a rapid descent into heroin addiction. Some catastrophic failure of will, or imagination, or better yet, the ticking time bomb of a character flaw. That can't happen now, Skip thought ruefully. Jimson's accomplishments were untarnishable by future failures. Jimson no longer had to worry about living up to expectations, or fulfilling his unbounded potential. Jimson would never have to walk around knowing that everyone thought he was a monumental fuck-up. No, Jimson would forever be the greatest golf talent the northwest had produced. Jimson would always be the one whose career had been tragically cut short. Well, fuck him.

The spotlight lit Skip up. He turned, shielded his eyes with his elbow, saw the police car. Fuck! The loudspeaker squealed, then crackled out instructions. Skip put his hands up. The officer got out of the car and walked toward Skip with one hand on the butt of his revolver and the other shining a flashlight into Skip's eyes. After the what-are-you-doing-out-at-three-AM-routine, the cop asked Skip for his identification. Skip reached for his wallet. Shit!

—Sorry, officer. I left my wallet at home.

—I'm taking you in.

—Look, Skip said, I'm just out for a walk. Here's my house key. Everything's cool. Just take me back to my house and I'll show you my wallet.

—Get in, the cop said, holding the cruiser's rear door open.

—Just trying to clear my head, Skip said as the door closed. They drove off.

—We've been having problems in this area, the cop said.

—Problems? Skip said.

—Yeah. So I'll take you home—*and* check that ID.

—No problem there, officer. Like I said, I was just out for a walk.

Skip placed the quarter under the rail of the pool table and rejoined Jessica at the booth. They'd be playing doubles against the winner.

—Thanks for coming, she said. I really needed to get out of the house tonight.

—Any night out with you is the night of my life.

—That's sweet, she said. But I'm still going to kick your ass when we play singles.

—I'll get us a pitcher, Skip said, and headed for the bar.

When Skip got back to the booth, Jessica was at the table slamming the cue ball into the rack. A well-spread break, but nothing went down.

—Hope you don't mind me starting, she said, but it was our game.

They played a middle-aged couple that, despite bickering over every shot, played well. On her turn, Jessica had a good run. The guy missed and left Skip an easy shot, but he rattled it in the pocket's jaw. Her next time up, Jessica had no shot and was forced to play defensive, pinning the cue ball behind another ball. Skip would get another chance at potting the winner. While the bickering couple argued over their options, Jessica offered Skip advice.

—Pool is like putting. Once you see the line, all you have to do is trust your stroke.

—I'll keep that in mind, Skip said.

When it was his turn to shoot, he was still slightly behind the fourteen-ball. Pinned by a mere sixteenth of an inch. He surveyed the shot from several angles. No go. He lined it up, but kept backing off. He waited until the other couple were arguing about something, then he used the tip of his cue to move the cue ball over a bit just before he slammed it down the table and sank the eight ball. The bickering couple jumped up from their booth.

—Shit, the guy said, that was a hell of a shot! I thought you had nothing.

—Me too, Skip said. He tried to appear shocked.

—You moved the cue ball, Jessica said. I saw you. You cheated.

Skip's heart was chunking as he waited in the trees, his breath misting in the cool night air. Through the leaves he could see into the window. Jessica removed the clasp from her hair, letting loose her ponytail. She reached back with both hands and pulled her blouse over her head and threw it onto the bed. She unzipped her skirt and slipped it down over her knees and kicked it free. Off came the bra and panties. She went into the bathroom, didn't come out. After a few minutes Skip saw steam billowing out of the bathroom and into the bedroom. He took a deep breath. Waited. He was rewarded when she came out of the bathroom wrapped in a towel.

Then the flare of a spotlight.

—Police! Hands up where we can see them, you sick fuck! Get your hands up! Now!

Buck bailed Skip out. From the police station they went to an all-night coffee shop, sat on stools at the counter, ordered coffee and breakfast.

—You're lucky she vouched for you, Buck said as he rubbed another cigarette out in the ashtray. *Damn* lucky.

Skip looked up from pouring syrup over his pancakes and grinned. Hey, he said, I told you I had her wrapped around my little finger.

Buck laughed and snorted, I don't think so.

Skip ignored the comment and started eating his pancakes.

—You know, Buck said, if you'd only get your act together I could bring you on as my assistant.

—You mean my game?

—Just don't end up a registered sex offender is all I'm saying.

Three AM. A light sprinkle fell. Skip didn't feel the chill; he'd worked up a bit of a sweat. He bent over and teed another golf ball. Swung deliberately. The ball arced up into the dark, and then tumbled down through the light cast from the clubhouse's dining room. Splash. The ripples pushed towards the rock wall in front of the eighteenth green, pushed towards the unlit portions of the lake he couldn't see.

Skip tried to laugh. Ha, ha. Sounded phony even to himself. He hit another ball into the lake. Ha, ha. Another. He counted the ripples. Another. He couldn't even fuck-up the way Jimson did. He was pretty sure that that was the only day that he'd ever seen Jimson laugh a real laugh. The day Jimson blew the course record. They'd been on the course late, playing the last few holes in near darkness. Jimson grinding hard, stone-face serious. When they got to the eighteenth tee, a short par three, the light shining from the clubhouse windows was the only light left. Jimson needed a par to break the record. Instead he chunked one into the lake. Skip expected a thrown club, a string of profanity. He didn't expect laughter. He didn't expect Jimson to hit the rest of his balls into the lake.

A police car slowed to a stop on the road behind the tee. The spotlight flashed on Skip as he emptied the rest of his golf balls from the pouch in the golf bag. Again he tried to laugh. Ha, ha.

—You again, the cop said.

—Just let me hit the rest of these balls into the lake, officer, will you? You can use a good laugh, can't you?

Acknowledgements

I wish to express my gratitude to the editors of the literary journals where many of these stories first appeared: You do it for love or you wouldn't do it at all and I appreciate your efforts. Thanks for choosing to publish my stories. *SmokeLong Quarterly*, *The Angler*, *Red Wheelbarrow*, *Word Riot*, *Scarecrow*, *Carve*, *Aethlon: The Journal of Sports Literature*, *Passages North*, *Timbercreek Review*, *Westview*, and *Thieves Jargon*. Thanks also for the Pushcart nominations. Eloise Klein Healy, Tara Ison, Karen Bender, Leonard Chang, and Darrell Spencer; teachers who helped me cut my teeth. To my mother and father, for being there when it mattered. Gary, aka the Conga King, whose friendship I prize; thanks, couldn't have done it without you. Jeff and Seth, cheers, mates. Therese, for sharing the journey and everything else, much love. The music of Shadows Fall, Killswitch Engage, Lamb of God, Chevelle, Metallica, Nirvana, Soundgarden, and Alice in Chains got me through the final draft. Thanks guys. I'm grateful to all the trees that gave their lives to produce the many reams of paper it took before these twenty stories made it into this book. No animals, however, were harmed during the production of these stories. People, though, that's another story…

SM

Born and raised in Seattle, Washington, Steven J. McDermott now resides on one of the San Juan Islands. His website is www.stevenmcdermott.com, where you can listen to him read the stories in this collection on the Winter of Different Directions Podcast.